On Our Backs

# On Our Backs
## The Best Erotic Fiction

Edited by Lindsay McClune

alyson books
los angeles | new york

MANUFACTURED IN THE UNITED STATES OF AMERICA.

THIS TRADE PAPERBACK ORIGINAL IS PUBLISHED BY ALYSON PUBLICATIONS,
P.O. BOX 4371, LOS ANGELES, CA 90078-4371.
DISTRIBUTION IN THE UNITED KINGDOM BY
TURNAROUND PUBLISHER SERVICES LTD.,
UNIT 3, OLYMPIA TRADING ESTATE, COBURG ROAD, WOOD GREEN,
LONDON N22 6TZ ENGLAND.

FIRST EDITION: DECEMBER 2001

02  03  04  05  **a**  10  9  8  7  6  5  4  3  2

ISBN 1-55583-652-6

**LIBRARY OF CONGRESS CATALOGING-IN-PUBLICATION DATA**
ON OUR BACKS : THE BEST EROTIC FICTION / EDITED BY LINDSAY
McCLUNE.—1ST ED.
ISBN 1-55583-652-6
1. LESBIANS—FICTION. 2. EROTIC STORIES, AMERICAN. I. McCLUNE,
LINDSAY.
PS648.L47 O5 2001
813'.0108353'086643—DC21                    2001034081

**CREDITS**
COVER DESIGN BY MATT SAMS.
COVER PHOTOGRAPHY BY MICHELE SERCHUK.

# Contents

# Preface

by Heather Findlay
editor in chief, *On Our Backs* magazine

## Apocryphal Story #1

Minneapolis, Minn., circa 1981, 4 A.M.: Two freshly mint-
ed feminists are driving down a deserted street in the city's
red-light district. Both of them are alive with the electricity of
their virgin feminist insight, that moment when the light goes
on, when "patriarchy" explains everything, when suddenly
the whole world looks different. They are also in love. The
short-haired brunette has known she is gay since forever; the
kinky-haired blond since she got hot for the woman sitting
next to her.

They are fueled, moreover, by the truly puritanical zeal of
the antipornography movement, the juice that sustained
many a young, post-bra-burner activist (including yours
truly). It's that zeal that landed them in Minneapolis's red-
light district, a Molotov cocktail in a paper bag sitting
between them.

As the adult bookstore approaches, Nan, the brunette,
presses the break softly. She nods supportively at Debi, who
rolls down the window on the passenger side, grabs the
homemade bomb, lights it with her ever-at-hand cigarette
lighter, and hurls it toward the storefront. Both the window
and the calm of a Midwestern night are shattered at once; an
alarm starts as the Buick speeds off.

Something else broke that night: Call it Nan and Debi's
innocence, call it political naïveté, call it their guiltless con-
viction that pornography was the root of all evil, the cause of
all violence against women. Like their first conversion, their
second was a radical reversal. Within a year, they'd got into
their butch and femme identities, experimented with S/M,

and found themselves in the self-imposed margins of Minneapolis's lesbian community. Soon Nan Kinney and Debi Sundahl quit their jobs, packed their bags, and moved to San Francisco. By 1984 they published their first issue of *On Our Backs*.

### The Money Shot Heard Round the World

It's hard to picture the climate then in the tiny, not necessarily representative but enormously influential clique we called "the lesbian community." Lesbian feminism had provided many of us (as it did Nan and Debi) a philosophical framework and justification for our desire. But that framework often felt as tight as a whalebone corset. For example, "lipstick lesbian" was an oxymoron; lipstick itself was a linchpin of the patriarchal beauty myth. Butches suffered from false consciousness and male identification. Not just sadomasochism, but any sort of top/bottom sexual dynamic, was the horrifying, literal translation of men's cultural power over women. As for pornography, it was the theory; rape was the practice.

One of the central mouthpieces for this take on sexual politics was *Off Our Backs,* a newspaper published out of Washington, D.C. This tiny monthly was put together by a brave and brilliant collective and did much to spread the news, particularly international news, of women's oppression and feminist resistance. But it wasn't much interested in sexual liberation. In fact, the collective regarded both gay politics and sex lib as "male-dominated." By the time Nan and Debi arrived in San Francisco, *Off Our Backs* had published numerous articles attacking the evils of pornography.

As a kind of mischievous pun, Nan and Debi decided to call their new magazine *On Our Backs*. The subtitle was also a citation, "Entertainment for the Adventurous Lesbian," which recalled *Playboy* magazine's subtitle, "Entertainment for Men."

With their puns and linguistic thievery, Nan and Debi had

already adopted the ironic, playful style that characterized the spunky new kind of feminism they helped found. Butch/femme, in their eyes, wasn't retro; it was a sexy, inventive "appropriation" of male/female roles. (The first issue's centerfold featured Honey Lee Cottrell as "Bulldagger of the Month"—another pun, this time on "Pet of the Month.")

S/M wasn't a literalization of male power; it was a lusty, brave, even intellectual foray into the limits of liberated desire, even if those limits were frightening and painful. As for porn, the theory was, well, if you can't beat 'em, join 'em.

The first issue of *On Our Backs* was the shot heard round the lesbian world. It helped, along with a 1983 conference at Barnard College on sexuality, to incite what feminist theorists now call the '80s "sex wars," the huge theoretical debate among feminists about the politics of erotica, sexual fantasy, and S/M.

As a magazine, *On Our Backs* made all these concepts available, accessible, and "real" to a wide, nonacademic audience. *On Our Backs* did more than talk abstractly about lesbian desire; it pictured it, narrated it, and discussed it without jargon or pretense.

Reaction was strong, immediate, and polarized. Many women's bookstores, from Northampton, Mass., to Santa Cruz, Calif., refused to carry *On Our Backs*. The stores that welcomed it, however, sold out in a flash. In subsequent issues, the controversy raged on in the letters to the editor. Dykes wrote in protesting the magazine's pro-dildo editorial, calling it "full of penises." Others wrote in to say *On Our Backs* was the most powerful affirmation of their sex lives they'd ever seen. In bars, dykes lined up over whether they were "Off" or "On Our Backs" lesbians. In the streets of Seattle, lesbians vandalized a bookstore and set fire to one issue, calling the "Dawn on Fire" cover (which showed a woman body-painted with flames) a depiction of violence against Asian-Americans.

## Apocryphal Story #2

Much of the magazine's success stemmed from the genius and inspiration of the founders of *On Our Backs*. But part of it too was due to lucky coincidence between *On Our Backs* and a technological revolution: desktop publishing. Desktop publishing made it possible to bypass an expensive typesetting bill by laying out your publication on a computer. Thus it allowed regular people to wake up one day and say—as did Nan—"I'm quitting my job climbing poles for the phone company to become a lesbian pornographer." The explosion of "niche" publications in the '80s was enabled in many ways by a little machine called the Macintosh.

My old boss Debi used to claimed that *On Our Backs* was the first publication ever to be laid out on a desktop computer. In 1983, Debi was working as a stripper at the Mitchell Brothers' theater in San Francisco. She was making good, if not spectacular, money, and it was mostly in cash. When she heard that some little computer company called Apple was putting out a desktop you could use to lay out a magazine and that Apple would be selling some hot off the assembly line at some new convention called MacWorld, Debi put $8,000 in small bills in her purse and walked down to San Francisco's convention hall. From a foldout table she bought one of these computers from a young, enthusiastic man named Steve.

I love this story. It's such a modern story, a story about how a technological advance meets a sexual minority and causes a major transformation. It's about how a major American celebrity met a minor queer celebrity and, without knowing it, changed things for dykes for good. It's also a story about the closer links back then between the world of sex workers and the lesbian community in general, *On Our Backs* in particular. Sex work literally made *On Our Backs* possible. Debi bought our first Mac with money she earned giving lap dances, and at the time many of our models were gay and bi gals Debi knew from stripping. Even today some of the magazine's favorite models look so good on paper because they do it live for a living.

There are so many other stories. Like the one Nan used to tell about landing their first account with Absolut Vodka, who bought the back cover of *On Our Backs* at a premium price and made it possible for the magazine to go color and quarterly. Back in those days national advertisers wouldn't touch gay magazines, erotic or not, with a 10-foot pole. But a handsome Frenchman named Michel Roux, who was the head of Absolut's now famous advertising campaign, saw value in the gay market and decided that Absolut, not Stolichnaya or anyone else, was going to "own" that market by buying everybody's back page. (It didn't hurt that Debi, still connected to the Mitchell Brothers, was in charge of entertaining Absolut's rep when he came to town.) Even by the time I joined the magazine in 1993, I remember waiting—the magazine laid out and ready to print—for Absolut's check so that we could print.

The old days at *On Our Backs* are so difficult to imagine from the perspective of today's gay world. In those days publishers like Nan and Debi didn't start with a business plan. They started with a vision—and lo and behold, that vision actually paid off, at least enough to hire a part-time editor, an art director, and a marketing director. It helped that the magazine's sibling, Fatale Video, benefited from a much higher profit margin on its products. Nan and Debi would put together a real lesbian porno video for several thousand dollars or less, make a master, dupe it for $10 and sell it for $30.

Today's gay publishers—and I know, because I'm one of them—can't afford to publish a magazine just because they have a passionate commitment to its content. They have to worry about competition, the Internet, attracting national advertisers, battling for position on an ever-shrinking independent newsstand, covering payroll, and homophobic actresses and politicos who won't give our editors the time of day.

*On Our Backs* faced some of that toward the end of its first incarnation. Like many great niche magazines (*Spy, Sassy, Future Sex*) during the mid '90s, *On Our Backs* began to have trouble reaching its readers and (with competition from other magazines and the Internet) keeping them. Management also went through classic lesbian drama: Nan and Debi had split with Susie Bright, who had been the editor since the beginning and had rocketed the magazine to fame. Then Nan and Debi split up with each other, Nan running off with a photographer's girlfriend, Debi getting married to a man. First, contributors stopped getting paid, then employees. A year and a half after I started as editor, Debi sold the magazine to her marketing director, Melissa Murphy, who managed to put out one more issue. In 1995 *On Our Backs* went belly-up until my company, HAF Enterprises (publisher of *Girlfriends*), purchased its assets and began republishing in 1998.

## The Fiction Behind the Truth

*On Our Backs* sparked a political revolution in lesbianism, but it also sparked a literary one. To illustrate this, I'd like to tell one last story.

When Lindsay and I began to put together the volume you're now reading, I had to go through volumes of paperwork from the early days of *On Our Backs*. I was looking for contracts and contributor information, but I couldn't close my eyes to the occasional evidence of scandal or zeitgeist.

The first page of my oldest volume, "Contracts 1987–88," was a piece of pink paper with a handwritten message from Susie Bright, then the editor. "Debi," it read. "These contributor payments are due out by the 25th [of May, 1987]. Susie." Below the message is a list of names—some of them recognizable, such as photographers Honey Lee Cottrell, Jill Posener, Phyllis Christopher, and Tracy Mostovoy, or cartoonist Jennifer Camper. Next to their names Bright had written their fees: Fifteen dollars for a photograph. Ten dollars for an illustration. Twenty-five dollars for an erotic story. The total editorial budget for the Summer 1987 issue of *On Our Backs* was $622.

As I crawled through the records, more big names popped out: a pictorial from Cathy Opie—who's been collected by the Whitney Museum and whose couples portraits sell for $7,000 in galleries. Della Grace, another major lesbian photographer—whose drag-king photos have inspired academic studies—made a cameo on *Sex and the City*, and her work has appeared in two gorgeous coffee table books.

As for the fiction writers, equally big names graced Susie's records. The table of contents of the very first issue of *On Our Backs*, published in the summer of 1984, reads like a futurist's "who's who" of lesbian letters: Jewelle Gomez (*Oral Tradition, The Gilda Stories*), Pat Califia (*Sapphistry, No Mercy*), and Susie Bright (*Susie Sexpert's Lesbian Sex World, The Best American Erotica*) herself.

Later *On Our Backs* published Dorothy Allison, whose *Bastard Out of Carolina* made her the community's most visible crossover literary talent. ("What She Did With Her Hands" was Allison's virgin appearance in print.) Also brought forward by *On Our Backs* to wide audiences at the time were Sarah Schulman (*After Dolores, Shimmer*), Sapphire (*Push*), and Lee Lynch (*The Swashbuckler, The Amazon Trail*).

The magazine's standard payment for erotic stories in those days was $15.

I'm not trying to make a point about inflation here. I marvel—and I hope that I can provide context so that you will marvel too—at the enormous need that *On Our Backs* filled in the days it first began publishing. And I don't mean just the obvious need, the need that most folks think of when they think of the function of *Penthouse* or *Hustler*. *On Our Backs* has fulfilled its fair share of those needs. But the magazine also fulfilled a deep creative need for lesbian writers.

In 1984, at a very crucial moment in lesbian herstory, great dyke talents were writing material they needed to get published, even if the payment barely covered sending an overnight package. And they willingly and delightedly sent these stories to an erotic magazine because sexuality was something that they—like many great straight artists—cared about representing. That *On Our Backs* did this as an erotic magazine is an amazing statement about the importance of— and overlap among—sex, literature, and the printed word to lesbian culture.

In 1984 *On Our Backs* was America's only lesbian magazine. Not just the only erotic magazine; it was the only one, period. There were a few, important newspapers and journals available—*The Lesbian Connection; Lesbian Contradiction; Common Lives/Lesbian Lives*—but none of these publications dedicated themselves as wholly, as did *On Our Backs*, to photography and fiction. None of them sported a glossy cover. And you'd be more likely to see *The Lesbian Connection* sitting next to feminist journals than gay and lesbian magazines such as *The Advocate*. But *On Our Backs* published regularly (quarterly until 1989, bimonthly since), supported national advertisers, and—despite resistance from some lesbian feminist bookstores—reached newsstand buyers nationwide.

Most important, it was the only place where dyke authors could publish fiction. Sarah Schulman, for example, whose "A Short Story About a Penis" *On Our Backs* published in 1987, wrote to the magazine in 1989 to say thanks for our being the first lesbian publication to print her short stories.

Eventually, *On Our Backs* published almost anybody who now stands tall in the modern lesbian canon: Robbi Sommers, who published a handful of erotic novels and short-story collections for Naiad; Karen Christa Minns, who wrote lesbian vampire novels and now a gardening book; Wickie Stamps, who served as a former collective member at *GCN* and editor of the gay men's erotic magazine *Drummer;* and Jess Wells, whose novel *The Price of Passion* came out to critical acclaim.

Today *On Our Backs* is still the catalyst for so many important lesbian literary careers. Its current editor, Tristan Taormino, traces her meteoric rise to fame back to the days when she sent *On Our Backs* "Bombshell," a short story about a lesbian stripper and the butch she seduces. Today Tristan Taormino—in addition to regularly writing a sex column in *The Village Voice* and best-selling how-to's as well as shooting an award-winning video series—gets to edit the very magazine that gave her a start. And, take my word for it, you will be hearing a lot more about Peggy Munson, whose story "The Long Parallel Tracks" you'll find in these pages. She's just finished an anthology on dykes and chronic fatigue syndrome, and her literary talents are clearly prodigious.

Enjoy. For 17 years now *On Our Backs* has survived as a vehicle for hot, high-quality lesbian fiction. May this be only the beginning.

# Introduction

by Lindsay McClune
former associate editor, *On Our Backs* magazine

I first discovered porn when I was 5 years old. I was tidying up my parents' room to surprise them when I happened upon their copies of *Penthouse* and *Playboy*. I was fascinated. I got to see all the parts of women I'd never seen before. Just seeing all those naked women in sexual positions made me feel turned on (or "real funny," as I knew it then) even as I vowed never to look at the magazines again.

I decided, however, that I had no choice but to confront my parents and let them know I was in on their dirty little secret. I sheepishly broached this subject with my mom while we were doing the dishes, and without flinching she said, "It's not a secret, and we weren't hiding it from you."

My mom had no idea what license she had given me then. Porn wasn't something dirty? It shouldn't be hidden? Twenty years later I found myself as an editor for a lesbian porn magazine, looking at naked pictures and reading erotic stories on a daily basis.

Associate editor at *On Our Backs* might sound like a dream job (don't get me wrong—I felt lucky to be around porn all day for 40 hours a week), but it was a job that was not without its challenges. As editors at the only national erotic magazine for lesbians, an enormous amount of responsibility fell upon us; we were one of the only gateways between tons of raw erotic fiction about lesbians and our 45,000 readers who expected the best.

In our yearly surveys, readers say that out of all of the magazine's content, they enjoy our fiction the best, second only to the photo spreads. (Apparently, lesbians actually read the articles and don't just look at the pictures.) As a result, an important part of the editors' jobs is to line up hot, sexy fiction for each issue.

This is no easy feat. *On Our Backs* receives dozens of submissions a month to be placed into a magazine that comes out every two months, with space for only two stories. With the pressure to keep up a certain standard for our erotic fiction, the editors read an awful lot of stories. (And a lot of awful stories. I don't know how many times I read a story where the vagina was called the "love flower.") Sometimes the editors encourage specific smut writers we know to submit their work, but most often the magazine publishes unsolicited stories.

*On Our Backs* looks for stories that are, firstly and most important, well-written. It doesn't matter how much sex goes on in a story; if it's badly written, readers won't enjoy it. By "well-written" I don't mean that the writer employs traditional "proper English." I mean well-executed stories that are rich in style and that have some sort of depth, whether they're written in the "King's English" or street slang. The so-called "lesbian" or "dyke" voice is hardly a traditional one and is still being defined. For example, take Red Jordan Arobateau's "Cum E-Z," a powerful story about a butch dyke who hires a hooker. The language is a harsh, and very hot, vernacular that challenges the concept that women cannot divorce emotion from sex.

Second, *On Our Backs* looks for stories that have explicit (and erotic/pornographic) sex in them, especially as it's the magazine's mission to counter the idea that all lesbians do is hold hands. Knowing that a lot of nonlesbians find lesbian sex an enigma, *On Our Backs* recognizes that lesbians can definitely achieve some hard-core fucking or lovemaking, and they expect their stories to reflect that.

*On Our Backs* also pushes for explicitness because it has always been the magazine's mission to bring lesbian sexuality out into the open, both to stimulate lesbian desire and to educate. When I first came out as a dyke, I found it difficult to find resources that taught us how to have sex. I knew all there was to know about heterosexual sex from TV shows and movies but for the life of me could not figure out what lesbians did in bed. Lesbian erotic fiction taught me a lot about what kinds of sex I was interested in and how to go about seeking it in a way that *Claire of the Moon*, not to mention straight romances, did not.

That said, with those two basic requirements satisfied, the fiction in *On Our Backs* also aims to represent the political issues current in various lesbian communities. Lesbians enjoy arguing about penetration versus no penetration, S/M versus vanilla, lesbian identity politics, and on and on and on. You need only read the letters to the editor in each issue to see that these discussions are still very much alive and that many lesbians still feel strongly about them. That's why we published, for example, Wickie Stamps's "Medusa's Dance," which addresses the use of the role of an abusive father in sexual power play. Abuse is a controversial issue when discussed in relation to lesbianism on its own, let alone when discussed in a lesbian sexual context.

Just as important, *On Our Backs* is committed to publishing fiction that presents diversity in terms of race, ability, geography, size, class, gender, and sexuality. The magazine looks for stories that represent more than one kind of experience, and the editors were pleased to be able to publish a story such as Stephine V. Wilson's "The Dead Air Between Stars," which describes the role of S/M in bringing sexual feeling to a disabled woman. It's incredibly difficult to represent the vast diversity in the lesbian community and to simultaneously appeal to that same community. *On Our Backs* understands that, as lesbians or dykes, we are all different from each other and have different experiences, sexual desires, and sexual styles.

Finally, the magazine's editors refuse to draw the line

between what is "lesbian sex" and what is not. Take, for example, Mil Toro's "Whips and Appendages," a science fiction story about a human female who falls for a female from a species whose bodies have many appendages. Toro's tale challenges the simple assumption that sex between two lovers with female bodies is lesbian sex.

These are the kinds of issues the magazine's editors take into consideration when selecting fiction. For this anthology, we relied on many of the same criteria. Making selections for this book, however, was not also without its challenges. Much of the material from the archives of the "old" *On Our Backs* was lost, which made it difficult to find contracts and author contact information. We have Diana Cage to thank for her many hours spent poring through the archives that currently exist.

We started out with more than 100 stories from both the "old" and "new" *On Our Backs*. With our space limitations, we were only able to select 36 stories. We made an attempt, in our selections, to represent the variety of fiction the magazine has published over the past 17 years, and we have placed each story chronologically in the book, listing the original publishing date with each piece. Because *On Our Backs* has always had a rigorous admission policy, the selections in this anthology really are the "best of the best." I hope you enjoy these pieces as much as we do. I hope they entertain you, make you think, but above all, make you wet. Here's to proving to the world that lesbians are not only having sex but are having fucking hot sex!

*Issue: Summer 1984*

## A Piece of Time
by Jewelle Gomez

*Her middle finger slipped past the soft outer lips and entered me so gently that at first I didn't feel it.*

Ella kneeled down to reach behind the toilet. Her pink cotton skirt was pulled tight around her brown thighs. Her skin glistened with sweat from the morning sun and her labor. She moved quickly through the hotel rooms, sanitizing tropical mildew and banishing sand. Each morning our eyes met in the mirror just as she wiped down the tiles and I raised my arms in a last wake-up stretch. I always imagined that her gaze flickered over my body, enjoying my broad, brown shoulders or catching a glance of my plum-brown nipples as the African cloth I wrapped myself in dropped away to the floor. For a moment I imagined the pristine hardness of the bathroom tiles at my back and her damp skin pressed against mine.

"OK, it's finished here," Ella said as she folded the cleaning rag and hung it under the sink. She turned around and, as always, seemed surprised that I was still watching her. Her eyes were light brown and didn't quite hide her smile; her hair was dark and pulled back, tied in a ribbon. It hung lightly on her neck the way that straightened hair does. My own was in short, tight braids that brushed my shoulders, a colored bead at the end of each. It was a trendy affectation I'd indulged in for my vacation. I smiled. She smiled back. On a trip filled with so much music, laughter, and smiles, hers was the one that my eyes looked for each morning. She gathered the towels from the floor and in the same motion opened the hotel room door.

"Goodbye."

"See ya," I said, feeling about 12 years old instead of 30. She shut the door softly behind her, and I listened to the clicking of her silver bangle bracelets as she walked around the verandah toward the stairs. My room was the last one on the second level, facing the beach. Her bangles brushed the painted wood railing as she went down them through the tiny courtyard and into the front office.

I dropped my cloth to the floor and stepped into my bathing suit. I planned to swim for hours and lie in the sun reading and sip margaritas until I could do nothing but sleep and maybe dream of Ella.

One day turned into another. Each was closer to my return to work and the city. I did not miss the city nor did I dread returning. But here it was as if time did not move. I could prolong any pleasure until I had my fill. The luxury of it was something from a fantasy in my childhood. The island was a tiny neighborhood gone to sea. The music of the language, the fresh smells, and deep colors all enveloped me. I clung to the bosom of this place. All else disappeared.

In the morning, too early for her to begin work in the rooms, Ella passed below in the courtyard, carrying a bag of laundry. She deposited the bundle in a bin, then returned. I called down to her, my voice whispering in the cool, private morning air. She looked up, and I raised my cup of tea in invitation. As she turned in from behind the beach end of the courtyard I prepared another cup.

We stood together at the door, she more out than in. We talked about the fishing and the rainstorm of two days ago and how we'd spent Christmas.

Soon she said, "I better be getting to my rooms."

"I'm going to swim this morning," I said.

"Then I'll be coming in now, all right? I'll do the linen." She began to strip the bed. I went into the bathroom and turned on the shower.

When I stepped out, the bed was fresh and the covers snapped firmly around the corners. The sand was swept from the floor tiles back outside and our tea cups put away. I kneeled to rinse the tub.

"No, I can do that. I'll do it, please." She came toward me, a look of alarm on her face. I laughed. She reached for the cleaning rag in my hand as I bent over the suds, then she laughed too. As I kneeled on the edge of the tub, my cloth came unwrapped and fell in. We both tried to retrieve it from the draining. My feet slid on the wet tile, and I sat down on the floor with a thud.

"Are you hurt?" she said, holding my cloth in one hand, reaching out to me with the other. She looked only into my eyes. Her hand was soft and firm on my shoulder as she kneeled down. I watched the muscles in her forearm, then traced the soft inside with my hand. She exhaled slowly. I felt her warm breath as she bent closer to me. I pulled her down and pressed my mouth to hers. My tongue pushed between her teeth as fiercely as my hand on her skin was gentle.

Her arms encircled my shoulders. We lay back on the tile, her body atop mine; then she removed her cotton T-shirt. Her brown breasts nestled insistently against me. I raised my leg between hers. The moistness that matted the hair there dampened my leg. Her body moved in a brisk and demanding rhythm.

I wondered quickly if the door was locked, then was sure it was. I heard Ella call my name for the first time. I stopped her with my lips. Her hips were searching, pushing toward their goal. Ella's mouth on mine was sweet and full with hungers of its own. Her right hand held the back of my neck, and her left hand found its way between my thighs, brushing the hair and flesh softly at first, then playing over the outer edges. She found my clit and began moving back and forth. A gasp escaped my mouth, and I opened my legs wider. Her middle finger slipped past the soft outer lips and entered me so gently that at first I didn't feel it. Then she pushed inside, and I felt the dams burst. I opened my mouth and tried to swallow my scream of pleasure. Ella's tongue filled me and sucked up my joy. We lay still for a moment, our breathing and the seagulls the only sounds. Then she pulled herself up.

"Miss—" she started.

I cut her off again, this time my fingers to her lips. "I think it's OK if you stop calling me 'Miss'!"

"Carolyn," she said softly, then covered my mouth with hers again. We kissed for moments that wrapped around us, making time have no meaning. Then she rose. "It gets late, you know," she said with a giggle, then pulled away with her determination not yielding to my need. "I have my work, girl...and I see my boyfriend on Wednesdays. I better go. I'll see you later."

And she was out the door. I lay still on the tile floor and listened to her bangles as she ran down the stairs.

Later on the beach my skin tingled, and the sun pushed my temperature higher. I stretched out on the deck chair with my eyes closed. I felt her mouth, her hands, and the sun on me, and came again.

Ella arrived each morning. There were only five left. She tapped lightly then entered. I would look up from the small table where I'd prepared tea. She sat and we sipped slowly then slipped into bed. We made love, sometimes gently, other times with a roughness resembling the waves that crashed the sea wall below.

We talked of her boyfriend, who was married and saw her only once or twice a week. She worked two jobs, saving money to buy land, maybe on this island or her home island. We were the same age, and although my life seemed to already contain the material things she was striving for, it was I who felt rootless and undirected.

We talked of our families, hers so dependent on her help, mine so estranged from me; of growing up, the path that led us to the same but different place. She loved this island. I did too. She could stay. I could not.

On the third night of the five I said, "You could visit me, come to the city for a vacation or—"

"And what I'm goin' to do there?"

I was angry but not sure at whom—at her for refusing to drop everything and take a chance; at myself for not accepting the sea that existed between us; or just the blindness of the circumstance.

I felt narrow and self-indulgent in my desire for her. An ugly black American, everything I'd always despised. Yet I wanted her; somehow somewhere it was right that we should be together.

On the last night after packing I sat up with a bottle of wine, listening to the waves beneath my window and the tourist voices from the courtyard. Ella tapped at my door as I was thinking of going to bed. When I opened it she came in quickly and thrust an envelope and a small gift-wrapped box into my hand.

"Can't stay, you know. He's waiting down there. I'll be back in the morning." Then she ran out and down the stairs before I could respond.

Early in the morning she entered with her key. I was awake but lying still. She was out of her clothes and beside me in moments. Our lovemaking began abruptly but built slowly. We touched each part of our bodies, imprinting memories on our fingertips.

"I don't want to leave you," I whispered.

"You not leaving me. My heart go with you, just I must stay here." Then... "Maybe you'll write to me. Maybe you'll come back too."

I started to speak, but she quieted me.

"Don't make promises now, girl. We make love."

Her hands on me and inside me pushed the city away. My mouth eagerly drew in the flavors of her body. Under my touch the sounds she made were of ocean waves, rhythmic and wild. We slept for only a few moments before it was time for her to dress and go on with her chores.

"I'll come back to ride with you to the airport?" she said with a small question at the end.

"Yes," I said, pleased.

In the waiting room she talked lightly as we sat: stories of her mother and sisters, questions about mine. We never mentioned the city or tomorrow morning.

When she kissed my cheek she whispered "sister love" in my ear, so softly I wasn't sure I'd heard it until I looked in her eyes. I held her close for only a minute, wanting more, knowing this would be enough for the moment. I boarded the plane and time began to move again.

*Issue: Spring 1985*

## The Succubus
by Jess Wells

*Could anyone see her hardening nipples? She swore there
was a tongue running 'round and 'round its crumpled skin.*

She timed her arrival to the corner well: without breaking her stride. Margarite stepped into the bus as the last
passenger entered, dropped in exact change, and slid into a
seat alone.

*There should be no reason for feeling flustered,* she
thought, a bit confused. Her clothes were clean and well-
pressed, her hair combed in place. Even her briefcase was tidy,
and she was well-prepared for the meeting she had called.

*Well, I'm not really flustered,* she puzzled, *but something
feels amiss, like remnants of a bad dream that delays my
breakfast, makes me forget where I've put the jam, or something. Silly, really.* Margarite smoothed the collar of her
tucked white shirt and its thin black bow.

There was...it was...wait, her forearm told her, it was her
breast. There was a burning, in her breast, like a mouth on
her nipple, and (she shifted in her seat) now a pinching feeling, was it...teeth on her nipple, no, of course not. Margarite
looked down at her blouse then glanced to the side (was anyone looking?). Could anyone see her hardening nipple? She
swore there was a tongue running 'round and 'round its
crumpled skin.

Margarite cleared her throat, straightened the crease in her slacks, and pulled her briefcase in front of her.

*Absurd,* she thought, the flush growing in her cheeks. *I'm on the 8 Market toward Sansome St., just like every morning.* But she swore there was a mouth on her breast, circling her nipple, taking bites.

The bus lurched to a stop, and Margarite braced herself with a hand on the seat in front, left it there to shield the excited breast. Maybe if she read the paper, she thought, but she didn't want to take her hand down. A woman with a large parcel edged past her seat, a young girl in tow. Businessmen, oblivious to everyone, pushed down the aisle. People were standing up now, holding the railings, their bellies at eye level, so Margarite stared straight ahead. She couldn't move, pressed against the seat by the busy lips inside her blouse. Her breathing deepened. She was pinned, trapped by the suck, suck, bite.

*I am not a prisoner*, she thought. *I am Margarite LeCarr. I am going to work like I would any morning. I slept alone last night, in pajamas, and I do not have...lips on my nipples.* The idea was absurd; never mind the feeling, the thought of it was preposterous. *I'll read some papers for the meeting— mind over matter*, she thought, and set down the briefcase between her legs and yanked out a folder. Ah, she could move from the back of the seat. Margarite smiled. *It must have just been...my blood or something.*

But the woman didn't get the folder open before the tongue flattened and covered her entire breast with wetness, wiggling a tongue point into the crease between breast and chest. Margarite gasped, looked sideways. Her breast was being lifted up, sucked. She felt the spittle running down her mound onto her belly. She could see it, she could; the surface of her left breast higher than the right, being held and now kneaded and squeezed. Margarite cleared her throat and pulled up her collar.

"Excuse me," Margarite said, as she gathered her things to her chest and scurried out of her seat. The woman beside her looked puzzled. Margarite pushed through the crowd, gasping and whining as her nipple was twisted. "Pardon...me...ah...oh, excuse, ah, coming through...back door!"

"Good morning, Mr. Taylor," she said as she stepped into the wood-and-chrome elevator.

"Good morning, Ms. LeCarr."

"Margarite."

"Tom. Hello, Harold," Margarite tried to steady herself. She turned. "Vivian, good morning, dear." Up the floors and out the doors, the workers held their attaché cases and their Styrofoam coffees, raincoats over their arms, a higher class of knit suits remaining as the numbers climbed.

In her office, Margarite set her briefcase down as if the journey had taken months. What was going on with her body? At 43, she had graying hair and crow's fee cut in toward her deep-set eyes. She had a round belly and wide thighs, long fingers, a regal carriage. But this morning she felt like a girl confused by her first blood.

Margarite poured herself coffee. Diane, her assistant, was already in: The phones were on hold, and Margarite could hear the file cabinets rolling back and forth. She ran her finger across her manila files but wandered aimlessly into the front office.

"Good morning, dear," she said softly.

"Good morning, Marge," Diane said with a grin, spunky, looking up from the folders to study the woman's face. Diane was 35, with hair as thick as a dog's and a nose that drew a viewer up its arching smoothness to her eyes. Constantly moving, Diane always looked like she'd gotten off the racquetball court, no matter what she wore. There was always a telltale pink in her cheeks.

The two women knew each other's lines and wrinkles;

they knew what puffy eyes in the morning meant. Diane had listened to the many stories of Karen leaving Margarite and moving East, and she had been gentle during those months of pain when Margarite stared out the windows and cried during lunch.

Margarite trained Diane and pushed for her advancement but often asked her to take her laundry to the first-floor cleaners. The two rotated breakfast and coffee chores with great ceremony, but this morning it only made Margarite feel worse.

"I forgot our breakfast," Margarite said softly. "I'm sorry, falling down on my job."

"Well, those blintzes are a hard act to follow," Diane said, flashing her brown eyes and giving her friend an out. When Margarite didn't take the bait, Diane scanned her face closer. "Bad dreams?"

"No," Margarite said hesitantly, averting her eyes. She wasn't sure what was happening. How could she explain this, even to Diane, who was her only confidant?

"Well," Diane said, shoving the file drawer closed, "no time for breakfast anyway, only 20 minutes before this fucking meeting."

"Right," Margarite said, and returned to her office, where she opened her curtains to the sun and plopped into her high-backed chair. Her coffee sat steaming on the file cabinet in the other room while she stared out at the willow trees, their tendrils languorously streaming in the breeze. They dipped and skittered across the morning.

This was not her imagination, she reasoned. And nothing unusual had happened to precipitate it. The night before she had not dreamed; she had not touched herself or slept naked. She had lain motionless—the perfectly smooth and tucked sheets told her—for eight hours and 30 minutes, the same celibate night she had lived for the nine months since Karen had left her for a new job and a new woman on the East Coast. Her body was something that sat behind her desk, sat at a café table, lay cold under sheets at night. It was better this way, easier.

Sex wasn't even something she thought about, except occasionally when she was in a crowd of lesbians and found herself imagining things—her hand against a woman's cheek while she stood talking about business, or the shape of the breasts on a woman across the room, or her hand slipping across the small of a woman's back, embracing, touching, kissing anyone in range. It happened rarely. She was just more controlled than that.

But this...this attention—well, it was wrong, it was bizarre. Next time she would have to be sure it didn't show. Margarite turned her chair from the window. *Next time?* she asked herself. *You're planning on it?* Margarite remembered the feeling of her breast being lifted, and a flush rose through her body.

*Now, what was this feeling? No, not again,* she thought, and smoothed the front of her blouse. No, it was not her breasts, but there was a tingling in her legs. Margarite sat back in her chair. Like the touch of a feather tipped with down, the sensation ran up her ankles to her calves and played behind her knees, bringing her blood up inch by inch. Suddenly it teased the curve of her hipbone and drew across the top of her thigh. Her mouth opened, and her eyes glazed over. It stroked the side of her neck; she lay her head back and gave her temples to it. *To what?* she thought. *To whom?*

It brushed her lip; she shivered and turned away, the feather proceeded, and the willows outside draped themselves through the air like a dozen soft boas. The feather took her back and forth, rhythmically, in long sweeps up the front of her body, then down her shoulders and across her buttocks, as if she were not sitting, as if she were not clothed, not on the 12th floor with things to do. Margarite swayed in her chair, eyes closed, the muscles of her neck standing out, red from ears to chin, little beads of sweat gathering under her nostrils. She allowed herself to be lulled into the rhythm.

Just then, her tormentor switched from feather's down to quill tip and dug into her shoulder. The pain burned her skin. Diane walked into the room with Margarite's coffee cup. The quill scraped from her shoulder to base of the spine.

"Margarite, you left your..."

Margarite shuddered. As she grimaced, the phantom plunged fingers into her cunt, up where it was wet from her bus ride. The pain drained from her shoulder to her vulva, giving her a bigger hole and a throb like a drum. She slammed her hands on the table.

"Ah, I'm not well," Margarite stammered, "I mean, I..." She watched Diane take inventory of her flushed face and unfocused eyes. *Oh, not here,* Margarite begged silently. *What am I saying? Not anywhere. Leave me alone.*

"I need to go home," she said, pleading.

"Home? You? But the meeting!" Diane replied, confused, shocked.

"Oh, yes. Well...you can handle it. Yes," Margarite said, brightening. "That will be fine. We've been over the proposals a number of times, Diane. You helped write them. It's a fine opportunity for the board to see—"

"Margarite," Diane said, warning.

"—to see how valuable you are." Now standing up and searching for her papers. "Really, Diane, this can't be helped," she said, not quite certain what she meant.

"Is it your stomach?" Diane asked.

"No."

"The flu? Your joints feel all right? Margarite, you're a wreck. You don't look sick—you look absolutely frazzled."

The two women stood silently while Margarite unpacked her briefcase, hoping its contents at least resembled the papers she had brought in this morning, trying to lay out the proper folders for the meeting. The stalemate continued, a tight silence in the office, until Margarite picked up her report and handed it across the desk. "Here, you'll need this."

"Oh, god." Diane paced with the width of the room, exasperated. "All right...I'll call you a cab."

Margarite sat back in the taxi, her beige linen coat draping on the seat, her legs crossed at the ankles. The cab plunged up Market Street, the reverse of the route she had just taken. *This is the first time I have ever taken a day off work for...nothing...for sex,* she thought. Margarite was incredulous. *In how many years of being sexual...* she thought. *And why now?* And how could she be expecting to...and so didn't that mean that she was an accomplice and so making love with...this phantom, this...succubus?

Yes, that's what it was, a succubus, a woman spirit who comes to seduce in a woman's sleep. She had read about them in reference to the saints. A nun locked in a convent cell—and denied the world except a view of the herb garden from her barred window—would be visited at night by the spirits of women. The succubus came when the nun had spent the day watching the bent backs of the novices in the fields, torn by the sight of women so far away while her pen and ink and scriptures sat idle. The nun would get to bed early, slipping under her coarse cotton sheet, still in her hairshirt. She would toss and turn. A touch would come to her; her temperature would rise; "No, no, I mustn't," she would murmur but would turn her buttocks to the moon. The succubus would laugh and, hovering above the length of her body, set her mouth on the nun's ass.

In the morning the nun, her eyes sunken from lack of sleep, her hair wild, would be found in the corner of her cell by the novices who brought her breakfast. Gripping the windowsill, her neck covered with black and blue bites, kiss marks, her shoulders and forearms also black and blue, the

nun would grit her teeth against her words. The novices, pro-
hibited from stepping inside the threshold, would stare open-
mouthed at the woman's bare legs and cold toes.

"Sister Angelina! Do you...require anything?"

The taxi that took Margarite home pulled smoothly into
the drive. She sat very still in the back.

" 'Scuse me, ma'am?"

"Yes?...Oh, of course...how much do I...oh, I see, $4.50."
Margarite fumbled in her briefcase. "Keep the change." She
leaned forward with the money and caught a glimpse of herself in the rearview: Her neck was purple with bites. She
dropped the bill onto the front seat and pulled up her collar,
her breath caught in her chest.

"Ah, ma'am, it's a bit short here. That's $5.50."

"Oh. Yes. Excuse me. Let me give you two more...thanks
again," she said weakly and slid out the door. She opened the
collar of her coat and pulled on her clothes, seeing just what
she'd expected: black and blue marks all over her shoulders.
As the taxi drove away, she stood clutching her lapels.

*What I see, I am*, she thought, *and what I think, I feel. Oh,
Goddess, this is very dangerous.*

Margarite stood in the drive looking up at the second floor
of the peach Victorian, where her curtains slowly blew in and
out of the open windows. It had been years since she had seen
her tiny front lawn in the daylight of a working day. She
opened the front door and climbed the polished stairs to her
apartment. Everything was as she had left it: the plants at the
top of the stairs, the French doors open to the front living
room, pillows just so on the green velvet sofa, armchairs, fireplace, candlesticks, closed and polished writing desk—it was
all the same, but so peaceful. Margarite felt she was disturbing something. She looked at the light on the polished floors,
the way the flowers looked in the afternoon, everything in the
room a different color than she saw in the evening. She set her

briefcase on the sofa, hung up her coat, her short heels clacking on the floor. She turned back to her living room. She felt like an intruder.

Margarite moved to the china cabinet by the fireplace and lifted down a tumbler, opened another cabinet for the scotch, and strode into the kitchen for ice. Back in the living room, she kicked off her shoes, plopped into an armchair, and set her feet on a square footrest. *I guess I work like my mother*, she thought. *Four years without a single break.*

Her mother would come home tired and disgruntled, and ease herself into her overstuffed chair with lace doilies on the arms. Mrs. LeCarr would fold her coat over the arm, pry her shoes off with her stockinged toes and sigh.

"Gite, baby," she cooed to the young Margarite, waiting by the television, "come rub Mother's feet, please, baby. I work so hard."

Margarite would turn on the television and hurry to pull up the ottoman. This was the finest part of the day. Mother worked so hard; she deserved attention, and Margarite was happy to give it to her. The little girl scanned the *TV Guide* every afternoon: What would Mother like? She prepared the woman's special chair, polished her table. When Mrs. LeCarr finally came home, the little girl would hold back, expectantly, waiting for her favorite phrase: "Gite, baby, come rub Mother's feet, please, baby." Flushed and silent, Margarite would hurry across the room, sit on the flowered ottoman at the woman's side, and grasp one of her ankles. She would knead and rub and hold the foot like a breakable object, like a lamp you rub to make wishes come true.

"Momma?"

"Yes, pet," the woman sighed, stroking her daughter's head but never moving her eyes from the set.

"I can't do a good job through these stockings."

"What dear? Oh, well, all right. You can take them off, Gite." The two had a special ritual. Mrs. LeCarr would remain totally still as Gite slid her little hand under the tight A-line skirt to her garter belt. Or the woman would slowly pull her skirt up to expose the clasp, one side at a time. The little girl's eyes took in every inch. Gite was so gentle, the soft warm thigh making her hands tingle. She grasped the black garter with both hands. Gite's body was hot everywhere, her nose overcome with the smell of her mother. She slid the sheer stocking down the thighs, dragging her little fingers along the flesh, over the knee, across the calf and off. Gite let it accordion-fold onto the floor. Mrs. LeCarr leaned on her other buttock to receive her daughter on the other side.

Now, with her hands on flesh, Gite would massage with a new vigor, rolling the soft skin between her thumb and finger, stroking the calves, pushing into the arches, pouring all the energy, the expectation of the afternoon, into her mother's skin. "I work so hard," her mother would say, "I deserve my..." whatever it was at the time: her Sunday sleep, her fancy food. Work made it right, and for Gite, hard work made this skin and touch and caress and woman smells possible; hard work meant Gite's hand slipping into the tight, hot space between the hem and the panty leg.

Today, in her own apartment, 43 and ill at ease, Margarite sat forward in her seat. *You do not fantasize about your mother*, she thought. Margarite glanced at the bruises on her shoulders and, setting her scotch glass on her knee, felt her shoulder blades for the beginning of the scratch. *You've never touched your mother above the knees, and you'd better not start thinking about it now, goddamn it.* Margarite leaned her head against the chair back and closed her eyes.

"Momma, I can't do a good job through these panties," she murmured.

"All right dear, you can take them off."

Margarite continued, "*Let me sit between your legs... You work so hard. Let me nuzzle inside your folds. I want to see*

16

*your head against your chair, I want spit sitting in the creases of your lips. My mouth on your cunt, my lips teasing your lips, fingers pulling your hair. Spread your legs farther—that's right—touch my ears with your thighs. Yes, yes, drape me back across the ottoman, my pigtails on the rug. I know the tops of these thighs to slip my hand around the back to your buttocks, one hand in back, one hand in front, wiggling into your cunt, I dive again, my fingers plunging, fist sucked back up where it belongs, fucking you...you scream for ME at night."*

Margarite opened her eyes. Wide. She was...good Goddess—she breathed—she was draped backward across the ottoman, the afternoon sun striping her belly and legs in her executive clothes. The scotch glass was spilled on the floor. The smell of a woman was heavy in the air. Margarite clambered off the floor with difficulty. Her hand...was wet. Viscous come clung to the webs of her fingers, curled into a fist. *It can't be,* she thought, turning in a circle, scanning the room for a woman she knew she wouldn't find. The succubus was in control and could make her fantasies more real than she had ever wanted. *I do not cry,* she thought, *but look at me...* She turned to the mirror. *I don't have sex, but I've been fucked on a bus, in a cab, in my office. I'm covered with bites and bruises and scratches and,* as she eyed her hand with suspicion, *I fuck.* She wasn't really in control anymore. She knew that now. Even though she felt she was totally in charge of herself, her cunt had always broadcast her need to her constantly, feeling so swollen and insistent that it was as if it walked a few inches in front of her. Now Margarite knew she had never been in control of her body—she had consistently denied its needs but had never controlled its desire. Now the succubus had taken away even her ability to deny herself. She was being fucked and—she smelled her hand—she was fucking. Truly now, she was living what she thought and feeling what she saw.

*Issue: Summer 1987*

## Exchange Highway
by Gwendolyn Forrest

*I leered at her body, trying to make her feel self-conscious about being caught out in the middle of nowhere with almost nothing on.*

So there I was, ridin' high in the cab with the tunes blasting, the sun comin' up real slow, and my cunt dripping from a full night's worth of fantasizing and trying to stay awake. All that coffee eventually did the trick, 'cause I was wide-awake, cruising without a car in sight, on my way to deliver a load of silicon chips or somethin, I dunno. California was still new to me, so I was takin' it pretty slow, just enjoying the scenery and the sensations I felt between my legs.

I was hot. I hadn't been with a woman since a whole month before, a pretty sleazy chick I'd picked up in a pretty sleazy bar—but we had a good time together. She even got me to stay another night... As a matter of fact, she was the bitch that stole all my stuff—my dildos, my harness, my cuffs, everything! I'm *still* pissed about that, and if I *ever* see her again... Well, never mind that. It was a while ago, and although it took me some time, I've been able to replace almost everything.

So anyway, there I was, daydreaming, when out of nowhere this chick in a red Mercedes sped by and cut me off so bad I had to slam on the breaks to keep from ramming right into her! I almost wanted to. With a whole fuckin' road to pass me on and no one else on it! Damned if that didn't spoil everything. I was mad as hell but had no chance of catching her. She was miles ahead of me before I could even catch my breath. So I calmed down, cursed a few dozen times, and got over it. There wasn't too much I could do anyway. And the fact that my cunt was even hotter than before helped, 'cause I started rubbing my crotch and thinking about how I'd love to shove a large dildo right up her ass!

A few miles went by, and I had just about forgotten about her when I spotted the same red Mercedes on the side of the road with the hood up. And standin' in the road was this long-haired bitch with big tits, wearing a blood-red dress and wavin' her arms like crazy. I reached over and put on my sunglasses. *This could be fun,* I thought.

I slowed down and practically drove right through the woman 'cause she wasn't about to move out of my way. I stopped hard, like two feet in front of her, and hit my head on the steering wheel. Off came the glasses. I looked up, and there she stood, only now her hands were on her hips.

I stepped down to get a better look at her. She was h-o-t! She had on this short, loose red thing that barely covered her luscious legs and allowed a hint of the body underneath. Her tits were large, but it was more the fullness that made you stare. Beautiful! But don't get me wrong—I'd swear there was smoke coming out of my ears. I was mad, and I saw a good chance for revenge. I decided to savor the feeling and assume full control over the situation.

I smiled at her. "Well, hello there, honey. That's a mean little drivin' machine you got there." I leered at her body, trying to make her feel self-conscious about being caught out in the middle of nowhere with almost nothing on. "Looks like you got a problem there, sweetie...you wouldn't be needin' a little help from me, now, would you?"

Her expression didn't change. "My car overheated. Fix

it," she said, slowly and precisely, enunciating each syllable.

"What?" I said. What a cunt. "Do I look like I have a Triple-A hat on or something?"

Her steel-blue eyes looked right through me. "You heard me, truck driver. FIX IT!"

"I'll fuckin' fix it!" I mumbled, but I walked toward her car anyway. I'd seen plenty of her type before. Sexually frustrated. Get 'em hot, strap on your dildo, fuck 'em good and hard, and then talk to 'em. Still, there was something in her voice that got to me. I wasn't used to being spoken to like that.

So I decided to be nice about it. I'm looking at her car, but I don't see any smoke or sign of overheating. I bent over to look at her radiator or something, and I felt two soft tits pressing against my back. Sent a shiver right through me. *Damn!* I thought. *This chick really needs it!* And I was fully prepared to give it to her. My way.

I played it cool and just sort of pushed back against her, making like it was the car I was interested in. I felt her hands grab my arms, pulling them back behind me.

I started to pull away, and I wasn't even worried 'cause I was sure I was at least twice as strong as her and definitely outweighed her. I don't know why, but my arms just couldn't resist as she pulled my wrists together, high behind my back. My brain was thinking the right thoughts, but my body just wasn't responding. I thought I heard her laugh, and in an instant I felt cool metal around my wrists and a distinct click.

My head jerked up. *What the fuck?* I thought, as I tried to pull my wrists apart. "What the hell do you think—" I started to say as she spun me around and slapped me full on the face. Hard. I was sure she laughed as she pushed me to my knees. I didn't even have the time to wonder how I let myself get in this position. I was actually scared. Maybe even shaking.

"Don't open your mouth until I tell you to," she said in the same precise way.

"Who the fuck—" I started. She slapped me again. Harder still.

"I can tell this will be fun for both of us," she said, laughing.

Well, I'll tell you, she definitely had me. Like I'd never been had before in my life. Now it was just a matter of what she wanted. I was still trying to get my hands free as she pulled me to my feet and dragged me to the trees next to the road. She was far stronger than I imagined, and I kept tripping over myself trying to keep up with her. Fifteen minutes later I was sure I'd never see my truck again. At least I was wrong about that.

When she finally stopped, I noticed she had this leather bag with her, but I didn't even have time to think what might be in it 'cause she grabbed me and kissed me full on the mouth.

"Be a good little cunt and get down on your knees for me," she said in a whisper. But I couldn't move. Shit, I couldn't even think! All I could do was stare at her, her kiss still wet on my lips, her scent permeating the air around me, making me dizzy. She groaned and pushed me down, her hands gripping my shoulders, until I was kneeling before her, her crotch inches from my face, blotting out anything else I might have seen.

"Mmmm..." she moaned, "I've had luck with truck drivers. Let's keep it that way."

I must have made some kind of noise in response, because she laughed and pushed my face into her crotch. The scent of her drove me over the edge. I had to have that pussy. I couldn't believe what I was feeling. I, a muscular butch truck driver, was on my knees in front of a gorgeous femme who had complete control over me. I loved it! Yeah, that's right, I couldn't get enough.

"Let me suck you, please...give it to me..." She pulled her dress up slowly for me as I licked her thighs, which were gradually being exposed.

"Ooh...what a good pussy you are. What a hot cunt you are. You want some pussy? Huh, little slut?" she purred as she teased her pussy in front of me. Her hair was light brown and barely covered her swollen, dripping cunt. She had the nicest-looking pussy I'd ever seen. Pink lips, smooth and even, and a big swollen clit. And the sweetest scent...I can still smell her. She knew I really wanted it, and she was gonna take her time giving it to me. I must've begged for 20 minutes before she pushed my face into her juicy sweet pussy. A second later she exploded, her hips bucking and her cunt grinding into my face, covering me with her juice.

She took a minute to recover, her hands still holding my head while I licked and sucked her drenched thighs. Then she put a hand under my chin and lifted my face until I was looking directly into those steel-blue eyes.

"I'm going to fuck you very hard!" she said, and pushed me down on my back, mounting me in one swift motion. She forced my legs apart with her own and slammed her pussy into my crotch. I moaned with the force of her, desperately wishing she would pull off my jeans and let me feel her pussy against mine.

"Mmmm..." she sighed as she ground her pussy against mine, fucking me with such force that we were actually moving. She had me pinned there, humping me furiously until she came again, screaming and panting, while I could only lie there helplessly trying to feel her pussy through my jeans.

Finally, she got up and stood over me, fully composed and leering down at me with those eyes. She dangled a key above my head—the key to the cuffs that encircled my wrists. She was smiling, almost laughing, as she tossed it into the air. It landed a full 20 feet from where I lay. I could only look on helplessly as she turned and left, her sweet ass calling a soft "goodbye" to me. And then I was alone.

Well. I don't know how long I lay there, motionless, listening to some far-off birds singing, feeling the cool wind on my body, my mind totally blank. But I must have somehow figured out that I should get up and leave, 'cause I remember trying really hard to sit up, and even harder to stand. My knees were weak. I kept tripping. Once I'd found the key I had a lot of fun trying to fit it in the hole using my bound hands. But I really didn't have much choice, and my mind wasn't on it. All I could see was her. On top of me, standing over me, looking down at me, laughing at me.

The next thing I remember is falling asleep in the cab, for almost 10 hours, until a cop woke me up and made me move. Then I drove to the nearest town and found a motel and slept some more. Who knows? That was one year ago today. One year. Doesn't feel like it. Could've been yesterday.

No, I'd never had nothing like that before, and not since, neither. Oh, I've had some women all right...more than my share, I suppose. But it's never been the same. And damn if I haven't come 365 times against her soft body, looking hard into those steel-blue eyes.

*Issue: Spring 1988*

## An Exploration
by Dorothy Allison

*Fisting is as savage as big cats rolling over each other in a jungle clearing.*

For years I didn't really understand it—the way women would look at each other's hands across the bar, the way some women's glance would trail up from the fingers to the swell of the knuckles, past the wrist to the forearm, and then look away suddenly if they saw me watching them. I used to hang out at the only gay bar in Tallahassee, Florida, and watch women stare as the tall, slim-lipped bartender would lift four beer bottles together, their pupils reflecting the cable-like tightening of the muscles from her wrist to elbow. I watched the other women lick their lips, look away and inevitably look back again, and I knew by their manner that it was about *sex*.

I'd look back myself, admire the bartender's jaw, black eyes and the curling short hair on her neck. I loved the way her hips moved, the way her tongue would peek out between her lips when she was counting change, but I didn't really see the power of her hands. They were small, finely shaped, and the nails were trimmed down and filed, but then most lesbians wore their nails that way. It was nothing special as far as I could see. I would look back to see what all the women were watching, but I couldn't quite figure it out.

There was a whole language in the subtle movements of women's hands on a shot glass, but for me it was like hearing someone speak French. Even what I thought I understood turned out to be mostly misunderstanding. A raised eyebrow, a direct glance, or a shy tongue appearing suddenly on a full lip were all obvious evidence of erotic interest, and I knew how to respond. But a woman who cracked her knuckles while looking into my eyes confused me. I suspected she might want something of me I might not want to give.

The older butchy women I liked best seemed to think that I would surely catch fire if they held me down and fucked me. I responded powerfully to being held down but not so well to fucking. Years of severe and persistent endometriosis had convinced me that nobody could possibly enjoy fucking. Well, one or two fingers perhaps, during that time of the month when you want to howl at the moon anyway, but not more than that, and certainly not with any kind of sudden or forceful movement. The kind of sustained and forceful fucking that made women with big powerful forearms so attractive was unimaginable to me. I was a master at coming by rocking on my partner's thigh or pulling my thigh muscles tighter and tighter while I sucked and tongued at my partner's clit. But fucking hurt me, and I'd only do it if my partner insisted, biting my lips and giving it up like a gift too costly to offer often. It wasn't until my mid 20s, well on in my life as a lesbian, that I finally had the surgery for what had plagued me since my adolescence.

Curing my endometriosis changed my life. After that, when the moon came on me, and a woman pushed three fingers into my wet and aching vagina, I got the shock of my life. There was no pain; there was a heated rush of desire. I wanted that hand. I wanted it hard. I wanted it fast. I wanted it as long as she could keep giving it to me. I remembered every bartender I had ever seen pick up a handful of cold bottles, and in the middle of an orgasm I laughed out loud. I had acquired the language.

"Speak to me," I told my lover. Without knowing what the hell I was talking about, she did just the right thing. She slipped another finger inside me and started all over again.

In the movie in my head, fisting is as savage as big cats rolling over each other in a jungle clearing. The instant of being entered is as abrupt and shuddering as a flying kick. In my bed, however, fisting is neither savage nor abrupt. It is slow, measured, enticed and enticing. My women take their time, sometimes to my great frustration. When I beg them to move faster and harder, they just go on taking their time, putting in only as many fingers as the drum-ring entrance to my vagina will allow. They work me up slow, making sure that I am as open and aroused as possible. It is slow, teasing work, getting a whole hand in my cunt. But if it were easy, I don't think I would enjoy it half so much. Part of the charge is the excess of the act.

If we have to work on it, then it's about submission. If it's easy, then it's more about the physical sensation. It's the overwhelming aspect of it, the being totally carried away, shouting demands, shrieking to be fucked. The fact that it's hard makes it better, more satisfying.

I don't react to fucking like a character in a jack-off manual. My women almost never get their fists going in and out the way it's described in cheap pornography. Once the fist is fully inside, the motion is a slow, sliding, back-and-forth movement with the wrist sometimes swiveling enough to turn the knuckles up, pushing toward that mythological G-spot where all the nerves leading to the clit seem to cross.

I don't spurt the way some women do. Push me hard there, though, and I might pee. That's excessive too, the idea that we are fucking so hard and so furiously that I will just pee all over us. I like that. I like the idea of being that far out of control. Even the moment when I am shocked and embarrassed has its enjoyable aspect. Just so long as we don't stop, and especially if I am told that she wants it, wants me to let myself go like that, the thought turns around and I'm proud of myself. We are bad girls together, enjoying ourselves.

The first woman I ever really fisted was a big butch girl—a tall muscly woman who left working on her motorcycle to polish my belt buckle, get me a cup of tea, and blush when I hooked my fingers in her belt. She had been flirting with me and my girlfriend, and we were both enjoying her enormously. It was my girlfriend who checked it out with her girlfriend and got us all together at a party later.

"What do you want?" I kept teasing that girl, enjoying the size of her, the stretch of her shoulders and the slow, gliding way she moved.

"What can you do?" she replied, looking down at us. We were both so much smaller than her. Well, what? I wondered, but my pride wouldn't let me show her any uncertainty. I squeezed her, pinched her, and ran my hands over her body as firmly as possible, enjoying every little sigh and quiver she made. I was looking forward to watching my girlfriend fuck her, but somehow when we had her lying back and her jeans off and her legs spread, it was my fingers that were teasing at her slippery labia. I slid my thumb inside her and felt around. It was smooth and open and welcoming. I pulled back and slipped two fingers in and looked up into her half-closed eyes. There was lots of room. I pulled back and went in again with three fingers, then four. Her next sigh was deeper, and she shuddered slightly in our arms.

I looked at my girlfriend. She was smiling and nodding, watching my fingers closely. I laughed and pulled back, cupping my fingers. I was going to push, slowly, feel my way tenderly, but the big girl had other ideas. It felt almost as if she reached for me with her whole body. My hand disappeared, sucked into the warm, enclosing glove of her. I gasped, and my girlfriend laughed. I wiggled my fingers and felt the walls of the surrounding vagina balloon out and in on my hand. I closed my hand inside her, and the big girl rocked on my wrist.

"Goddamn!" Everybody around me laughed. I had never felt anything so extraordinary in my life. I tried to remember everything anybody had ever done to me that I liked. All right, I told myself and started moving my hand, the motion flowing from my elbow while I watched her face. When she started moaning and rocking with excitement, I let the muscles in my upper arm go to work. I felt my whole arm working. I wanted to do it right. All of my senses came alive. I needed to feel every motion she made, smell her as she got hotter, hear her guttural cries and slow grunting "Please," I wanted to shout, but that would have distracted me. I tried instead to speak the language of her body. I felt a hot sweat break out all over me, and every time I looked to the side I saw a proud, happy smile on my girlfriend's face.

"This role reversal stuff," I told her, "I like it a lot."

"Uh-huh," she laughed back at me. "I can see that."

I know remarkably few women who enjoy anal fisting. But there was a time in my life when I became quite accomplished at it. Not that I listed being fisted up the ass as a goal—I just had lots of fantasies about anal sex, and I told a woman I was seeing at the time about those fantasies. Natalia was much older than me, and we had been playing schoolgirl and governess. When I was the governess, Natalia was my toddler who needed to be washed tenderly, powdered down, sometimes have her temperature taken—"Turn over, baby"—and invariably be nuzzled gently until she orgasmed in my arms. When I was the schoolgirl, I was a stubborn adolescent who accumulated countless demerits and had to be taught how to wash behind her ears and between her thighs. After weeks of this play and lots of talk about our mutual fantasies, Natalia decided she would like to play out one of hers and see if she couldn't train her schoolgirl to enjoy having her ass used.

"For me," she begged, feeding me warm baklava and cold dry wine. I didn't know if the butterflies in my tummy were from her suggestion or the snack, but I agreed. Thus began a period of about three months in which I spent at least two nights a week lying belly-down on her big oak bed stand while she whispered threatening enticements into my ears and slipped magic greasy fingers up my butt. She took her time getting me used to her manipulations and refused to tell me just how many fingers had done what at any one time. Regardless, it didn't seem to take very long until I was comfortable enough with what she was doing to climb up on my knees and start pushing back at her thrusts.

"That's my girl," Natalia would purr, and reward me with the fast, slippery swipes at my clit that always made me come.

Finally, one evening Natalia asked me to come early and have dinner. She served raw oysters, lots of wine, and a big salad, and after dinner sent me off to clean myself out and lie for a while in a hot bubble bath with a glass of cognac while she did some tidying up. When Natalia came for me later I was pink all over, giggly, and very tipsy. She was wearing her highest heels and the black jacket with the high collar and the tight-fitting sleeves. Without a word she wrapped me in a big towel, bundled me into the bedroom, and plopped me face-down on an enormous pillow on the floor. Before I could hiccup in confusion she had my wrists tied to a ring in the floor.

"Ma'am?" I tried, unsure which game we were going to play.

"Be still," she said sternly. "Don't think, just relax. I want something from you, and tonight I'm going to get it." She poured a pool of thick, creamy lotion into her palm and began to massage my ass, her blunt fingers pushing dollops of cream up into my butt. I hiccuped, giggled, and after a moment wiggled my ass at her. She laughed, slapped my thighs, and, leaning forward, placed a small, silver, bullet-shaped object in my hand.

"Take a deep breath of that," she told me, still pushing at my ass. I did, and was rewarded with a slow spiral of pin lights that rose from the base of my nose up to my brain. The room got hot. I got dizzy, and a beehive started buzzing in my ears. I had never done poppers before, didn't know that was what I was doing. I just knew I was suddenly high and horny and desperate to push back at her pushing hands.

"Ma'am," I wailed, and she purred back at me, "That's my girl," while her hand worked its way steadily into my butt. She hurt me, and I screamed at her. She laughed at me, and I howled at her. But she'd had all that practice and knew every crevice, every rudimentary panic, every movement I would make in response to every movement of hers, and nothing I did or said or cried stopped her. After a while she wasn't hurting me, she was guiding me, whispering soft words while her fingers played tickle-touch so deep inside me I wanted to burp. I was gasping and begging and coming every little while as easily as a big sponge choo-choo train would fall off a cartoon trestle. Everything was slow-motion, overwhelming and marvelous.

"Fuck me, ma'am. Oh, fuck me," I kept begging her.

"Oh, I am," she kept telling me. "I am. I am. I am."

The sun was coming up when she slid her hand out of me finally and completely. I burst into tears and tried to grab her with my thighs. I wanted it back, that full, marvelous, scary, wonderful feeling. She had pulled the slipknot loose on my hands hours before, and I was free to be coaxed up into the bed to wrap around her and fall asleep, but groggy as I was, I didn't want to sleep. Even if I couldn't move, I wanted to do it again. I pulled her hand up, cradled it to my cheek, and ran my fingers along her forearm. I dreamed of bartenders; slow-eyed, grinning butch girls; and big cats rolling over the jungle floor—big cats with wide, wide mouths, great hanging wet labia, and muscly, tapered forepaws. That woman spoke my language; what she could do with those hands. Oh!

*Issue: Spring 1988*

## "December 25th Uncensored"
by Dot Cogdell

*"You sure are a cute little devil," she said, then punched me in the stomach. "But how tough are you?"*

It started out as just another day. I mean, just another December 25th, which may as well have been October 1st or Friday the 13th. I woke up, ran the tub full of hot water, and gulped down three bowls of peanut butter Cap'n Crunch. I got in the tub, at which time my eyes opened wider than I've ever known. The water was scalding me to death. "Goddamn it," I yelled, and sprang out of the tub quicker than a thousand ants could cover a picnic blanket. I stepped over to the refrigerator and flung the door open to shiver for 10 minutes in front of the freezer. I also opened all the windows in my house only to immediately slam them shut. "For crying out loud, it's the dead of December," I whined. I stared at some children playing outside. A wonderful feeling came over me, and I ran back to the tub. Just before reaching it, however, my body went flying cockeyed straight—I mean, directly—for the sudsy water. No, I wasn't making a heroic Wonder Woman leap—I tripped on my towel. My mouth opened wide, and I swallowed a ton of Mr. Bubble.

At that point I realized I could die a painful death in my bathtub and nobody would be the wiser. But what extravagance just for a little old bath. Reluctantly I got out of the tub and dashed for the passion of my life—the full-length mirror in my bedroom. Upon greeting myself in the mirror, I remarked, "You good-looking thang, you. Don't you ever die." (After saying that every morning I usually remember my mother saying how I'm getting to look more like a little boy every day.) I laughed out loud. I pressed my breasts against the mirror and chuckled, "Look, Ma, no balls." I gazed at my feminine fluff and added, "My god, I've been castrated." But I reminded myself not to play that, or as Ma has warned a billion times: "Girl, the Lord is going to strike you down for that foolishness." And I knew that she meant Pa was the Lord, so I stopped.

I stood in front of the mirror naked as a drumhead. For a moment I got homesick. But even through the homesickness I could see that in the mirror before me stood the sexiest Black woman known to femalekind.

I turned the radio on and began to dance around the room, making sure I could still see myself in the mirror. Eventually, as all good things must come to an end, I had to get dressed this 25th day of December. I put on my red underwear, beige socks and bra, a dress shirt with a Shetland wool vest, a black tuxedo jacket, my best slacks, and my new brown patent-leather shoes. My hair was pulled back into what my mother calls a "masculine ponytail." I went outside but discovered it was colder than I'd thought, and I was still hungry. Back into the house I went and put my overcoat on. But it didn't match my snazzy dress pants so I took it off and ate three apples and another bowl of Cap'n Crunch.

I called a couple of friends on the phone, and the three of us went to the movies. They were dykes too, so hanging out with them on the 25th day of December made the evening more bearable. We saw *Crimes of the Heart*. After the movie, Barb, Cathy, and I went to shoot pool at the Riviera. The Riviera is a lesbian hangout where one can find women of all ages, types, and, someday, races. Anyway, it was here that I discovered that all lesbians are not named Barb and Cathy. They're all named Terri, with various spellings. There was nothing happening at the Riv, so Barb and Cathy left. I stayed because I had just won the table and I NEVER LEAVE AFTER WINNING THE TABLE.

I was about to shoot an easy shot lined up with the hole in the side pocket, when in walked this striking Annie Lennox look-alike. Our eyes met and we both smiled. She walked past me and said, "Hello, there." I nearly creamed my jeans. A few people laughed and somebody yelled, "Are you going to shoot or not?"

I put the ball in the side pocket and continued to ogle the flamboyant blond. I went and sat beside her at the table. But people immediately yelled, "It's your shot, Braxton!" The nerve of those people calling my given name out loud in public. They know I go by B-Jay. Anyway, I reluctantly left the blond's table and went back to the green table and cleared the last three balls in succession.

Some women asked me to let them have the table, and, of course, I said no. But the blond came up and said, "Oh, let them have the table and come dance with me."

Everybody within earshot began cheering, "Yeah, go for it, Braxton!" The Terris who wanted a turn at the pool table were dancing around in circles.

The blond lady who was standing close to me took me by the hand and led me to the dance floor. The music was loud, and we were slow dancing. I was getting warm all over, and she was getting closer and closer to me. I could still hear people cheering "Go for it" and "Grab the gusto" and "Do it." We were the only people on the dance floor, so everything we did was noticeable and commented on.

We went back to her table, because people were getting crude with their comments as well as being voyeuristic. She said, "I'm Sasha," and offered her hand out for me to kiss.

"I'm Braxton. But people call me B-Jay." I kissed her hand.

"You sure are a cute little devil," she said, then punched me in the stomach. "But how tough are you?"

"What?" I asked, rubbing my stomach.

She stood on my feet and said in a pleasant voice, "Are you tough, sweetie?"

I looked her square in the eyes. God, she was gorgeous. "I'm tough enough for the important stuff," I said, and pulled myself up so that I seemed taller.

She smiled, "Well, have you ever handled a whip?"

I looked at her again. A whip! I thought she must be the dyke my mother warned me about. I laughed. "You're kidding."

She lifted one foot off mine and stomped hard. "Does it look like I'm kidding?"

"Get the fuck off me." I pushed her backwards. She fell to the floor on her butt. I extended an arm to help her get up. She smiled, and her warm beauty made me melt all over again. "You're all right," I said, and helped her to her feet.

She grabbed me by the collar and pulled my body close to hers. "My wife is out of town for four days. Let's party."

"Your wife! Is she an S/M mama who's gonna strangle me for seeing you?"

Sasha laughed. "My wife's a pussycat."

"Probably more like a jungle wolf," I mumbled. "Listen, it's dead in here. I'm going to Perry's," I said as an after-thought. "Care to come with me?

"You bet." She bit my hand, and I yelled.

She laughed. "A live one. And sexy too. I'm driving with some friends, so I'll meet you, O.K.?" Her eyebrows formed a raised hyphen.

"Cool," I said, and went to round up some friends to drive over with me just in case this blond Sasha bombshell was a *real* killer.

"You'd better show up." She pinched my breasts hard.

"I will," I said, and gave her a knee to the crotch. This was scary but exciting as hell.

We looked at each other and smiled. She rubbed her crotch and pushed me to my knees. "Kiss it and make it all better."

I did. I looked up at her from my knees and thought, *Damn, she's sexy and kinky as hell.*

"I'll meet you at Perry's," she said as she pulled me to my feet. We kissed, but it was just a peck.

In the car on the way to Perry's I thought about being with Sasha. I wondered just how rough she was going to be with me. And whether or not to ask a friend to play chaperone. *Heck of a December 25th*, I thought. *And certainly the most exciting I've had in a long time.*

Well, my group arrived at Perry's before Sasha's did, and we went directly to the dance floor. All five of us. Perry's was practically standing room only, and there was so much energy on the dance floor that it shook the room. I felt the bass of the music trembling in my chest. We grabbed three tables and put them together so that we had a seating arrangement for 15. The gay men and the straights try to save seats for their friends, but we lesbians always reign supreme and manage to have three or four large lesbian table sections in the bar.

Sasha's group arrived with a loud ruckus, and she immediately came over and sat on my lap. We kissed, a little more than a peck, and ordered drinks.

I introduced her to my group, and she introduced me to her group. We had two empty chairs at the table, but we knew they'd soon fill up.

Sasha was bigger than me and wouldn't stop squirming in my lap. At one point, she jumped straight up and plopped back down. "Hope I'm not squishing you," she said, and ground her fist into my crotch.

"Not at all," I shrieked, wondering if she broke my clitoris.

"Braxton, let's dance." She grabbed me by the armpits and dragged me to the dance floor.

I screamed all the way there. I pulled her by the belt loops of her 501s. All lesbians wear 501s or at least own a pair. She laughed, and I, as if gobbling a grape, bit her cheek. "Don't ever call me Braxton without my permission."

She kissed me hard on the lips. I pulled back to keep her from tearing the lips off my head. Then she slipped her thigh between my thighs and lifted me off the floor. Sasha must have bounced me for half an hour on her thigh, because I felt my pelvis going numb.

"Do you cum in chocolate?" she asked me and finally stopped bouncing me.

"Come to the bathroom with me and you'll find out." I was grateful to have both feet back on the floor.

We walked hand in hand to the john. I put my hand out to open the door, and Sasha shoved me into the small room. She bent her blond head forward like she was about to reluctantly scold a child. "May I call you Braxton?" she asked in a calm, passive manner. But even through this new manner of hers, I knew she was as innocent as sin.

"Yes, you may," I answered, as if granting permission to a schoolgirl. I was scared to death of this aggressive, genteel woman.

She gently rubbed the back of my hand and whispered in my ear, "I have to pee-pee."

I took her to the stall, pulled down her pants, and sat her on the toilet. "Does that feel better?" I asked, and stroked her hair.

She nodded, then stood up with her legs straddling the commode. "Here." She stuck a wad of toilet paper in my hand. "Wipe, please." She sounded like a little toddler and was arousing the hell out of me.

I wiped her ass, and she grabbed me and threw a French kiss down my throat. "Better?" I asked again after she released me.

"Braxton, do you want to come to my house?" She was being charming and innocent again. I was shaking in my pants.

I led her by the hand to the sink, and we washed our hands. "We'd better just go dance," I said, thinking that my mother would have a heart attack if I went home with this woman and wound up in the obituary column: *Young Black lesbian dies of welts from rider's crop. Police amazed to find the victim wearing a smile and little else.* I giggled out loud.

"What is it?" Sasha was still playing toddler, and her voice was timid and small, but as provocative as a sleigh ride.

I laughed. "I was just thinking...My mother would shit a brick if she knew we were—" She gave me a hard look. "Uh...'bout to have this much fun."

Sasha dried her hands on my pants, and we ran out to the dance floor. The music was Top 40 and loud. Sasha bounced me around on her thigh some more. "I wasn't joking about wanting to fuck you," she said, and stopped jumping around.

"I'm really not into violence, especially S/M," I said.

Sasha caught my arm. "Braxton, I wouldn't hurt you." This was the first sign of her charm and gentleness returning. I mean her real charm, which had previously got me looking in her direction.

"Sasha, I've never been with an S/M woman, and I'm not into pain at all." She started to say something, but I stopped her. "Dance with me."

I put my arms around her neck, and she put her arms around my waist. "I've never been with a Black woman, so we're even."

"This makes us both virgins of a sort."

"Do you want to fuck me? I thought you wanted me when we were at the Riv."

"If you take me home with you and promise to be gentle with me," I said, "I'll agree to cum peacefully!"

"I'll go easy for your first time with an aggressive dyke."

"No ropes, whips, rider's crops, chains, sticks, none of that stuff—just fucking."

"All right, nothing too kinky."

We looked into each other's eyes. I kissed one corner of her mouth and then the middle and proceeded to tongue one lip at a time. She started climbing my body, and both of us slowly pressed into each other's muffs. We gyrated to the music. When the music got faster we dry-humped to that rhythm as well.

I was more than warm. I felt my pussy dribbling with want for her. "You're turning me on," I said, though that was obvious to her about 10 songs ago.

"The feeling is mutual. Say goodbye to your friends, and let's get the hell out of here." Her breath was low and hot.

I grabbed my coat off a chair. Sasha arm wrestled me for the right to put her coat on. I was saying goodbye to my friends, yes—all the Terris with various spellings—and Sasha waved her group and stood in front of me and pulled my arm. "Can't I finish saying goodbye?"

"Let's have a fucking happy evening." She nibbled my ear, grabbed me by the arm, and hurriedly led me toward the door so all I could do was wave to the rest of my friends from across the room.

We went to her place, and before the front door was closed we were both naked. We sprinted to her bedroom and dove under the covers. Then we sprang out and went to the bathroom to wash our hands, brush our teeth, and wash our faces. We jumped back into bed.

Sasha climbed on top of me, and we started moving up and down against each other gently. I drew a deep breath. My breathing was getting faster, and so was Sasha's motion. She started thrusting. "Let's see how tough you really are."

She was bucking pretty hard, so stopping was out of the question. In fact, I would have been in danger had I let go of her. I yelled every time she bucked. The ceiling was getting low.

"Damn, this is fun." She bucked hard. "Ride her, cowgirl." The two of us and the mattress went crashing to the floor.

"Sasha," I whispered, trying to alert her that we were on the floor.

"Oh, I like it when you say my name," she said, and kept bucking. The mattress was bouncing on the floor.

"Sasha," I said a little louder and thought about unwrapping my arms from her.

"Say my name some more." Her voice rose three octaves, and she thrust and bucked harder.

"Sa-ha-she-ha!" I hollered.

She bucked one final time and said "Wow!" in a high-pitched voice.

"The mattress is on the floor!" I told her.

"You're right. It is." She looked at me with an "I've got a secret" grin. "Shall we?" We both looked at the mattress on the floor, picked it up, and placed it back on the bed frame. "I've got some handcuffs," she cheerfully announced, and took a couple of steps toward the closet.

"Oh, no, you don't," I said, and put my arms around her waist. "None of that stuff. Just fucking, remember?"

"Thought you might have changed your mind."

"Come here," I whispered.

She was already in my arms, so she faced and kissed me. I relaxed in her arms, and she tackled me on the bed. "You have nice shoulders."

"Thank you," I giggled, because Sasha was tickling me. She abruptly stopped and grabbed me by the muscle between my neck and shoulders so hard I jumped. "You're still feisty."

I pushed her arms off my head. "Knock that off."

She pinched my buttocks hard, and I yelled. "I didn't know you were so sensitive."

"Sensitive, hell. That hurts."

She moved close to me, and I relaxed in her body warmth. "I'm not going to hurt you," she assured me.

"I'm not giving you the chance."

"You're a wimp, aren't you?"

"Didn't we have this talk before?" I asked, and rolled over so that I was on top of her.

"Refresh me," she demanded, and rolled on top of me.

"At the bar?"

"The bar? The bar?" She pinched my buttock, and I pushed my butt into hers.

"Perry's."

"Oh, that bar." She arched her back. I slid up and down her body.

"Yeah, that bar where you said you wanted to fuck my Black ass."

"Wanna arm wrestle?" she asked.

"No!"

"Let's just plain wrestle."

We came to all fours and flipped and turned each other upside down. Every so often we'd make contact at, let's just say, points of interest. When we got to hands and knees, Sasha straddled my head, and before I could blink, her pussy was touching my lips. It's really difficult to have meaningful cunnilingus when the cunt approaching one's lips is pulsing up and down at 90 miles a minute. We grappled on the floor, and she took a huge bite of my breast.

"Shit!"

"Now, that little nip didn't hurt you." Her fingers were crooked like claws, her teeth half bared under a devious smile.

"Sasha, you promised to go easy with me."

"Fooled ya." She sprang toward me and pulled my earlobes.

"You S/M maniac, fuck fair or I'm going home."

She twisted my arm behind my back until I yelled uncle, aunt, niece, somebody—anybody. "Are you scared, Braxton?"

"Truthfully?" I asked, looking up without moving my head. "I'm getting a smidge afraid."

"Good." She pulled my arm back until it resisted. Somehow she got me into a headlock. I kicked her in the shin with my bare heel, and she let go of my arm.

"Stop it."

The golden-haired white woman assumed the stance of

a ninja. "Fight like a dyke," she said, and came charging straight at me.

I mentally apologized to my mother for all the times I played with the Lord. "Sasha, I'm not into this."

She set herself for a drop kick. Her body was flying toward me. I was suddenly faced with a life-or-death decision.

"I can take you," she said from mid air.

I grabbed her arm and flipped her over. I don't know how, but she did three somersaults, and I wound up holding her over my head. I let her fall to the floor. I stared at her naked body. "Oh, shit." I felt for her pulse and checked to see if she was still breathing.

Sasha was not only breathing, she was in a state of high arousal. She got on her knees, clasped my hands, and said, "Make me your slave."

"Your what? Sasha, are you all right?"

"You're the only person who's been able to tame me." She bowed her head.

This was getting to be too much, even for me. I knelt in front of her. Our eyes locked. I stroked her cropped blond head. Her hair was soft and wet from sweat. "Sasha, all I wanted was for you to rummage my bones."

"Yeah, I only wanted you to fuck my lights out too."

I picked her up in my arms and carried her to bed. She looked into my eyes all the way there.

"Hi, I'm Braxton. But people call me B-Jay, and I'd love to fuck your lights out," I said, and gently lowered her.

"Pleased to meet you. I'm Sasha, and I'll help you fuck my lights out."

I kissed her lips. "No torpedo-thrusting." I nibbled the corners of her mouth and swept my tongue down her chin and lightly brushed her throat from side to side.

"I don't know how you put up with me. My wife thinks I'm too rough, so we hardly ever have sex."

"Good things are worth waiting for," I said. My tongue,

still roving, found its way to her juicy breasts. I wrapped my lips around her nipple and lightly sucked the tip until it was erect. I felt my clit swell as Sasha kept working her pelvis back and forth.

"Braxton, I'm really sorry about that rough stuff."

I kept sucking and nibbling her breasts. My tongue flowed down and over her rapturous body. It made way to her hairy, moist pussy. I parted her labia with my fingers. My tongue slid into the little pee hole and lapped the already dripping love juice. She made a guttural moan. "You...ah ha...saw a wild side of me to...night...mmm. I'm not...always like that."

I tongued her clit, and her hips went back and forth in rapid, hard thrusts.

"Oh, you taste good," I said, and pushed my tongue into her soft pussy hole.

"Go deeper...come...Oh!" She clutched my head and dug her fingers into my scalp. I screamed and she came.

We lay face-to-face for a second, both breathing hard and fast. I, on top of this sensuous blond, her body warm, firm, and supple. Every muscle in my tummy woke up as she rode my mound. "You feel so good," I said as our bodies slipped and smacked from perspiration.

"Sasha, ohhhh...aaaaooooh...Shhh...shut up and fuck...Ooooahh..."

"Bra...aaa...xxx...ton...Ohaaah...Merry Christmas...you're aaahhh...the best..."

We bumped and ground and went in and out of each other all night long.

*Issue: Summer 1988*

## My Woman Poppa
by Joan Nestle

*My woman poppa is 13 years younger than I, but she is wise in her woman-loving ways.*

You work at a job that makes your back rock-hard strong; you work with men in a cavernous warehouse, loading trucks while others sleep. Sometimes when you come to me while I work at home, you fall asleep in my bed on your stomach, the sheet wrapped around your waist, the flaming unicorn on your right shoulder catching the afternoon sun.

I just stand and look at you, at your sleeping face and kind hands, my desire growing for you, for my woman poppa who plays the drums and knows all the words to "Lady in Red," who calls me sassafras mama—even when I am sometimes too far from the earth—who is not frightened of my years or my illness.

My woman poppa who knows how to take me in her arms and lay me down, knows how to spread my thighs and then my lips, who knows how to catch the wetness and use it and then knows how to enter me so women waves rock us both.

My woman poppa who is not afraid of my moans or my nails but takes me and takes me until she reaches far beyond the place of entry into the core of tears. Then as I come to her strength and woman fullness, she kisses away my legacy of pain. My cunt and heart and head are healed.

My woman poppa who does not want to be a man but who does travel in "unwomanly" places and who does "unwomanly" work. Late into the New Jersey night, she maneuvers the forklift to load the thousands of pounds of aluminum into the hungry trucks that stand waiting for her. Dressed in the shiny tiredness of warehouse blue, with her company's name white-stitched across her pocket, she endures the bitter humor of her fellow workers who are men. They laugh at Jews, at women, and, when the Black workers are not present, at Blacks. All the angers of their lives, all their dreams gone dead, bounce off the warehouse walls. My woman grits her teeth and says when the rape jokes come: "Don't talk that shit around me."

When she comes home to me, I must caress the parts of her that have been worn thin, trying to do her work in a man's world. She likes her work, likes the challenge of the machines and the quietness of the night, likes her body moving into power. When we go to women's parties, I watch amused at the stares she gets when she answers the traditional question "What do you do?" with her nontraditional answer, "I load trucks in a warehouse." When the teachers and social workers no longer address their comments to her, I want to shout at them: Where is your curiosity about women's lives, where is your wonder at boundaries broken?

My woman poppa is 13 years younger than I, but she is wise in her woman-loving ways. Breasts and ass get her hot, that wonderful hot that is a heard and spoken desire. I make her hot and I like that. I like her sweat and her tattoos. I like her courtliness and her disdain of the boys. I mother her and wife her and slut her, and together we are learning to be comrades.

She likes me to wear a black slip to bed, to wear dangling earrings and black stockings with sling-back heels when we play. She likes my perfume and lipstick and nail polish. I enjoy these slashes of color, the sweetened place in my neck where she will bury her head when she is moving on me. I sometimes sit on her, my cunt open on her round belly, my breasts hanging over her, my nipples grazing her lips. I forbid her to touch me and continue to rock on her, my wetness smearing her belly. She begins to moan and curves her body upward, straining at the restrictions.

"Please, baby, please," my woman poppa begs. "Please let me fuck you." Then suddenly, when she has had enough, she smiles, opens her eyes, says "You have played enough," and, using the power she has had all along, throws me from my throne.

Sometimes she lies in bed wearing her cock under the covers. I can see its outline under the pink spread. I just stand in my slip watching her, her eyes getting heavy. Then I sit alongside her, on the edge of the bed, telling her what a wonderful cock she has, as I run my hand down her belly until I reach her lavender hardness. I suck her nipple and slowly stroke her, tugging at the cock so she can feel it through the leather triangle that holds it in place.

"Let me suck you," I say, my face close to hers, my breasts spilling out on hers. "Let me take your cock in my mouth and show you what I can do." She nods, almost as if her head is too heavy to move.

Oh, my darling, this play is real. I do long to suck you, to take your courage into my mouth, both cunt, your flesh, and cock, your dream, deep into my mouth, and I do. I throw back the covers and bend over her carefully so she can see my red lips and red-tipped fingers massaging her cock. I take one of her hands and wrap it around the base so she can feel my lips as I move on her. I give her the best I can, licking the lavender cock its whole length and slowly tonguing the tip, circling it with my tongue. Then I take her fully into my mouth, into my throat. She moans, moves, tries to watch, and cannot as the image overpowers her. When I have done all I can, I bend the wet cock up on her belly and sit on her so I can feel it pressing against my cunt. I rock on her until she is ready, and then she reaches down and slips the cock into me. Her eyes are open now, wonderfully clear and sharp, and she slips her arms down low around my waist so I am held tight against her. Very slowly she starts to mover her hips upward in short, strong thrusts. I am held on my pleasure by her powerful arms; I can do nothing but move and take and feel. When she knows I have settled in, she moves quicker and quicker, her breath coming in short, hard gasps. But I hear the words "Oh, baby, you are so good to fuck."

I forget everything but her movements. I fall over her, my head on the pillow above her. I hear sounds, moans, shouted words, know my fists are pounding the bed, but I am unaware of forming words or lifting my arms. I ride and ride harder and faster, encircled by her arms, by her gift.

"Give it all to me. Let it all go," I know she is saying. I hear a voice answering "You you you you," and I am pounding the bed, her arms, anything I can reach. How dare you do this to me, how dare you push me beyond my daily voice, my daily body, my daily fears. I am chanting; we are dancing. We have broken through.

Then it is over. We return, and gently she lifts me off her belly. I slide down her body, rest, and then release her from the leather. We sleep.

Yes, my woman poppa knows how to move me, but she knows many other things as well. She knows she will not be shamed; she knows her body carries complicated messages. My woman poppa, my dusty sparrow, I know how special you are. Your strength, both of loving and of need, is not mistaken for betrayal of your womanness.

*Issue: Winter 1988*

## Loved I Not Honor More
by Rebecca Ripley

*Their eyes locked, suddenly alive with a passion more demanding than Stern had ever felt for a civilian.*

Stern woke, stiff and shaken, and swore she would never again captain a spaceship on a military mission. Nothing paid a ship captain better than troop transport work, but it was beginning to wear her soul. No matter how limited her official responsibilities, she always got involved in planning and often in fighting. This mission had left her drained, discouraged, physically and emotionally exhausted.

She unstrapped herself, hands moving on automatic, and forcibly focused her bleary eyes, squinting first at the clock. The readouts showed the ship still on course. Regulations required the captain to ensure that the ship was secured for space and that all other personnel safely were in storage before going into storage herself. That was Stern's next job, but it had to wait. Her body had its own priorities, too long ignored.

She walked down empty hallways to the galley, where she gulped protein goo on a tasteless wafer, washing it down with heavily sugared coffee. At the shower room door a blue "In Use" indicator momentarily surprised her. She had assumed the four survivors of the marine detachment were sacked out in their own quarters. She shrugged and opened the shower door.

Before her one of the four nozzles hissed out a cloud of floating droplets, half-hiding a short, brown, muscular body. It was Gonzalez. A temperamental, egotistical kid, merciless in her judgments but rock steady in a fight. During the mission she had treated Stern with decreasingly hostile respect.

Stern nodded and went about stripping off her filthy uniform. Gonzalez grunted a greeting back, slopping sap on her short black hair.

While they were both toweling off, Gonzalez suddenly turned to Stern. "You did good, for a civilian."

A reprimand rose to Stern's lips, but she stopped it. Gonzalez's clear voice held no sarcasm, her wide sculptured lips no sneer. Her deep-set eyes reflected only honest admiration.

Stern looked at Gonzalez as if for the first time. Her gaze wandered across the young woman's strong face, her compact body, and back up to her electric brown eyes. Gonzalez, Stern realized with a surprise, was a strikingly handsome woman. She hid it with her usual rough manner. Stern couldn't mistake her intention in dropping the mask.

The tension that still gripped Stern lightened up a little. Her job kept her lonely, professionally remote, and her tall frame and severe face made her seem aloof. It was more than a mask. Unlike some captains, she never fraternized with any of the troops her ship carried. Even so, she needed human contact.

"You did well too," she said with a slow smile, "for a bunch of grunts."

Their eyes locked, suddenly alive with a passion more demanding than Stern had ever felt for a stranger. She tricked occasionally, casually. But this wasn't tricking. An irresistible tide flowed through her. It obliterated memories of scorched, cratered battlefields, of lifeless forms left on poisoned worlds. Stern didn't fraternize with the troops. The thought flew away as their lips met.

Desire so strong it felt like need propelled them onto, into, around each other. Crumpled towels and tile made enough of a bed. They pressed only lightly on the hard deck, careless of how they lay on each other. Stern wrapped herself around Gonzalez and came quickly against her leg, shuddering, head thrown back, a fast, needed release. Gonzalez began to stroke her more slowly, but Stern shook her head. "My turn." Need still drove her, a force stronger even than sickness. She dove for Gonzalez's cunt like a desert-parched woman finding a bottomless well.

She licked soft, then hard and steady, teasing, insisting, until Gonzalez's breath caught up with the rhythm of her tongue. She held her there on the edge till Gonzalez gripped Stern's head and pushed it down against herself, coming hard, cursing softly.

While they sprawled entangled, breathing slowly, the door creaked open, and a low, slightly hoarse voice, said, "Starting without me?"

Gonzalez laughed, and Stern opened her eyes to see Jones, the little marine pilot, still wearing rumpled, sweat-splotched fatigues and the reflective shades she never took off. Jones was the type that turned Stern on, remote and cocky, a challenge. She felt a fleeting, automatic lust for her.

"Just warming her up," Gonzalez said lightly, but with a sensual undertone. She turned on her elbow to look matter-of-factly at Stern. "It's share and share alike in the Corps."

Stern heard the challenge even before she caught the meaning. These two wanted to make it with her. Together. Her first thought was to tell them to stuff it. She picked her own women. She could live with the lingering sexual tension. Preserve her professional distance.

Anger must have shown on her face. Gonzalez, still lying easily on the deck, snapped a salute and leered half-jokingly, "At the Captain's pleasure, of course."

What the hell. Stern's distance was already lost, and she didn't need it back yet.

"Right," she said decisively, putting more than a hint of command in her voice. She swept her eyes over Jones, who stood, feet planted apart, looking tough, with a know-it-all smile. "Go wash up, and I'll take you under consideration.'

When Jones came dripping out of the shower, Stern sized her up, watching her slip into a clean tank top, covering her firm little breasts with a neat, efficient gesture. She was broad-shouldered, short-legged, long-waisted, with an opaque round face and mousy brown hair, as pale and plain as Gonzalez was brown and beautiful. And as distant, even secretive, as Gonzalez was open and vibrant. Reflective like her shades.

"Over here," Stern ordered, suddenly shy when Jones obeyed, dropping down next to her on the deck. Where did you begin with two women?

Gonzalez leaned over Stern to grab at Jones's shades. Jones swept her hand away and twisted toward Stern. Stern barely dodged, came back and grabbed Jones's waist, while Gonzalez got her legs. The three of them tussled a few minutes, competing eagerly for the first squeezes. Jones was a biter, leaving Stern starred with fresh bruises. As soon as she got Jones down, Stern gave back as good as she'd gotten.

At last they slowed into a sensual rhythm, with Stern nibbling her way down Jones's shoulder, whisking one hand down her belly. Gonzalez flopped onto one of the benches against the wall, watching.

Stern pushed up Jones's tank top and cupped one barely round breast. Jones made a scarcely audible gasp as Stern rolled the stiff nipple between her fingers. She raked her fingernails down Jones's belly, then stroked back to uncover the other breast. Jones gasped again, louder, then snapped into action. She pulled Stern close with both strong arms and kissed her dizzyingly, rolling on top, thrusting her furry wet cunt against Stern's thigh, her leg pressing Stern's clit.

The moment of truth. "Not yet," Stern whispered, raking Jones's back. "I have plans for you."

"What plans?" Jones shot back, grinding expertly against her. Stern steadied her voice. "I'll show you."

Hands against Jones's shoulders, she forced her onto her back, then looked down savoring the moment. Jones hadn't tried to stop her.

Their legs twined together while Stern pursued her strategy, pushing softly against Jones's cunt, stroking up her body to her face, her hair, her eyes. Stern picked her time, then reached firmly for the wraparound shades. Jones made no move to resist. Stern sent them slowly tumbling through the air to Gonzalez, who casually caught them grinning.

Jones's shallow, close-set eyes were a deep, clear green. Alive with lust, Stern urged her legs apart with one hand, still holding her gaze. Jones took in four fingers, eagerly, her muscular, round legs flung carelessly apart. The smile melted into a moan.

"If you want more, you have to ask for it."

Jones pulled her cool together. "I can take it, ma'am. I'm a marine."

Stern began to work her thumb in, then stopped and slid it back out when Jones flushed, a red cascade tumbling down her face to her chest. Stern let her hand back in to explore the rings of internal cunt muscle, noting which spots made Jones jerk and shudder. She lazily stroked the pink little clit with her thumb until Jones's every breath was a moan. Stern pulled her hand slowly, then pushed back in, aiming her longest finger for the hottest spot, until Jones grabbed her arm with both hands, forcing it in and rising to meet it. Stern's cunt clenched its own demand as she pushed in all the way.

As Jones's belly started to rise and her legs began to tremble, Stern pulled out, to a groan of frustration, waited a beat, then eased herself full-length on top of Jones and went back into motion, riding her hard. Jones bucked against Stern, arms and legs clutching, and threw them both onto their sides.

Stern grunted as the corner of a bench struck her shoulder. She sat upright, clutching the bruise.

"You've gotta hold *on*, mate," Gonzalez called mockingly from the sideline.

"You OK?" Jones asked in a blurry whisper.

"Let me show you just how OK," Stern said, ignoring the fading pain. Jones flashed her old smart-ass smile as she grabbed Stern's legs with her own. Stern clamped Jones's wrists, holding herself up on her elbows, watching desperation and then relief wash all the hotshot-pilot look from her face. Jones groaned, and Stern stopped for a hard kiss. She forgot her shoulder. Power radiated from under her ribs, and she went over into her own orgasm.

Jones shuddered to a slow stop. Stern stroked her side and got no response. The girl was out, and Stern was barely there. She rolled onto her back to let some of the sweat dry, then lazily reached to pet Jones's damp hair, curling slightly in the steamy air. After a few minutes, Jones, eyes still closed, neatly pulled her damp, crumpled tank top down and sat up on her elbows, blinking.

"Hey, Jonesie," Gonzalez called.

Jones reached out her right hand. Gonzalez tossed her the shades. They fell slowly, rotating, and Jones picked them out of the air and put them back on. Stern smiled to herself and shook her head at the on-again, off-again cool.

"All right, you Venusian whores," Jones said, "I'm gonna get some grub."

Half an hour later they were settled in the galley around an instant dinner. At first they shoveled quietly away. Stern hadn't thought she could still care enough to get this hungry, to even taste what she ate. She had been wrong.

After a while they slowed down, sprawled comfortably on the benches, downing the last scraps, licking fingers. Too full for anything except coffee and talking. Gonzalez and Stern did most of the talking, trading stories of sex they'd had, boastful and animated. Jones didn't talk much except to reinforce Gonzalez's stories of shared adventures. After half an hour, Stern began to feel sleepy. Maybe she'd get some normal sack before cleaning up and stripping for storage.

Gonzalez, leaning close to Jones, punched her arm. "You know who the best sex ever was with?"

"Naw, who?"

"With you, asshole!" Gonzalez sang, reaching for Jones in a mock attack. Stern felt a moment of stinging hurt feelings, then shrugged it off. It made sense. If they fucked each other a lot, they knew how to make each other feel good. Hearing it might have bothered Stern half an hour before, but her natural reserve had returned with physical satisfaction.

Jones met Gonzalez's attack, laughing. They wrestled like young dogs, rough and fast, hitting the deck harmlessly. Like kids, they were completely absorbed. Suddenly they were fucking, humping each other's thighs, kissing. It wasn't the hard way Stern had kissed Jones, nor the driven way she had kissed Gonzalez, but something softer than she'd expected from either of them. Gonzalez's square hand rested on Jones's butt, her lips pressed to her neck. Jones's tight little smile dissolved, then reformed, serene and ecstatic, while Gonzalez watched with a look of pride and tenderness that made Stern feel wintry inside. How long since anyone had looked at her that way? Or since she had looked that way at anyone?

"Goddamn, you're good, Jonesie," Gonzalez said softly, thrusting her cunt against Jones's leg. Jones clasped her, pressing her knee, taking her home. The curve of her shoulder bent over Gonzalez showed everything her face tried to hide. Those two were in love.

Either of them could die on any mission, incinerated or shredded right next to the other. Could they afford to know they loved each other? Could they let themselves in for that much pain? No, Stern decided, they were soldiers. Sex was so routine, so communal to them, it must be a kind of camouflage.

No fuck could mean that much. They could allow themselves pleasure, but not softening, nothing that might attach them to life. And she had been getting like them.

Jones's knees went lax, and she slid to the deck. Gonzalez rested for a breath, then gathered her up and stroked her awake. They lay satisfied in each other's arms. A hell of a place for young love to take root, Stern thought in disgust. A hell of a way to live.

"Come on," she said, more roughly than she'd meant. "We'd better get ready for storage."

Gonzalez raised her head abruptly from Jones's shoulder, with a puzzled, even wounded look, so suddenly vulnerable it surprised Stern. Jones turned toward Stern open-mouthed. For half a second they hesitated, then snapped to the discipline of their encapsulated world and scrambled obediently to their feet.

Stern felt ashamed. It showed how the job had gotten to her. But the job was no excuse. There was no excuse for carelessness with power.

The marines were used to jumping when ordered. They were used to taking what they could get, when they could get it, in the chinks between their duty hours. They couldn't afford to know they were in love because all they ever had was the moment. And Stern had taken one moment away from them, snapping her rank like a whip. She hadn't even given them enough credit to expect them to care.

Whether or not they cared didn't matter. What mattered was Stern's self-respect. Petty selfishness didn't become her dignity as a ship's officer or as a human being.

She made herself smile, waving her hand down, a gesture to wipe away the order. "Forget it, there's still time. Carry on."

Gonzalez broke into a grin. One good-looking woman, Stern thought again.

"Sure will, Captain," Jones said, circling Gonzalez's waist with her arm. Stern looked at them, hiding a rush of longing. She had entered military life nearly as young as they had, but now she was a civilian contractor, not a soldier. She could quit anytime. They couldn't until their enlistments were up. They didn't want to, but that didn't change the fact that they couldn't.

"You in with us?" Gonzalez asked expectantly

"No, thanks," Stern started to yawn. "I'm wiped out. Gonna get some sack. Be ready for storage—" She glanced at the time. "—at 1400 hours."

Ten hours of freedom. Her gift to their unacknowledged love. On impulse she added, "This is my last troop-hauling trip. I'll be switching to shorter runs. Be home a lot. Look me up if you get the chance."

"Thanks, Captain," Gonzalez said quietly. Jones echoed her with a happy "Yeah." Stern felt satisfied. She had shared what she could with them. She gave them a dismissing nod and turned toward the door and her future.

*Issue: March/April 1989*

## Faith
by Home Girl

*I'd push into her cunt and ass, and she'd dance on my hand.*

"A faithful friend is a strong defense."

She shared with me that little bit of wisdom she got from a fortune cookie she opened on New Year's Eve 1987. She got it at a closet party she went to after a fast fuck with me. Everyone at the party was a woman. Eight of them. At least four passing for straight, including her and her "girlfriend," who'd been going at it undercover for 15 years, and two of their friends who were tearing each other up in public ways that disappointed lovers, not girlfriends, do. But no one, you understand, was a lesbian.

She hated the word, but she loved me. I was her freak. The genuine lesbian who ate her out even when she was on the rag, even the first time we made love. That first time, I was acting out a wet dream I'd had about her, lying between her legs, tonguing her and looking up into her hard face, pulling her legs and ass around my shoulders. It woke me up with all the force of a wet dream: heart pounding, sweating bullets, throbbing sex. I was defenseless with her. She fucked my soul before we ever laid hands on each other.

We were friends from work. We had a lot in common. We were both white trash. Catholic school background. Same high school, in fact, even though we'd never crossed paths there. She had graduated a year ahead of me. A baby butch even then, she was basketball co-captain. I was a brain. When we met, we were in our 30s, making progress from nowhere, but not fast. Ambitious, smart, but lazy.

When she let herself go with me, she was loose with her love talk, but still stingy with her love, with no guts for trouble, a coward about feeling queer toward me, about being queer herself. If I believe her, I made her feel her cunt like nobody else, man or woman, maybe even her long-nailed self. I meant to fuck her.

She was the first person to ever make me want to wear handcuffs. And I did. I grabbed her hands with my cuffed hands, after she locked them, and ran the bonds over her neck and back while she did me. I wanted to hurt her with the passion I felt.

Sometimes now I want to make her feel sorry for the way she fucked me over. There may be no way back to the fortune cookie, because we went way beyond friends.

We got to fucking at work and in public with abandon—slapping each other, leg fucking, hard kissing. At work, for chrissake, with her in her cop uniform, with me playing at being a professional.

We sparked each other in a hotel bathroom, in dark corners, at the beach, in parked cars, in other people's houses, under her mother's nose, in public garages. There was one time we went at it so long and with such recklessness in a garage that a car pulled up behind us and flashed its headlights. Once on a beach, with cops coming in on one side and wild boys on the other, we were in each other's pants, wiggling around on the front seat. One of the boys pulled up right next to us and called, "Hey, John!" We froze.

"Bug off, you bastard," she growled back, digging deep down in her throat for an appropriately raspy voice. Yeah. She handled it like the pro I know she was.

We could have been the best of friends, the wildest of

lovers. But faithful? No, we never could have lived up to that fortune cookie's wisdom. She—who went down on her knees to lick me, who begged me to do her, who spread on all fours in front of me, who rode my fingers while I reamed her cunt and ass, who loved me so hard—doesn't talk to me now. She doesn't want to see me. She came out of her closet, screaming, laughing for joy, and then slammed the door in my face. I want to believe it meant something, that I meant something to her.

She was a coward. But her sex was so strong. She kissed hard and with talent. I'd push into her cunt and ass, and she'd dance on my hand. We talked tough love to each other. She was wild.

But then it started going weird. Loving me meant fighting for her passing way of life with the other "girlfriend," who was crying, fighting, and threatening her. For months we'd pull apart then rush back headlong at each other. Finally, there was a lull in the drama. We were sitting in her car. We were tense. At this delicate moment she reached over and rooted in my winter clothes for some skin. She fingered my hand. The feel of her skin and her sweat slammed me. I shut my eyes and moaned. The woman had a direct line to my cunt. I wanted to undo her. To get rid of the half-ass, white-trash clothes, the high-heel sneakers, to get her going with my lips on her ears, in her armpits, in the palm of her hand—get her hot and then, for payback, back off.

She beat me to it. She cut me off cold. She skinned me. I hope the thought of me bothers her, that I fuck her up. Girl, you reamed out a new way to my heart. My heart flew out the hole to you. You threw it back in my face when it got tough. I want to remember the exhilaration I felt with you, the mainline pleasure. I'm not sure I'll ever get it as good again. I'll probably look for someone like you, or even for you, for a long time. Maybe a better dresser, with good teeth, quicker—someone who could up me. Unlike you, you lying, half-ass, cowardly player. I miss you. I miss your company. I miss your fuck. I miss believing in you. You should have kept your faith.

*Issue: March/April 1989*

## Cactus Love
by Lee Lynch

*She kissed me again, and I smelled the iced coffee and felt her sweat and the heat of our bodies in the trailer's hot air.*

Until Saturday I'd have bet my bottom dollar I was a washout. It had been 10 years since I touched my last woman. I just didn't have the energy for love. Too much like walking barefoot onto a cactus in the dark.

Then Van came, with her youth and her brains. I hired her to run the retail end of my cactus ranch. That left me free to spend all of my time on the growing, the watering, and—well, soon I ran out of things to do. I'd watch that young body run around enjoying the heck out of life. That was October, right after her breakup with Ivy, and already she was back in the saddle.

I can see her standing in the bright sunlight outside my trailer, one foot on the metal step, saying, "I'm going down to the bar tonight. Want to bet I find a lover by Christmas?" What'd she do then? Went out and got one. I confess the girl's been an inspiration to me. I decided to go out and get one too.

That's when I met Patsy.

Whoopee! I feel like dancing with my cactuses.

Patsy is older than me by a couple of years, but she doesn't look like anyone's cute little grandma. Van called her the

Matriarch, from the way the young ones at the bar would chew her ear.

I watched Patsy.

I liked looking at her, sitting straight as a ruler's edge at the bar. She's part Irish, part Zuni Indian, tall but very skinny. Her bones are so broad and strong looking you'd think she was some desert wild thing. Maybe that's what put me off at first. I'd always been one for younger, femmier types. But Patsy, she's beyond all that. She's not butch, not femme. She's no garden-variety female at all. She's a monument. I could listen to her talk about her life all night...

But it wasn't listening I did that first night.

She had about as much stomach as I did for that smoky, loud joint with its watered-down country jukebox. She always left around 11, just before it got real loud and wild. I'd decided after the first few times I saw her that I wanted at least to talk to her. The next time I went to the bar, I dithered and dithered. Before I know it, it's 11 and she's leaving and I can't think of a thing to say to her anywhere as good as "Would you like to dance?" I'd missed my chance. So I let it go another week.

But you know, she started coming into my head a lot that week. When I was in bed at night I'd imagine her, with that long, strong body next to me on the white sheets. I imagined the life story she'd tell. And I imagined her hands on me. I'd noticed them when I was next to her at the bar ordering drinks. The beginnings of arthritis: a little stiffness, knobbiness. Still, you got the feeling that it wouldn't stop her. I could feel the seasoned fingers on my hip, on the parts of me that were never this cushiony for my earlier girlfriends. I kind of just ran her through my head, to see if I'd like it, or if I only wanted her because we were close in age. I'd get wiggly at the thought of Patsy's touch. Not many women can seep into my head like she did, in the dark.

So the next Saturday night, I asked her to dance. She

looked down at me and said nothing, nothing at all. But there was a little smile that puckered the corner of her mouth. And those brown eyes like polished jasper looked like they were laughing. Then she swept me out there and danced me around those young couples like she'd put me on wheels. I never felt so light on my feet. That darned woman took my breath away. I never wanted the dance to end.

I asked her back to our table. Van was sweet-talking her lover-to-be, so they didn't pay us much attention. Luckily, it had taken me 'til 10:30 to buttonhole Patsy. By this time it was getting on toward 11 P.M. I told her about my business, asked her if she'd seen a cactus ranch by moonlight.

"Well, no," she said, laughing. "I can't say that I have, or ever heard such a barefaced line."

It turned out she lived near the bar and didn't have a vehicle. I drove her out in Pickup Nellie, my old white Chevy. We parked behind one of the hothouses. Wonder of wonders, there was a moon shining down. Not quite full, but full enough. The moon looked like it was pounding up there, in time to my heart. The night was pretty darned hot for November.

We walked out on the desert a ways, without flashlights. She was wordless, quiet-moving. I was just enjoying the company, come what may. Big patches of yellow desert broom like earth moons glowed at our feet. We didn't go too far so as not to disturb any critters.

On the way back she took my hand. I thought I'd melt right there at her feet, like some little teenaged person.

"You want to come in?" I asked when we reached my trailer house.

"I didn't come all this way to turn around now," she replied, her teeth white against that sunburned-looking skin. There was a dog tooth missing. I thought of her moist tongue seeking out that empty spot, all around inside her mouth. Holy Toledo, I know I'm a goner when ideas like that creep up on me.

Patsy squints when she talks, like she's measuring you. "I've been noticing you at the bar," she said, over some iced coffee I threw together. "You're not my type at all."

I had to grin. "You're not my type either."

She nodded. "If there's one thing I've learned in life, it's that you have to take things as they come. It doesn't do to fight your spirit; it always gets its way. If it wants to go changing taste in women at the ripe old age of 69, well, then, I'm ready."

"Same here," I said. "I never wanted another girlfriend. All that heartache. But—" and I told her about Van's coming and about the blood that got stirred up in my veins. "I could take the lonesomes," I told her, " 'til I started wanting again."

"I hear you. I sit in my little apartment and tell myself I'll stay home with the cat, read a good book, watch the TV. I don't need that bar. It's not the liquor that draws me; half the time I order milk, trying to put some flesh on these bones." She lifted her arm so I could see the scrawniness under her striped jersey. "Maybe I feel useful there. The kids come and pour their hearts out to me. Sometimes they think they want to get me into bed, but to tell the truth, their energy drives me up the wall. I'd never get any peace."

She paused and set down her glass. "I'm thinking, little Windy Sands, maybe I could stand a change of pace."

I told you the lady was big. Those arms were long. She reached clear across my narrow tabletop. Now her eyes were like some wise bird's looking into mine for—I don't know what—some sort of sign, I suppose. Then she kissed me, a little shaky, from that distance, her hands kneading my shoulders. And I kissed her back, giving her everything I had to let her know it wasn't just the kids who wanted her.

I stood. Led her to the bedroom still with her hands on my shoulders, like she couldn't find her way without me.

"I guess we both know what comes next," I said, laughing. "But I'll keep the light out if you don't mind."

"Why, because you've got an old body?" she asked. "Hell, it's not even as old as mine!"

"Yeah, but you're slender as the needles on a piñon pine."

"I'm skinny, you mean. And I have scars."

She switched the light on. I saw her scars. An artery taken out of her leg for heart trouble. Gut trouble where she'd been sliced open a couple of times. That took my mind off me: I was whole, even with this body round and pale as another earth moon.

We lay full against each other, like we were hungry. Like we were on fire, and by pressing ourselves together we could put it out.

We held like that. We held like that for a long time. It felt so good, but it didn't put out my fire. The longer we held, the hotter I felt. I wondered if the same thing was happening to Patsy, but I knew I wouldn't find out 'til I reached between her legs, and it was too soon for that, old hands at this stuff or not.

After a while I started rubbing against her and rubbing against her, just the way we were, pressed together. She kissed me again, and I smelled the iced coffee and felt her sweat and the heat of our bodies in the trailer's hot air. Her skin felt slick, and marked like the moon. We kissed and pressed into each other. Then, swift as a crafty old rock dweller looking for shade, she wriggled her arm between us. Oh, she found out I was raring to go. I heard her exhale. I don't know for sure that she was excited before then, but hot ziggety if that didn't do it for her.

She took her lips from mine and started kissing and licking my neck and my face, her tongue in my ear, in my mouth. I rode the heel of her hand like she was some fine horse taking me out across the desert under the blue Arizona sky, taking me up a mountainside, green and lush like it gets over the east end of Tucson. We rode so fast I could hear the leaves stir from our passage until the sound of a rushing waterfall began to grow. She stopped so I could see, so I could feel, so I *was* that water falling from the mountain. Falling down and down and down and—

Ten years of bottled-up pleasure. Everything spilled out of me.

What I said after that was, "I'm too darn exhausted to turn over. Can we talk for a while?"

"Sure thing, Windy, if you have the breath to talk. Was that too much for you?"

"Not enough," I panted, "not hardly enough, Patsy."

It was the first time I heard that laugh of hers. The mysterious-sounding, low, back-of-the-throat laugh that reminds me of Frank Sinatra singing about "come-hither looks" in my younger days.

She began then, telling me about the place where she was raised in New Mexico. I tried to listen, but sleep glided over me like a red-tailed hawk onto a tasty pocket gopher.

I was out long enough for the moon to follow us to my bedroom, right inside the trailer window. Patsy fell asleep too.

Oh, the moonlight on that body. Patsy was less than slender; she was as bony as an ancient saguaro turned brown and ribby. Hips, shoulders, rib cage, and all made her like a cradle I just fit into. My hand waltzed over the juts and hollows of her. I felt weak—from exertion? Lust? Maybe all I needed was a little snack. No, I couldn't leave the sight before me, the white moonlight on the deep-toned body. She was handsome as all get-out.

It didn't take me long until one of my caresses woke her. She opened her eyes and groaned for me. I plunged in, wondering if she'd ever had babies—she was so big. Plunged in one finger, then two, then a third. She made herself smaller around me. I was too short to reach up and kiss her. I stroked harder, deeper, softer, slower, quicker. She brought her hands flat across my shoulders and drummed and drummed as she came.

"If I smoked," she said after a while, "I'd say that calls for a cigarette."

"Cigarette nothing, a 10-gun salute!"

We settled for my snack.

She sat up, all grins like a little kid going to a party. We padded to the kitchen bare-assed, dragged every darn thing out of the icebox we could find and had ourselves a feast.

Patsy didn't stop beaming the entire meal. What am I talking about? Looking at the gap in her teeth, the mussed gray hair, at those brown eyes like mirrors full of desert roads and pickup trucks, honky-tonk bars and jukebox-dancing women, full of 69 years of love and disappointment and love again—ah, jeez, I knew I'd found somebody who was going to make all of the mess and bother of love worthwhile.

*Issue: Sept./Oct. 1989*

## Erotic-Go-Round
by Susie Bright, Martha Courtot, Judith Stein, Jewelle
Gomez, Joan Nestle, Barbara LaRue, Sarah Schulman,
Elizabeth Pincus, Jan Stafford, Jess Wells, Mickey
Warnock, Rebecca Ripley, and Pat Califia

### Introduction
### by Susie Bright

Since my first Lesbian Fiction Clit-Quake, I've had the
pleasure of reviewing and publishing some of the best lesbian
literature I've ever read by women whose names have become
familiar over the past five years as first-rate contemporary
writers. I asked a few of my favorite writers to play a little
game with me for our fifth anniversary issue. I would send
out one sentence to the first writer, who would write a page
and leave her last sentence hanging.

Then I forwarded her last couple of sentences to the next
writer on the list, and they would continue with their own
erotic episode. No one would see the whole story or the list
of writers involved until it was completed.

Note that each piece of the story is credited to its author
along with the title of their most popular work from *On Our
Backs* and the issue that it appeared in. The author's credit
appears at the end of their contribution.

✣ ✣ ✣

If she hadn't bent over so far, she would have missed the
most powerful moment of the evening. Still smarting from the

whipping that Brenda administered to her backside, she was able to see, through the spread in her legs, an amazing assemblage of women, all naked and sweating under the lights. Their bodies gave off an odor of intense desire. Muscular legs moved toward her, encircling her. Women's hands lifted her off the floor. Some rubbed oils over her entire body, in every place where the whip had been, into every opening. The oil, heated by her own body, began to sting and fill her with a sensation to which she could give no name. Resisting the urge to tremble, she defiantly looked up at the circle of women. Not one had a naked face. Each was covered in a mask so complete, a mask of animal skin or bird feathers or some wild untamed thing, that she could not have remembered that under the masks were women; their brown and blond and black cunts were not facing her at eye level. The leopard woman, whose green eyes took her over and over again, scraped one of her long nails across her breast. A hawk-masked woman moved close to her, grabbed her hair tightly, and forced her to her knees. As the women moved closer, she could smell their heavy scent, a scent of Southern desire, desire that has been attic-bound too long and must have release, regardless of the consequences. It was the woman with the mask of a snake that would bring her into her own particular edge of pleasure and panic. The Snake-Woman's eyes were hooded and dark. Her hands moved roughly over her body, arousing her and withdrawing. Brushing her masked face against the surrendered...

—**Martha Courtot**
("The Telephone," Spring 1985)

...body of this woman, now crazed with fear and desire, the Snake-Woman suddenly realized that she had felt these feelings before, long, long ago. When she first knew of her desire for women, she had felt this same terror, this same desire. But not so intensely since that first time with a woman,

15 years before. Snake-Woman was torn between the heat of the moment and the fire of her memories. At the same time as her physical self moved toward the object of her lust, her mind drifted back to the first time her flesh pressed against the flesh of another woman.

It had been hot then, just as today. The burning sun had warmed Snake-Woman's skin just as it had today. She felt that same combination of languor and intense energy then as she did now, and she knew its source. Then, just as today, there was a throbbing between her legs, a tropical storm around her clitoris with floods of liquid heat pouring from her cunt. Then, as now, her desire was stronger than her fear, as she moved forward.

Snake-Woman's body pressed into Teshneh's waiting arms, and the rush of the physical sensation brought her back to the present moment.

Now her mind jumped from her first love to the woman in front of her. Snake-Woman was overwhelmed with the woman's heat, her softness, her taste, her strength. Their embrace became even closer, harder, their lips pressed together fiercely. Suddenly Teshneh thrust her tongue hard into Snake-Woman's mouth and probed deeply, hard and soft, hard and soft. Snake-Woman felt light-headed, dizzy; she wondered if she might faint. As if she knew, Teshneh pushed hard, and Snake-Woman was falling, falling backward. Still locked in Teshneh's embrace, lips still locked to Teshneh's warm mouth, Snake-Woman landed on the softest of beds. She was pinned down hard under Teshneh's large, soft body.

Snake-Woman freed one arm, then the other, and reached around Teshneh, stroking Teshneh's back, her head, her ass. Teshneh used her knee to part Snake-Woman's legs and shove her big thigh into Snake-Woman's cunt. Snake-Woman marveled, "Her thigh is so soft...so soft." Snake-Woman reached to grab Teshneh's breast and Teshneh responded...

—Judith Stein
("What Happens One Time," Summer 1984)

...by slapping Snake-Woman's cheek once, lightly but hard. Then Snake-Woman saw Teshneh grab six purple silk scarves.

She knew their significance and knew also she would be helpless now. Not before Teshneh's considerable physical and mental powers; and certainly not helpless before the strength of the lushly colored yet delicate vestments she now felt brushing her dark nipples. Snake-Woman was helpless against her own desire, and although Teshneh worked quickly, Snake-Woman growled with impatience. Left wrist first, tight against the mahogany, then right ankle, leaving her in an awkwardly vulnerable half-submission. She stretched her limbs giving Teshneh room to make the bindings even tighter. She sucked in her round stomach as one lurid sash was tied tightly around her waist.

"Eyes?"

Snake-Woman pondered the question for less than a second—to see the acts that fulfilled her desire or to perceive in darkness, allowing them to surprise, mystify, embellish themselves with their invisibility?

"Yes."

The room became lavender then black, and again Snake-Woman's throat rippled with a low sound. Later she would try to savor each move, languish in desire; first she simply needed—wildly. Needed in her head, her cunt.

"Now!" she commanded.

She felt Teshneh's weight as she dropped down and nuzzled between her heavy thighs. Teshneh's hands were broad and strong. She pulled apart the cunt lips as if they were tissue paper and sucked roughly at the red hard knot. Her tongue and teeth pushed and probed, bit and tormented. Snake-Woman began a soft, rhythmic moaning that pushed her further into desire. Her hips vibrated as Teshneh grabbed the scarf that bound her waist and held on as if riding a horse. Snake-Woman...

—Jewelle Gomez
("A Piece of Time," Summer 1984)

...screamed as she felt a purple orgasm sweep from Teshneh's mouth through her cunt, all the while aware of the others watching, but she did not care as her hips rose and rose again to take all the pleasure from Teshneh's lips. She wrapped her hands around Teshneh's head, pushed her deeper and deeper into her wetness. The others pressed closer, aware of the wonder they were seeing, the outpouring of Snake-Woman's lust on Teshneh's lips. They breathed in and let out gasps as if it were their collective body that was finding its release. Teshneh, aware of Snake-Woman's ways, lifted herself up and covered her lover's body with her own. "I know what you still want," she whispered to the turned head. First one finger and then more entered Teshneh's cunt, to milk the last pleasures from the coming. Snake-Woman moaned, her nails biting into Teshneh's back, as she pulled every muscle toward those fingers. They played against her walls, the contractions throwing them both up, higher and higher, until with one mighty squeeze Snake-Woman fell back onto the pillows. Teshneh rolled to one side, sweat covering her body. Another approached Teshneh and gently spread her legs, and then as if she were offering a benediction, she slowly licked the resting woman into her pleasure.

The quietness that had fallen over the group was suddenly broken by the booming...

—Joan Nestle
("The Three," Spring 1986)

...voice of Beeba. "There is still much for them to do. Turn over, Snake-Woman, and I will make your ass sing."

The paddle came down like a cat off the roof. Snake-Woman's eyes filled with tears, and she strained her hard clit against the mattress, yearning for distraction. Her face was muffled in a pillow, but in her mind she could see her ass cheeks plumply turning pink to red to white-hot. Her clit was growing like a sponge. With her fingers she could press it to orgasm in a moment. But her fingers could only press against the steel of the bed frame she was bound to. It was unbearable.

She would bite down and count, count, count—numbers are infinite, but the spanking had to stop sometime. It had to. She would count to a million if she had to, but she wasn't going to let out one little groan, one peep of sensation. She wouldn't give her the satisfaction.

But breathing was another matter. She had to get some air.

She raised her head to inhale, but the words poured out instead. She couldn't hold them back any more than she could stop the sweat spreading across her breasts or trickling down the crack of her stinging bottom.

"Fuck me, please. I can't take it if you don't fuck me! I can't!"

Her arms pulled helplessly from the posts of the bed. Goddamn it, if she didn't feel something big and strong inside her she would tear these cuffs apart. The pain rushing in between her legs was pumping her up, like Hercules; she would destroy everything if she wasn't satisfied.

Her tormentor grabbed her long hair at the neck and bent over to whisper in her ear. "Once I start fucking you I won't be able to stop. It won't matter if you cum once, twice, or not at all; it won't matter if the cream runs down your legs or the friction is too much to bear. Your pussy is just too pretty, and my fist too hungry, to stop for anything."

Snake-Woman nuzzled her ear against...

**—Barbara LaRue**
**("What Is It About Straight Women?" Fall 1985)**

...the hot mouth. She could barely spit out her answer: "I...don't care!"

Her lover heard her. She reached down to replace the dangling clitoris, and then all was in order. After decades of work, locked up in her laboratory, Dr. Muriel K. Starr had finally achieved what no one before ever attempted or desired—her own personal monster. Dr. Starr had created the perfect lesbian with sexual powers and imagination far beyond those of mere mortals. And now her creation was ready to be unleashed upon the unsuspecting world.

The doctor took one last look at her sleeping, darling monster. By tomorrow morning the anesthesia would wear off, and then, just as the sun was rising, her creation would begin a new era of human history. Locking up the laboratory, the doctor stepped out into the early morning air. It was 1 A.M. There was enough of the night left to rush home for a short nap and then be back in time for the awakening.

Walking the streets that late at night meant entering a particular state. There were objects everywhere. There was no free space. Her apartment looked poor. Her couch felt old-fashioned. The refrigerator was filled with mayonnaise, cocktail sauce, Canada Dry, Hershey's chocolate milk, and boxed corn muffins. There was no electricity in the bathroom, bedroom, or kitchen.

*I've let my life go to pot*, she thought. *All for my monster. But now I'll get my reward.*

Then she lay down, crossed her hands on her chest, and looked at the wall. All night the doctor lay there listening to the muffled snap of mousetraps echoing in the alley...

—Sarah Schulman
("A Short Story About a Penis," Winter 1986)

The anesthesia, however, had a mind of its own.

The anesthesia knocked me out, all right, but not with that lulling, euphoric calm I'd been led to expect. No way. It sent me reeling, pitching pell-mell into an agonizing void—like I'd been broadsided by a Mack truck and flipped onto a bed of nails. Reminded me of the time I'd followed the comely Lulu into a beckoning alley and run smack into Lulu's steady, Pansy. Pansy wasn't in the mood for an "open relationship."

I chuckled, then winced, as a zipper of pain shot up my left flank. Gasping into consciousness, I suddenly realized I was on a bed of nails. Holy Morticia.

My eyes fought for focus. I was in a crummy office, a boxy little room with peeling linoleum, faded mustard walls, and a film of dust on the sagging window ledge. Through the cracked pane, a flashing neon martini glass lent a pinkish glow to the decrepit surroundings. I spied an ornately framed document to the right of the window. It read "Sue Slew, Private Heat."

I turned my head, blinking. There she was, in the flesh, a hulking chinless lass in a fedora, leaning precariously on the edge of a rickety card table.

She laughed.

"That doesn't look like a real private eye license," I blustered, struggling to roll off my prickly perch.

"People will believe any ruse so long as you treat 'em right." She strolled my way, knocking me playfully back onto the nails.

"What am I doing here?" I demanded.

"I was hired to investigate you." She ran a wormy finger up inside the leg of my satin culottes. "You know, I'll find out all your secrets."

I froze. Sue Slew cracked a snaky smile. She looked me over, eyes rheumy in their cavernous sockets, and asked, "So, my little filly, what do you do for fun?"

—Elizabeth Pincus
("Monday Nights," Spring 1987)

My ex-lover's sarcastic query and her use of her pet name I hated irritated the hell out of me. I knew her envy of my new relationship and my idyllic life on Bora Bora fueled her sarcasm. I decided to feed her envy with my answer.

"Well, let's see," I said, tossing my red mane of hair to tease her. "This morning I paddled my surfboard out to my lover's private island. I went for a swim. The clear water sparkled beneath me as the sand reflected the sun. Each object below—moon coral, tubeworms, urchins—was cause for concentrated study and wonder. Tiny yellow millet-seed butterfly fishes nipped at my fingers.

"The water was warm, and the slight current washed over me. I floated on my surfboard facedown, my legs and hands dangling in the water. There was an occasional nibble from one of my yellow friends. I thought about a woman I loved in San Francisco. I thought of hiding in the park with her and the wind whipping fog through the eucalyptus. I could not see us as we were: clasped together, urgent in our need. Instead, I viewed the scene through an infrared lens. Around us it was cool, green, and we were burning in a dark red aura of heat into the film. Our movements caused the aura to undulate. I felt our passion in my throat and loins quite separate from the heat of the sun on my back or the coolness of the water on my hands and legs. I touched my cunt with cool, wet fingers and gasped as they slid through the warmth that the thought of her had created. My face was pressed against the board. My fingers moved slowly, so slowly that the board barely moved in the water, and my nibbling friends did not dart away. My fingers were quelling the passion, not unleashing it; their slow, delicate strokes rhythmically recalled the feeling of entering her, feeling her cunt tighten around my fingers and then give way. I gasped in release and felt the pulse spread through my body and dissipate. The infrared scene faded. The sound of the surf caressed my body.

"Suddenly I was thrown into the water. I heard the clicking first and then high-pitched laughter. My erotic thoughts had drawn the dolphins. The horny little devils."

—Jan Stafford
("Bizarro in Love," Spring 1985)

My ex-lover glared at me and muttered, "You were thinking about that bitch you cheated on me with, weren't you?'

I put my hands on my hips but decided not to sneer. My visit to the seamstress could hardly be called cheating: I had been surrounded by packing boxes marked JOHNNY WALKER, a couple of mismatched glasses, and a half-empty box of baking powder; that was all she'd left behind in one of her whirlwind flights. I'd given up at that point, thrown it all into boxes I found behind the bar, and moved into a second-story flat. There I was, again, wrapped up like a chipped cup in the newspaper of another divorce. I sat on a Tanqueray box and swigged a beer. That's when I saw the seamstress—across the driveway, downstairs in a bay window. The seamstress was a small woman, the sleeves of her white shirt rolled up, a yellow tape measure around her neck, and a pincushion strapped to her wrist. She walked slowly, looked closely at a woman in a tight blue dress who stood on a platform with her arms straight out to her sides, eyes closed. The tailor held the tape measure as if it were a lapel, crossed in front of her client, so her chest was slightly higher than eye level. I shifted in my seat at the thought of her inspection. The seamstress looked the woman up and down, reached up and ran her fingers along the neckline of the dress, then along the darts. She cupped the woman's breasts, smoothed the bodice. I put down my beer. *What sort of a fitting is this?* I wondered. The seamstress gathered a row of the bodice between her fingers as if to tighten the fit, but pinched the cloth at the nipples with a steady grip. I stood, then smoothed the front of my shirt. The client tilted her head back then dropped her arms and reached for the seamstress. But she quickly moved aside and disappeared into the shadows of the room, leaving the woman in the dress to run her own hands down her ribs and step off the platform.

Hours later, after I had unpacked the kitchen, I approached the window from the side rather than boldly face front, and the seamstress was there again. Same pincushion, same tape measure, but different client. This woman was standing on a chair on the platform, with only her legs and the hem of a full-skirted flowered dress visible. The seamstress circled the client, bunching the hem in the palm of her hand, checking for stray fabric. Standing to the client's side, she stopped, then turned her face up to my window, lifted the flowering material, and slid her face inside the woman's skirt. I stepped back from the window but reconsidered my plan to hang curtains.

As dusk fell, I crept back to the window. The seamstress was alone this time, boldly facing the windows and my apartment. She knew she had my attention. She ran her fingers along a needle and thread, snapped it taut, and slid the needle through the button panel of her open shirt. With a long, expansive gesture she reached over her shoulder and slipped a stitch into the back of the shirt. She pulled it so the shirt opened and exposed her breast and a tight brown nipple. The seamstress stitched the side of the shirt to reveal her torso, the black thread pulling across her ribs. With each motion, I inhaled and watched the cloth. I pressed my hands against the glass. She stitched a sleeve to a collar to expose a shoulder, gathered the button panel to frame her belly, and as I leaned forward against the glass, she stitched the hem of the shirt through the darts, with motions so slow I thought the metal must be grazing her skin. The cloth raised to show a sculpted hip and a dense triangle of hair. Bound now with thread and stretching cloth, she held the needle as if asking for direction. I picked up my house keys, the curtains better mended than hung...

—Jess Wells
("The Succubus," Spring 1985)

...and headed out the door toward the car, when my lover Christina called down from the bedroom window.

"Leavin' so soon?"

I looked up at her and smiled. "I gotta go to work, babe," I said, opening the car door.

"Well, come up for a sec. I got something to tell you."

I closed the door and headed back upstairs to her. She lay there naked on the bed, legs propped open. "You mean to tell me you're leaving without fucking me goodbye?" she cooed, running her hand along her inner thigh to her cunt.

Subtle as usual.

"I'm going to be late...again," I grinned, taking off my jacket.

Christina slipped two fingers into her cunt, stroking it as I got undressed. I lay down on the bed and pulled her to me gently, kissing her softly.

She pushed me back suddenly. "What are you doing?" she asked.

"Making love to you, what else?"

"No, no." She laughed, rolling over and opening up the nightstand drawer full of our toys. She pulled out our favorite, the seven-inch, ahem, lifelike dildo and lube, shoving them into my hands. "I don't want you to be too late for work," she giggled.

I shook my head at her and squeezed a glob of lube on the tip of the dildo, spreading it up and down the length. Christina positioned herself on the bed. I sat between her open legs and rubbed the head of the dildo back and forth over her swelling clit...

—Mickey Warnock
("Donna 15," January 1989)

"Cut the crap, you two!" Foss ordered good-naturedly. Her long freckled face was flushed, her eyes twinkling.

"Yeah!" Halvorson echoed. "We're having a strength contest, not an orgy."

"Why not?" Kresge ran her tongue over her lips and a quick hand up Halvorson's muscular thigh.

"Aw, hell, I forgot." I pulled a sheepish face and kept on rubbing Weaver's clit. It peeked from among her thick dark curls, looking me right in the eye.

"I'm just warming up." Weaver slid her hands over her tits and down her long body. "You never said a contestant can't warm up."

"You're overheated!" Halvorson laughed. "Come on!"

"Here's the meter. Put up or shut up." Foss sat up and thrust out the sphincter strengthener she had kiped from the base infirmary. It looked like a crooked turkey baster, with color gradations all along the tube.

"OK, OK." Weaver took it and ran her tongue all over the bulb.

"Try that on me next," I said hopefully. Weaver just pushed my hand away and slid the bulb slowly up her cunt. The tube stuck out in front. She stood over me like a goddess with a glass dick.

Kresge leaned forward, arms pushing her tits together. Foss counted down: "Three, two, one, squeeze!"

Before my admiring eyes, the glass dick turned red, clear to its end.

"All right!" I cheered. "Grip of iron!"

Weaver slid the meter out with a slimy popping noise and a self-satisfied look and sat back to watch the rest of us.

Foss held out the dice. I rolled two fives, Kresge got a four and a five, Halvorson a two and a three, Foss a three and a six.

"Halvorson. Front and Center!" Foss snapped. "Cunt-testing position, assume!"

Halvorson stood up and spread her thick legs the regulation shoulder-length apart.

"Boiled lettuce Halvorson," I jeered.

Halvorson tossed her head and gave me the finger. "That was a practice run."

Weaver stretched up her sinewy arms and smoothed back her silky hair. "Need help warming up?"

"Hey," I piped up. "That's my job."

"Both of you shut up and watch an expert." Halvorson

slipped the bulb up her sweet blond cunt, which I'd never been able to get near, and grinned rakishly. "Start counting, Foss."

—Rebecca Ripley
("The Initiation," Winter 1988)

Foss said, "Fuck that! I've always hated oral sex anyway. What's erotic about getting pubic hair down your throat?" She took a dental dam out of her wallet and dropped it on the girl's belly. "You need this more than I do, buddy. But I wouldn't be in your place if I had the Hoover Dam in between me and that raunchy thang."

Her archenemy flipped the square of latex into the dirt. "You're all sour grapes and hot air, Foss. She's mine now," she boasted. Then she plastered her face against the girl's crotch.

Foss laughed. "You're making a lot more noise than she is. You idiot. She wants a hard hand, not a soft tongue. You'd get a lot more out of the bitch if you'd keep her mouth busy."

Her rival's only response was to redouble her lingual labor. Foss said, "Hear that? You'd better get off quick. The Cennobites are coming, and this is the last time anybody is ever going to suck your pussy."

The roar of a dozen motorcycles filled the wooded clearing. Their riders wore the same bike-club colors that hung from Foss's shoulders.

"Yo!" she yelled. "Right this way, buds. Happy Birthday, Merry Christmas, have yourselves a party." To the girl, she said, "Hope you know how to say your prayers. Having some calluses on your knees would be a blessing."

Foss's rival came to her feet, reaching for the knife she had in her boot, but the blond on the ground was quicker. She snatched the blade from its hidden sheath and tumbled her admirer into Foss's arms.

The Cennobites descended up on the buxom little traitor and began to rip, cut, and tear off what little clothing she wore. Soon she was strung up between two saplings, making the acquaintance of every single biker, and squealing, "Harder! Faster! Use two hands!"

"As for you," Foss said to the defeated foe beneath her heel, "since you like licking clit so much, start softening up your mouth on this dirty old boot of mine."

The results were not all she had hoped for. "I have a feeling you aren't trying to be all that you can be," Foss said reproachfully. She slid her belt out of its loops. "How many strokes do you think it's gonna take for you to get promoted to something sweeter than that greasy steel toe? Start counting now!"

—**Pat Califia**
(**"The Vampire," Fall 1988**)

*Issue: Nov./Dec. 1989*

## Computer Blue
by Mickey Warnock

*She's looking for a gay Brooke Shields.*

"Lonely? Looking for that right one or just wanting to get rid of the wrong one? Tired of your friends playing match-maker? We can help! We are Sappho's Computerized Dating Service. Simply fill out the questionnaire below and mail $50, check or money order, to..."

It figured I'd get this in my post office box today. As a subscriber to a lesbian magazine, I was on every gay mailing list from here to Rhode Island. Yet it also figured that at this time in my life I was alone and single. Sappho's seemed to know this.

I spent the last of my No. 2 pencil on their final questions:

12. Type of personality you are seeking:
    a) romantic (candlelight dinners, soft music, etc.)
    b) fun-loving (wine, women, song and dance)
    c) couch potato (beer, the ol' lady, videos)

13. Femininity/social attire:
    a) "36-27-33" (no comment)
    b) "guppie" (gay urban professional)
    c) butch (Yes, we can find a "Joan Jett" for you!)

"You did what?" Justine laughed, shaking her head.

"I signed up for a computer dating service," I repeated, a little more quietly.

"What, are you desperate? Those places are a rip-off."

Leave it to loving and understanding friends.

"No, I am not desperate...just seeking some adventure."

*Meanwhile, at Sappho's Computerized Dating Service, our hapless heroine's matchmakers are hard at work, searching for that right one.*

"Shit! I just spilled my Coke in the disk drive."

Fizz...crackle...pop.

"Oh, no! Who were you matching?" the other Ms. Cupid asked, quickly wiping off the keyboard.

"This one here, number 0501. She's looking for a gay Brooke Shields."

"Wait a minute. Number 0075 hasn't had a good match in a while. Let's get these two together."

Ms. Cupid looked at the other. "You're not serious, are you?"

"Well, what do they expect for 50 bucks?"

I rewound the tape of my answering machine when I got home from work and began to search through the fridge for dinner.

"Hi, uh, I hate this machine. It's me, Justine. Call me later..." beep...click...beep... "Hello, dear. It's Mom. Call me when you get home..." beep... "The name is Anastasia, compliments of Sappho's. We got a date. Meet me at the corner of Pine and Market Friday night at 9..." Beep.

The jar of mayonnaise fell from my hands, hitting the floor with a crash. It was now time to panic.

"They got you a date already? They must have seen the desperation."

"Shut up, Justine. I'm nervous enough as it is."

"Well, who—or shall I say, what—is it?"

"I don't know. All I know is her name is Anastasia, and I have to meet her downtown Friday night."

"Anastasia?"

"Don't ask."


It was going on 10 minutes after 9 as I sat at the corner, waiting for the mystery date. A blue Chevy Malibu pulled up and stopped in the middle of the street. I couldn't make out the person inside, yet I knew she was looking over at me. Whoever it was lit up a cigarette.

"You must be zero-five-zero-one," she said, taking a drag.

"Are you Anastasia?" I asked.

"Yep. Why don't you come over so I can get a better look at you."

I walked slowly to the car. She opened her door at the same time and got out to face me. There she stood, all six feet of her. I couldn't help staring at the light-blue Mohawk she sported, the black leather jacket and mini-skirt, and the gold hoop in her nostril.

"Well, do you want your money back?" she asked.

"This, uh, is a surprise I wasn't expecting..."

"Yeah? So who were you expecting, Brooke Shields?"

"I, uh, I..."

"So, do you want to go dancing?" she asked. She guided us into her car and shoved a Dead Kennedys tape into the stereo.

"Yeah, sure. Uh, where to? The I-Beam? Kennel Club? Maybe the Babybrick?"

"Babybrick's closed down. I know where we can go." Anastasia smiled at me in a strange way, not calming my nerves at all.

She turned down Fifth Street, heading to the waterfront, where we pulled in front of what appeared to be an abandoned warehouse. I stayed in the car when she got out.

She poked her head inside. "Well, are you coming or what?"

"Where are we? I know this isn't a club."

"Didn't you pick 'B' for question 12?"

"What do you mean?" I asked, confused.

"B, a fun-loving type of woman."

*That same evening, back at Justine's Friday night poker game...*

"So, where's Karen tonight?" Mo asked, picking up two cards.

"She had a date." Justine threw a chip on the table.

A small slit opened on the front door of the warehouse. A pair of suspicious eyes looked us over.

"What's that?" a gruff female voice asked.

"That is my date. She's OK. Let us in," Anastasia said, passing a ten to the eyes.

The door opened to an enclosed gateway. A red light glowed overhead, and a flight of stairs was in front of us, leading to another closed door. Loud punk music thumped through the wall behind it.

"What is this place?"

"Bitch," spat the crew-cutted, bulldyke bouncer who was the pair of eyes that had let us in.

I turned to Anastasia, wondering what I'd said wrong.

" 'Bitch' is the name of the club," she laughed.

I followed her up the stairs. Two Anastasia look-alikes walked out, practically shoving me out of the way as they made their way down. We walked into a darkened converted loft barroom. The music hit me with a roar.

"You wanna drink?" she screamed to me.

"I'll take a Bud," I yelled back.

Anastasia disappeared into the crowded bar, leaving me with over a hundred pairs of eyes in leathers, ripped Levi's, and spiked hair, checking me out. I looked down at my own clothes, a pair of jeans and a polo shirt.

"Mohawk her!" someone shouted. A small crowd started toward my direction. I ran over to Anastasia, who was heading my way with the beers. The motley crew of lesbians ran past me to a girl cringing in the corner with her leathered lover.

"It's her 21st birthday," Anastasia said, handing me a beer. "It's a tradition around here. How old are you anyway?"

"23," I choked.

"You look so surprised by all of this," Anastasia screamed in my ear.

"I never knew this type of lesbian lifestyle existed."

"Karen, not all of us are w-o-m-y-n."

At that moment a woman dove off the stage, smashing onto our table. I leaped up to see if she was all right, but she had already jumped up and made her way back into the slam-dancing crowd of flinging limbs and hair.

"Do you wanna dance?" Anastasia asked.

"Uh, nah. I've never been too much for dancing."

"Well, ya wanna get outta here?" she sighed, putting out her cigarette.

"And go where?" I worried, although I knew nothing could quite compare to this.

"How 'bout my place?"

"Uh, sure, why not?" I smile weakly, then finished my beer.

Mo threw her cards down on the table. "I'll bet the next hand that Karen gets laid tonight."

"You got a death wish or something? No one gets laid on computer dates," Justine said, shuffling the deck.

"Is it a bet or what?" Mo replied, bypassing the sarcasm.

"It's your money."

Anastasia opened the rear door of her car, motioning for both of us to get in.

"I thought we were going to your place."

"Welcome home," she laughed, pushing me inside. She closed the door behind her, climbing on top of me.

"What are you doing?" I yelled, trying to push her off me. "We're in the backseat of a car in some godforsaken place."

"Oh, come on. You do this sort of thing, don't you?" she said, stroking my breasts, kissing my neck.

"Well, yeah, but we just met and I..." I tried to say, until she covered my mouth with her hand.

"No talking. Just lay back and take it like a woman," she said. I stared at her wide-eyed. She was serious.

What the hell. I pulled her down and let her kiss me some more.

"Mmm," she moaned, tearing my shirt in half at the collar.

"Uhnn...you're so aggressive," I panted, as she sucked on my tit.

"Eliminates obstacles."

"Justine, how are we going to know if 'it' happens with Karen, anyway?" Mo asked, relighting her cigar.

"Well, it's been about a year since she's had any, and if she does, she'll be singing it from the rooftops tomorrow morning," Justine calmly replied, sorting out her hand.

"That move is going to steam up the windows," I winced, Anastasia's semi-dry fist slowly entering me.

"Well, sorry, it's spit or nothing. I forgot the lube," she said, pulling my leg over her shoulder.

She stroked her fist carefully inside me. I moved with her until I stretched enough to allow more freedom of movement. She rubbed my clit with her other hand, keeping up the pace with her pumping fist.

I gripped the seat as Anastasia went full throttle within me. "God, slow down, girl," I groaned.

"Oops, sorry. I was just thinking of my favorite Sex Pistols song."

"Well, let's just concentrate on Barry Manilow for now, OK?" I sighed, lowering myself back onto the seat in relief.

"Well, it's going on midnight, Jus, and Karen hasn't called yet. It's about that time of night when those things are happening," Mo smiled slyly.

"I thought it was 2, when the bars closed," Justine yawned, opening another beer.

"It's blue," I said, surprised, staring at Anastasia's pubic hair with her legs over my shoulders.

"Well, whaddaya expect?" she laughed, pushing my face against her. For a treat such as this, I was expecting maybe blueberry-flavored, but I settled for the usual.

I parted the lips, flicking my tongue against her clit and then inside. Going in and out and back over. Anastasia grabbed my hair, arching forward in a deep groan as I buried myself within her, sucking intensely.

"It's going on 2. You might as well pay up," Mo said, open palm extended.

"Oh, come on, Mo, she could be dancing for all we know."

"So, can I have your phone number?" I asked, looking up from between Anastasia's legs as she lay smoking.

"I already gave it to you," she said, passing me the cigarette.

"When?" I asked, puzzled.

"I wrote it on your ass while we were sixty-nining."

"Well, what do you think?"

"I don't know. It's hard to tell while she's sleeping."

Mo walked around the bed, inspecting me as I lay there

peacefully. "I can't see any hickeys or lipstick smears any-where," she whispered.

"Maybe it didn't happen," Justine hoped with a smile.

"You wish. She was out until 4 this morning, Justine. Something had to have happened," Mo said, lifting my blanket to get a closer look.

"I say we wake her up and ask."

"Christ, Mo, it's 7 A.M.," Justine yelled, jarring me fully awake.

I rolled over with a groan to blurry images of Justine and Mo standing over me. "What the hell?" I mumbled, looking at the clock.

"How did your date go?" Justine asked, fingers crossed behind her back.

"You guys broke into my apartment to ask me that?"

"Come on, tell us," Justine said. Both hands had crossed fingers now.

"You've got to be kidding," I said, rolling over and pulling the blanket to my shoulders.

"Wait a minute." Mo reached for the corner of the sheet that half-exposed my ass cheeks. "What's 826-9742?"

"News at 11," I smiled, falling back asleep.

"Pay up, Justine."

*Issue: May/June 1990*

## Obsession
by Martha Miller

*The first thing I want besides a cigarette in two weeks and it's a straight woman.*

I am in the Laundromat. Sun falls across a row of harvest-gold washing machines and a heaping ashtray that sits on a table nearby. I pace like a caged feline back and forth through that patch of sun. I watch particles of dust swirl in the sunlight, then eye the ashtray. I will empty it, I think. I pick it up and throw the whole thing in the trash.

My name is Zoe Murdock, and I haven't had a cigarette in 10 days. There are a thousand things I could tell you about myself, but right now that's all I can think of.

I've washed and put away all the ashtrays at home and given away my half-empty carton after trying for days to throw it away. I've bought another pack, agonized, and given it away too. I've chewed gum till my jaws ached and drank so much water it's hard to stray 20 feet from the bathroom.

My best friend, Emily, quit a year ago.

"When will this damn headache go away?" I ask her.

She says, "Drink water."

"I feel irritable. I'm having mood swings."

"Drink water."

"Just what do people who don't smoke do after sex?" I demand.

"You're so irritable, no one can get close enough to you for sex," she says. "Don't worry about it."

I worry anyway.

I'll tell you what I think they do. I think they get up and go to the bathroom because of all the water. Then they lie in each other's arms and bore themselves to sleep talking about not smoking, because it's all they can think about.

I call Emily in the morning.

"This is hard," I complained.

"Yes," Emily agreed. "It is hard."

"I'm angry. Everybody said it would be easier by now."

"It's like childbirth," Emily said. "You forget how hard it was."

It's like childbirth all right, I think. In more ways than one.

I notice things now.

Once, years ago, the house I was buying needed a new roof. I started looking at roofs, noticing their shapes, their colors, their state of repair. I noticed sizes and shapes of shingles. I drove down the same streets and saw the same houses in a different way. Now I notice smokers and nonsmokers. I know who they are. I notice movies where no one smokes and movies where everyone smokes. And I'm reduced to throwing away ashtrays in the Laundromat.

I am suddenly ashamed. I look around. I am alone except for a young woman who's just come in. She's sorting clothes on a table while her baby babbles to her from a car seat that sits next to her wicker laundry basket.

I reach into the trash barrel past empty detergent and bleach boxes, past gobs of lint, ashes, and cigarette butts to the place where the ashtray has fallen, and pull it out.

I sit on the bench and try to read an old Sunday newspaper someone has left. But I find myself watching the woman stuffing laundry into the washers.

She is plump, attractive. Her hair is dark, gleaming, brushed back into a long bushy ponytail. She measures soap and pours it into each of the four washers. She looks up, sees me watching, and smiles.

I smile quickly and look away, nervous. There's a candy machine. Quickly I realize that if I don't buy candy I will fish the cigarette butts out of the trash and eat them. I go to the machine, and even as I drop the coins in, I am aware of how tight my jeans feel, aware of the slight roll over the waistband. I get a Diet Pepsi too.

As I pass the woman on the way to my patch of sun, she says, "Excuse me?"

She's stunning.

"The baby's sleeping, and I need to use the john." She jerks her thumb toward the bathroom door. "Could you keep an eye on her for a second?"

"Sure," I shrug.

I am eating my second Snickers and am halfway through my Moon Mullins when the baby starts to fuss.

I go through these phases where I feel like I don't have my skin on. Every nerve is exposed. The baby's cries vibrate against my bone marrow, echo in my skull.

I look over the funnies and wait. The baby's cries build to screams. I stand, rub my trembling chocolate-and-newsprint-covered fingers on my jeans. The bathroom door is still closed. The baby's fists are shaking in the air, its face all red and wet. Why doesn't she hurry up?

I walk closer and see that the kid's T-shirt says BABY-WOMAN. I think about that for a minute, then pick her up gently, jostle her a little, and pace. Her cries grow soft. She rubs her wet, warm face on my neck.

I turn and see the woman standing near the bathroom door. She walks toward me smiling. "Thanks," she says.

I pass the baby-woman to her and walk back to my bench. I want to say more, but I can't think of anything.

My wash is finished, and I start pulling it out of the machines. I notice a wet spot on my T-shirt where the kid drooled.

I squeeze two loads into one dryer and return to the bench. I look toward the woman again. She holds the baby in one arm and unbuttons her yellow blouse with the other. I feel a surge. She unhooks something and a breast is free. The baby-woman clasps onto it, sucking softly. They look peaceful, the woman sensuous. She watches her daughter, intent, smiling.

I try not to stare. The eyes of the woman and the baby are locked. They aren't aware of me, but I'm aware of me. I shift in my seat. Nice work, Zoe, I think. The first thing I want besides a cigarette in two weeks and it's a straight woman.

I look at the box of Tide near my plastic laundry basket. The air is warm. I rub my sweaty palms together. My lips are dry. I want a cigarette. The woman's breast is white and full. A blue vein makes it seem transparent. The baby sucks, kneading with tiny perfect fingers.

I press my thighs together, wanting to stop on some level, and feeling that if I move, stand, or walk around, the spell will be broken.

The dryer thuds to a stop. The washing machines end their cycles one at a time. The room is warm, humid, and quiet. I sit perfectly still. Flecks of dust float in the sunlight. The woman looks up, meets my eyes, and smiles. The baby-woman is asleep.

In the week that follows, I often think about that moment. In my fantasy the woman places the sleeping baby in the car seat and comes to me, her yellow blouse hanging open, both breasts swaying loose. I stand and take a step toward her, then wait, uncertain. When she's close enough that I feel heat from her body, she stops. I drop to my knees before her.

Now my obsession has a double edge. I want the woman and the cigarette. I move through the week muddled and con-fused. I see a detective movie where everyone smokes, where all the women's breasts are full and have soft curves. Every time I pass my laundry basket I feel a twinge.

I don't have that much laundry and finally decide to wash sheets to make a second trip. It's the same time of day. The place is crowded. No nursing woman. I convince myself that she was an apparition, a dream. I feel depressed.

"You've got to get out," says Emily. "When a lesbian starts looking at straight women it's well past the time to get laid."

I agree.

Saturday night we go to the bar. Cigarette smoke hangs over crowded tables. I take a deep breath. Everyone is smoking.

I ask Emily to dance. I want to move around, get a better look. Her lover, Tess, waves us on, and we make our way to the dance floor. The music is loud. Rhythmic. I look at each table we pass. There are 26 smokers. Will I ever be attracted to a woman with a cigarette again? Have I cut my already slim possibilities even slimmer? Am I doomed to wander Laundromats looking for a straight woman?

Emily is much smaller than me and very thin. I think we look ridiculous. She's a good dancer, though. After a few minutes I've worked up a sweat. I feel better. I look around the dance floor and spot Grace near the corner. Her permed red hair is wet with sweat and sticks to her forehead. She's dancing with a short plump woman who looks familiar.

I feel like I've been punched in the stomach. For a moment I'm sure it's the Laundromat woman. I tell myself I'm wrong. This has happened several times since that Sunday. I've got to cut it out.

The plump woman dances with erotic grace. She's wearing a pair of faded bib overalls. Her round bottom moves in seductive circles. She swings her long bushy ponytail from side to side, snaps her fingers to the beat. Light gleams in her auburn hair. She turns.

It's her.

I've stopped moving. Other dancers bump into me; I've violated the ritual. Someone says "Hey!" as I start walking between couples toward Grace and the woman.

"Hey, Zoe!" Grace calls to me and waves.

I am looking only at the woman. The song has ended. Couples are leaving the floor. I've forgotten Emily entirely.

"Have you met my cousin Holly?" Grace asks. "She's staying with me for a few weeks."

I nod at the Laundromat woman, grab Grace's arm, and pull her aside.

"Excuse us," she says to Holly as she's pulled away in my grasp.

I turn to her. "You brought a straight woman to this bar?" I demand.

"Holly? She's not straight." Grace is puzzled.

"But the baby..."

"You know her?" Grace asks.

"I've seen her with a baby. And I'm sure it was hers."

"Yeah," Grace nods, looking around. "It's hers. She and her ex-lover wanted a baby. They split up shortly after it was born. She's really a cute little—"

"Lover? How do two lesbians make a baby?" I insist, just like it's my business.

"Don't ask," Grace wrinkles her nose. "It's got something to do with a M-A-N." She spelled the word.

"You're the woman from the Laundromat," Holly's voice comes from behind me.

I turn. My knees feel weak.

A slow song starts.

"Dance with me," she says in a tone that makes me wonder who will lead.

I pull her to me and spin her around, just so we'll get it established early. She fits in my arms perfectly. My mind is Silly Putty. My heart pounds in my throat.

"I've been thinking about you since that day at the Laundromat," she says.

"Really?'

"Yeah. I had you spotted."

"Really?" Come on, Zoe. You've got a bachelor's in communications!

"It was the lavender SNAKE 'N' SNAKE T-shirt—and the way you walk."

I nod. I am not going to say "really" again! I remember the hand-painted BABY-WOMAN T-shirt.

We dance. She moves gracefully. It's like we've danced together a thousand times.

"Come home with me." It slips out. "I mean, it's smoky and crowded here." I stammer. Try to recover. "I mean—"

She places two fingers on my lips and says, "I'll just get my things."

We say goodbye to our friends and leave. The whole thing takes five minutes. The ride to my place takes 10. My fear grows with each moment. God, how I want a cigarette.

At last, I say, "Look, do you have a cigarette?"

"No," she says. "I quit when I was pregnant. And now I'm nursing."

I remember the breast.

"I quit three weeks ago," I tell her.

"Wow! That's great."

"It's still pretty hard some days."

"Are you drinking lots of water?" she asks.

I laugh. "You know," I say at last, "I never thought I'd be a nonsmoker."

"You never will be a nonsmoker. You're an ex-smoker. There's a big difference."

I look at her. Part of her face is illuminated by the street-lights. "I'll have to think about that," I say.

An easy smile spreads across her face, then is lost in the shadow.

In my small crowded bedroom I slip the blouse off Holly's shoulders. She's unzipped my jeans and has a hand inside already.

Martha Miller

I stroke her auburn hair, so soft, clean. I slide my hands to her bra. It's damp at the nipples. She unhooks the thing, and her breasts are free.

I drop to my knees. I'd done it so many times in my mind that it seems we've been lovers forever. She smells of sweat and talcum. I slide a hand between her thighs, stroke her mons, separate the labia. My mouth finds a nipple. It's moist. Sweet. Her cunt feels wet.

We stretch out on the bed. I slide two fingers inside her, press her clitoris with my thumb. She draws up her knees. I slide in a third finger.

"I want to go down on you." Her voice is a whisper.

I stop, rise on one elbow, and look at her.

"Let me go first," she says hoarsely.

My cunt feels on fire. I think I'll probably come before she gets there. I lie back, and she kisses a trail down my belly, separates my labia, and boldly presses her tongue to my clitoris. She's a master at cunnilingus. The feeling is intense, immediate. I rock my hips slightly. Quiver with excitement. A tingling sensation spreads through my thighs. Coming is quick. Exhilarating. Exhausting. I am drowning in a wave of ecstasy.

My reciprocation is slower. Methodic. I linger over her full breasts. Nuzzle. Caress with my lips. Her nipples are firm and wet. They taste like warm sugar. She gives my head a gentle push. I take a deep breath and move down, toward her sweet cunt. I savor the taste and smell of her. I feel a perfect connectedness. Rightness. The way I felt with my first woman. I drink her in. Linger.

She comes slowly. Holding me to her. I think I might smother. I'm briefly grateful for my added lung power. I want to touch and kiss her more. She pushes me away.

I move up on the pillow next to her, hold her. She curls up in my arms, a perfect fit. For a moment I feel something is missing. Something I can almost but not quite remember. Then I'm lost in rapture.

"Damn," I say, "I'm glad you're not straight."

"Well, I'm glad you're an ex-smoker." That beautiful, easy smile spreads across her round face, and I remember the thing I'd forgotten. There seems to be no place for it now, no way to make it fit.

Holly's lips find mine. We taste of sex and smell of each other. I think about the Laundromat, the patch of sun, the dust swirling and settling. I remember the rooftops and that I only looked at them for a while, until my own roof was fixed. I lie back and relax. Maybe for the first time in three weeks, I'm glad I'm an ex-smoker too.

*Issue: May/June 1990*

## Low and Inside
by Gina Dellatte

*Jamey slapped her big carpenter's hands to her thighs. "You're real brave, aren't you, little sister?"*

I clapped the bottom of my cleats together over the locker room wastebasket. The caked infield clay slid between the points. I grinned. What a game!

My shoulder ached, and my muscles burned. Taking a hit from that bitch Jamey as she slid into third was worth it. And so was colliding with her in the base path while she tried to field a grounder in front of me. The big dyke's reputation was for playing it rough.

I had spent my entire career in the league trying to avoid her, until I realized that the burning rush I felt every time our bodies came together was not totally unpleasant. But she was such an arrogant shit! I'd be damned if she'd ever find out what I was thinking.

Today we'd played so well against our hard-hitting rivals that the local radio station had kept the captain behind for an interview. That was me. So now the locker room was empty, and I could play the game in my mind without interruption. I could remember a win with the same intensity that I could recall good sex.

In fact, winning turned me on.

Maybe I could find a hot number at Stoney's tonight, while the welcome blush of sexual heat still coursed through my body. Sitting on the bench before my open locker, I started to undress, contemplating a plan for the evening's hunt.

Before I could settle into some serious fantasizing, though, my attention was diverted by a faint clicking noise. I tried to identify it, but for endless moments it eluded me. Suddenly a lanky, muscular woman appeared from behind the row of lockers. My stomach leapt.

"You're in the wrong locker room, Jamey." I balled my hands into tight, angry fists.

She leaned disdainfully against the cinderblock wall and announced in her resonant alto voice, "I thought I might find you here, hot dog."

"If you came to start with me," I said quietly, "I'm not in the mood."

Jamey slapped her big carpenter's hands to her thighs. "You're real brave, aren't you, little sister?" She was one of the few people who could call me little. At nearly six feet, Jamey was two inches taller than me and outweighed me by 40 pounds. And she was a handsome woman.

I turned my attention back to my locker, tossing my socks in the laundry bag. Meanwhile, warning bells were going off in my head. Her take-charge attitude kind of turned me on, but I was also afraid of it. Femmes were her style...and mine too.

"You know, Trish," she chuckled, "you look so butch scooping up rockets at third. I've been wondering for years just how butch you are."

I sighed, wiping my sweaty palms on my thighs. "I'm not following you. I'm not sure I want to."

"Oh, you want to, all right," she breathed, taking a couple of steps toward me. Her bright-green eyes flashed. "Let's go."

"What?" A fight could be fatal for me. Jamey snickered. "You find something fucking funny?" I asked, my hair beginning to bristle.

She feigned fear. "Oh! Big tough dyke, huh? Come on, baby butch. Teach me a lesson."

Though I was well aware I was in for a stomping, I charged her. Bravado, si. Brains, no. The surprise attack allowed me to take her down to the cold stone floor. I held her around the waist squeezing tight, just able to hold on. My face was buried in her shoulder. She smelled pungent, of sweat and infield dirt and sex. She'd probably gotten some from that cute little left fielder as some sort of incentive before she came to harass me.

Jamey was growling. "You little bitch! When I'm through, you won't know what hit you!"

True to her word, she turned the tables effortlessly as I grappled for a hold. Jamey tossed me off her and pounced, pressing me facedown onto the floor. She climbed on. Enraged, I grunted like a caged animal and bucked hard to get her off. Her leg pushed between mine so that when I jerked, it mashed my mound against her thigh.

"What're you going to do now, sweetie?" she hissed into my ear. The sensation raised gooseflesh on my neck in spite of my rage. I turned my head enough to look in her face. Her eyes were bright. She was getting off on this.

"Jamey, goddamn it!" I begged, my resolve caving in.

"What? What do you want?" Her eyes were unsympathetic.

"Let me go!"

She laughed, that fucking snicker again. "Aw, my heart bleeds for you. But I don't think that's what you want. Is it, Trish?"

"Yes!"

She jammed her leg up more firmly into me. "Is it?"

My head swam. This time I didn't answer. I couldn't. Jamey kept up a running commentary as she stroked my pussy with her thigh. "I know women like you, Trish. Seen 'em all my life. So butch. So hot. With a gaggle of little femmes mewling and squealing for you at every turn. But that's not what you need. You need a good fuck. Not by some frail, sympathetic hand, but by someone who knows what it means to fuck... Someone like me."

In a swift move, Jamey pinned both of my wrists above my head. It was easy for her; her little speech had totally deflated me. She'd read me so correctly, so categorically, that I was soaking wet with a throbbing clit. I could never make it easy for her. She knew that. But she also knew from the rhythm of my breathing that she was in.

She alternated the beat of her thigh with humping against my tight ass. With her free hand she reached beneath my body and squeezed my breasts roughly. My nipples stiffened beneath her palms. The pain was delicious. Just as I began to enjoy the friction, she maneuvered down to unfasten my pants. I pressed my hips to the floor and squirmed.

"Stay still, bitch!" she ordered, biting my neck for emphasis. Eventually her efforts succeeded, and she shoved her hand down the back of my pants and began tugging them down. Cool air hit my butt. Jamey squeezed the hard flesh in her fingers, murmuring, "I see why those bimbos drool over you."

I was reduced to helpless writhing. Even if Jamey hadn't been holding my wrists, I probably wouldn't have fought her off. She pressed her finger into my ass hard, without the benefit of any lubrication. Tears sprung up in my eyes. Before I even had a chance to cry out, she withdrew and moved on.

Jamey spread my juices around with her fingers, wetting her whole hand in them, then pausing to taste me. She brought a finger to my mouth and coated my tongue with my own wetness.

"See how good you taste, Trish? You're so wet. Too bad a good eating's what you need. I wouldn't mind doing that for you either."

Jamey returned to probing my pussy with her skilled fingers, strumming on my clit, making forays to enter me. I struggled to my knees and elbows as she mounted me, still maintaining a headlock. I bit her forearm and sucked on the salt of her perspiration, lost in the experience. If my friends had seen me then, they'd have sworn I'd flipped my lid.

"Hang on, baby," she told me. "You're in for a hot ride." Abruptly, Jamey thrust two fingers into my wetness. My vaginal muscles contracted, holding onto her, her fingertips tapping the bulbous head of my cervix. This was all new, all mysterious to me, and I fought the urge to scream out in pleasure.

She built up luscious friction by thrusting heatedly into me, her thumb pressing my aching clit. My pussy felt raw and wonderful as she fed me three, then four fingers. I was completely full. The sensation made me heady. My body wanted more.

I met Jamey's thrusts with my own. She ran her other hand through my hair and wrapped a leg around my thigh. Her crotch was wet, and she kept in tempo with me. No longer able to stay up on my knees, I fell prone, on the verge of a powerful orgasm.

"Oh, come for me, baby," Jamey growled into my ear. "Come on, take it. I know you want it."

Waves swelled and crashed over me, and I cried out as if wounded. My body spasmed, muscles rippling, and a great gush of juices covered the hand Jamey had buried in me. I heard myself calling her name over and over, reaching for her hand to wrap her arm around me. Jamey shuddered too but held me tightly to herself.

Quiet blanketed us. Jamey lay on my back, breathing heavily into my ear. I could neither move nor think; both required more energy than I could muster. I just wanted Jamey to hold me, kiss me, take complete possession of me.

In a moment Jamey got to her knees and hauled herself to her feet. Eyeing me arrogantly, she straightened her clothing. I rolled into a supine position to look at her. The exposed areas of my ass and back stuck to the cool tile floor. Her eyes held the most triumphant look I had ever seen. Feebly I tugged at my clothes.

She started for the door. "Later, baby."

*Issue: Nov./Dec. 1990*

## The Dead Air Between Stars
by Stephine V. Wilson

*You've got to tell me how it feels.*

After the accident my body faded away in pieces. In the hospital there was the numbness, but numbness itself is a feeling, and in time even that vanished. Now there is only my head, neck, and just a hint of my shoulders; the rest is nothing.

I know the body is there; I see it in the mirror. It is sitting in the wheelchair with the motor that buzzes too loudly. It is still quite firm; the exercise machines take care of that. I am still beautiful. But the body doesn't move; the body doesn't feel. It's not mine anymore—it's a fancy piece of baggage along for the ride. But the baggage isn't heavy. It's empty space that I'm carrying—the dead air between stars.

I am the best bottom in this city. I can do any scene. But there's got to be a big mirror around, and you've got to tell me how it feels. You've got to describe the cool wetness you feel as you apply the lubricant to your hand. You have to let me see you do it; make it a dance. Make your voice as beautiful and precise as the best symphony. Describe the viscous heat you feel as your fingers enter my cunt one by one. Move out of the way; want to see it in the mirror. Tell me about the contours of my womb; if you reach back far enough, you'll find it. When your fist is inside me, move it around slowly. Think of your fist as a baby's head, savoring that last warm wet hug before it's born. Give me your hand now. I want to smell it. Did you make me bleed? Good. I want to taste it. That lovely warm salt. Eat me now. Kiss me afterward. Don't be afraid. I need to taste myself. Make your mouth dance with mine. Put all that you are into your lips and tongue; this is the only way I can truly know you. I will kiss you until the last of me has faded from your lips like a song fades on the wind. I will thank you for telling me about that weightless stranger that floats beneath me.

I buzz in my chair through the throng of women at the festival. My lover walks beside me, her hand resting on mine.

"You have beautiful hands," she tells me. "Your fingers are so delicate and thin, the skin so smooth."

I stare ahead at the women. The leather girls are beginning to look cliché—leather this, leather that, knee-high leather boots and leather masks in the dead heat of August. Some women jingle as they walk with their cuffs and key rings. Even my lover looks like last year's news in her black leather halter top, with the spider tattoo above her left shoulder blade.

Then I see her: a tall, tan woman with delicate movements. She wears nothing but a leather belt that falls just over her hips. The belt has a small suede pouch that rides on her left hip; a dagger is stuck in a leather sheath on the other side. Her body is covered with geometric designs done in raised scars. I would like to know who did them; they move with her perfectly. Her head is shaved, and as she moves closer I notice she has made no attempt to hide her femininity. There is no macho tightness in her face, no pursed lips; no cold, cruel eyes. She is beautiful, and as far as I can tell, alone.

"Lookit that," I say to my lover.

"Yeah, lookit that," she says curtly. I can tell she's jealous. She leaves me in the crowd.

I follow the almost naked woman. She walks in slow motion, and to watch her move is mesmerizing. I buzz along about two feet behind her. I watch the cool sway of her hips, how the sweat-slicked scar pictures dance with the sunlight.

"You are following me?" she asks, turning. She has a deep voice with an accent that's hard to place.

"I sure am, honey. Who wouldn't?" I smile very slowly. I have learned to speak with my face.

She looks at me, then the gray chair I'm sitting in. There's no double take, only the acknowledgment that it's there. Looks promising.

I'm wearing a tight white T-shirt, no bra. I've been sweating a little, so my nipples show. The jeans I'm wearing are tight too, and her eyes follow the curves of my hips and thighs. Her stare is making my mind swim with pictures.

"Man, you are beautiful," she says.

"You ain't too bad yourself."

"Do you mind if I push you?" she asks with nervous courtesy.

"No," I tell her. "Run your hand across my face. I want to feel you." I smile, trying to melt her with my eyes.

She moves behind the chair, leans over, and passes her hand across my cheeks. It's so soft, the fingers so delicate. She smells dark and heavy, like the deep woods on a humid day when the clouds have tried to rain but can't. She pushes me through the crowd. I close my eyes so I float even more and lose all sense of distance. I lose that chatter of women and hear only the sound of her breathing and the wheels rolling over gravel. I submerge myself in her smell and dream of the wild jungle.

She has taken me to a clearing on the edge of the festival grounds. No sounds here except the birds and buzz of flies. She lifts me out of the chair and holds my face close to her breasts. I run my tongue along the tiny hills and valleys of her scars. I taste her salt. She lays me on the ground. I feel the prickly grass at the back of my neck. I look up and float in a pale blue haze of sky.

"Lean over me," I say. "I want to taste you."

I hear her take off the belt, hear the belt hit the ground. Then she straddles me, her beautiful cunt taking up my whole view.

"Closer. You won't smother me."

She comes close enough so I can taste her. Her juices bounce on the tip of my tongue. Her lips are pierced with two tiny gold rings. The metallic taste alternates with the smooth gentle taste of liquid salt, seawater without the edge.

"Closer," I breathe. I pull the rings with my teeth. She moans above me. "Spread your lips, if you can. I want to stick my tongue inside you."

So she spreads her lips, and I feel her fingers hard against my face. My tongue finds the hot center dripping with nectar, explores the dark slippery inside. I feel her convulse with pleasure.

"Kiss me. Drink yourself," I tell her. "Drink yourself from me."

There is no mirror here by the clearing so I will have to dream my body. I tell her to give me scars like hers. Carve something, I tell her, carve life into my skin. She straddles my torso and holds the dagger, bringing it down to my body. I dream the kiss of cold steel on skin.

"Tell me about my body. Tell me how it feels."

She describes my body as the knife takes its journey. With her accent, the description becomes a chant, a ballad of the physical. With each line a piece of my dreambody is born.

"You are bleeding," she tells me. "Just a little."

"Let me taste it."

She holds a finger to my mouth; I lick off the blood. Now the body I dream has flesh, where before it was just the dim memory of light. She chants my body like a landscape; my dreambody becomes as solid as the earth.

"Oh, honey, you are so wet," she tells me, "and you taste so wonderful. You melt in my mouth like maple sugar candy."

I dream of coming. My dreamcunt opens like a flower, deep-purple petals bursting like the sun. Her tongue flickers in my mouth; I drink my own juices. I smell my dampness on her lips.

Then there is a whisper of sweat on my forehead, and I am floating once again. I open my eyes and see her backed by the pinks, purples, and oranges of early evening.

"I've never done anything like this before," she says. "You are so beautiful." She carries me back to my chair.

When the wounds healed, I spent hours in front of my mirror, looking at myself and dreaming of her.

*Issue: Nov./Dec. 1991*

## Cum E-Z
by Red Jordan Arobateau

*Hunting sex was a drop in the bucket, throwaway cash.*
*Yes, tonight she would go down to the street.*

Rusty was an entity unto herself. Hands in blue-jean pockets
as she walked through the door. Black leather jacket, blue work
shirt underneath. Sex warm in her crotch as she sat down on the
barstool, unzipped her jacket.

Watched the women a few feet away shooting pool; one
willowy brunette in jeans, feminine—imagined taking her
home, into her bedroom, unbuttoning her blouse. Woman
lying back naked for her, pillow under her butt and...fantasy
faded as a fag jostled her elbow.

"Excuse me, dear."

Hot music played, and dykes and fags moved back and
forth along the bar, on the dance floor—not a lot of
women, and all of them in couples. Rusty's face white,
tense, reflected in the barroom mirror. Rusty wanted some
good hot gash. Could taste it—cunt rising to her aware-
ness like bubbles in the glass of beer in her hands. Rough
worker's hands. The faggot bartender slapped a white
towel, passing time with the guys. Little action for a dyke
with no lady.

All that day at work in the machine shop, she'd been thinking about cunt. Wanted to go someplace where there was a

willing girl and take her pants off and push her on the bed and give her hot sex.

The satiny black leather jacket kept out the cold but not the cold inside.

How difficult it was with women. Sometimes they wanted you, sometimes not. Sometimes they loved you then broke your heart. Climbing the mountain was so difficult. Couldn't it just be easy sometime? Just simply E-Z?

The clock on the wall said 12:45. The calendar said 1973. People played darts, and drafts blew through the door. Pool players looking like the Potato Eaters in a Van Gogh painting, studious at their game. How many times had she sat here, watching the clock hands crawl through the night, the calendar pages flip through the years? How many times, sitting in bars exactly like this, holding a white hand, a woman's hand, reaching her rough fingers up to touch hair that fell lightly to a shoulder, her boots on the rungs of the barstool, saying words, almost begging, and all her efforts leading to nothing?

Painted faces. Some plain. Fancy blue jeans. Painted white women, bitchin' women, femmes with style. Earrings and bracelets. She watched them dance, tits jiggling, she the voyeur on the outside looking in. Music played, dim lights in a gay tavern on Main Street USA. Conversation lilting, falling, occasional bursts of laughter.

Blue jeans shifting on the barstool. When had she last had a climax? Rusty could have it every night—either this way, a pickup in a bar, which was chancy, or a call girl coming to her home, which was expensive. Or the street.

Rusty had a good job—welder. Hunting sex was a drop in the bucket, throwaway cash. Yes, tonight she would go down to the street.

The street is an addiction itself. Outside of the drugs and sex and money and power is the street itself. The Life is an addiction. Hard to get it out of your blood.

The denied have sex in the street.

Risk of disease; she'd been fairly lucky so far. Had been to the clinic only once. Didn't have all the information, but the risk was one she must take. Going down on the wild side, cautious and armed. Was it worth it?

Hands of the clock spun to the final point: 2 A.M. California tavern closing time. She picked her last dollar up off the bar and went out into the night. Riding the streets in her truck. Hunting.

A grid of gray deserted streets punctuated by motels, lights of fast-food joints. Hunting for a female who meant nothing to her. A thing. Meat. A slut. A piece. They came in colors— white or black or tan. A piece of meat with a taste for brown sugar and no broken hearts afterward. Whore's face, inter-changeable with the rest. A hundred in a dozen American cities Rusty had passed through. A world where dates don't last five hours, but 25 minutes. Satisfaction.

Cum E-Z. Don't have to get to know her. She's here for your cash. Simple, basic, animal. No embarrassment. Don't have to try to force her down, don't have to get her drunk or melt her with your savoir faire. Two ships passing in the night—one services the other, and the other pays. Rusty wasn't down here for romance.

Near a liquor store she saw whores, but as the truck got closer she saw an ugly face, 30s, same age as herself, but worn down much worse by time. Moved off quick, for there are younger ones. Young and fine. Red lights caught a tired whore waving her hand after a missed chance.

Hard hands on the wheel, hair blowing back. Eyebrows fuzzy as she peered through the windshield. A recent mem-ory drove her back to a certain place, near the overpass. Empty street. All traffic, all society's intervention, gone. Heart of the city empty. Anonymous. Now it was person to person. Time for people of the night, the denied, to work out their trade.

Rusty kept a gun under her seat—.45-caliber automatic,

black steel, oiled and loaded. Violent thoughts flooded through her system, buoying her spirit. She sat there, parked just past the freeway overpass. Radio playing: "Baby get off, baby get off, you know you want to get off." Rusty rubbed her pale hand across her face, stretched stocky shoulders under her jacket.

Suddenly, movement in the rearview mirror. Out from the overpass, five women, walking fast. They came over to the truck; Rusty rolled the window down halfway.

"Say, baby, are you dating?"

When they saw she was a woman, two turned away in disgust. Three dark faces clustered in the window. "Honey, I'll go with you. I like women."

"You want to see me, baby? I'll treat you right."

Then she saw that one. First time, the girl had wanted to know what Rusty wanted of her. Now she knew.

"You," Rusty said, pointing at the girl, looking her dead in the face. She leaned across the expanse of the seat. Fingers lifted the lock on the door. "Yeah, you. Come on."

Girl got in, carefully arranging her leather coat. The others turned away, disappointed, smacking gum and puffing cigarettes. Proceeded to stroll back to their job. Girl was cold. A nameless woman of the night. Three feet of leather seat separated them.

"You still at the same place?" Rusty asked.

"I got a room at the M—. It's paid up until the third."

They pulled up to the hotel. Moonlight twinkling down on a billion bits of broken glass in the gutter. A few old cars out there, discarded. Bloodied steps to the entrance. A fire escape hanging in space. Front vestibules open. A quiet hotel. Once it had been famous. Dignitaries, recording artists, show people had stayed here. Most units vacant now.

Rusty, hands in pockets, got out of the truck. Hooker didn't say nothing and neither did she.

In the beginning Rusty had been embarrassed, being a

female when the hookers expected male tricks. Now she thought, *Going to give her some good hot cock action.*

Rusty could give it to her. Pornographic visions building low coals in a furnace. Hooker down on her knees, still in high heels, dress pulled up around her waist, exposing half her body, cunt and thighs and stomach naked. If she couldn't take it, if cunt was too bitter a taste, she'd leave the cash on the dresser and get the hell out, laugh about it down on the stroll with the others.

But they seldom laughed.

Risky, this scorn and ridicule she might face. But the risk only heightened the pleasure. The idea that they didn't like being with a woman made it even better in a perverted kind of way, gave her a sense of power, increased her dominance.

The girl went up the cement steps. "You go in first. Sometimes the clerk's still awake with his nosy eyes looking out that window to the lobby."

Hunched in her jacket, Rusty went into the empty lobby, crossed the old tile floor. Dusty. Footfalls of her boots, hands crammed into her pocket, fingers on a knife, ready to flick it open if any funny business lay ahead. Quiet. Walked. Heard the door open behind her, the girl coming in.

Row of elevator buttons up to 8. One last look at the lobby and Rusty closed the grate. Floors dropped away. Went up the shaft to the fifth floor. Eyes straight ahead, legs spread, boots planted in the corridor. Waited. Heard the elevator creak again. Anticipating the girl, Rusty got hotter.

The two went down the hallway. Rusty strode along beside the girl, who wore a long leather coat, expensive, arms crossed over her chest protectively. Rusty's hands shoved in the pockets of her jeans, short hair pushed back. Collar of her leather jacket turned up.

Light fixtures in the hallways, some missing. Worn old rug turning to string on the edges. The two walked. Her body was ready, desire burning in her loins.

Noticed the girl's tits and ass, the way she moved. Not a lot of time. Couldn't afford talk, didn't want to talk anyway. The feeling of impersonality, of nothing between them and nothing to remember but a hot lay.

Stopped in front of a door. The girl already had the key out. Rusty had learned a long time ago, way back in some other city, be ready when you get there. Not a lot of time for what you can afford. No warm-up. No foreplay. So be ready when get-down time comes.

Door closed behind them. Worn green rug under their feet. Room overlooking the street five stories below, hookers walking up and down. Bare gray walls. Window cracked, years of dust on it. Drapery not moved for eons, till they tear the place down or remodel it for a whole new clientele, and the tricks and the trade would be gone. Cold. Rusty would probably keep her jacket on.

Hooker sat on the bed. "My little room," she said proudly. It was her trick pad, not her residence.

*She don't want to fuck*, Rusty thought, and this heightened her sense of lust—taking a woman who hated being with a lesbian. *She don't want me. That's all the better. But she has to accept it if she wants my money.*

The bed was perpetually made. People played on it, not in it. They got laid; different pairs, coupling, uncoupling. Rusty looked out the window as she unzipped her fly for the thousandth time, remembering a thousand other dates, relationships, tricks.

Exhilaration. Freedom. No bonds.

The girl peeled off her stockings.

Rusty was paying more than a male trick: $40 cold cash on the dresser.

"You gotta take your dress all the way off this time. I want to look at your tits."

"I don't want to muss my hair."

"I'm payin' you 40 bucks. I want you to take your dress off."

Girl looked at the butch. Dull brown face. Lipstick glistening.

Rusty looked back at her, pulling down her pants. "All the way off. I want to look at your tits while I fuck you."

Silence.

"It'll make me get through faster," Rusty added.

"All right."

And she was taking it off, over her head, her brown flesh sweet, small breasts of a girl-woman.

Rusty sat on the side of the bed, untying her boots, hair tousled. "And I want you to put your arms around me this time, put your hands on my ass. At least when I start to cum."

"You get everything the other tricks get, baby."

"Just hold me when I cum, OK? Put your hands around my butt."

"OK," the girl said coarsely.

"But I like the way you move your hips," Rusty added.

"Hurry up, baby. I got to get back out there."

Disdain. That's what the girl felt for women in general, and a lesbian, the lowest of all, not being a man but doing what a man does to her. A lady lover. And here she was, lying down for one. The girl gritted her teeth, set to work.

Rusty could have lain on her back and let the girl suck her off, but she wanted to see her on her knees. Curve of her shoulders, on her back, her brown ass squatting on the floor at Rusty's white feet. Couldn't enter that mouth with her tongue—hookers don't kiss—so she put her sex there instead.

Looked down at the girl under heavy lidded eyes; these were secret thoughts. The girl began, wrapping her hands around her thighs and butt, beginning to suck cunt. The girl knew the reason and the game. It was just a game. Moving Rusty's curly hairs, licking her tongue up and down her cunt, burying her lips in it, sucking it.

*So she's gonna take it*, thought Rusty. *The way I smell, the way I am.* Rusty started groaning with pleasure, her hips moving forward and back, pushing into that mouth. A shudder went through her body.

The whore serviced her excellently. A professional.

As she ground into the girl's mouth, spasms ran through Rusty's body. Stood over her, held her curly head, fierce, like a possession, with ringed hands. Examining the merchandise, glad she'd bought it. The slope of the shoulders, breasts, butt, her feet. Knowing she was paying more than a man. Taking a moment to appreciate, to savor.

Tipping her face up to the ceiling, her mouth flew open and a moan escaped, deep and low from her soul. Her hips moved forward of their own accord into the girl's mouth. A shudder went through her body in the final moment.

Hips stopped. For a frozen moment the hooker looked up at the butch standing above her. Sound of the wind in the night outside. Breeze-teased curtains on the window.

Rusty sat on the bed. Hooker got up from the floor, wiping her mouth, face wet with her own saliva and Rusty's discharge. Went to the bed, and Rusty took her in her arms, held her a moment. Then Rusty pushed her down on the rough quilt that hadn't been turned back by an actual sleeper in over a year.

Rusty looked at the girl. Her lipstick had worn off. Soon she was getting between the woman's thighs, fucking her.

Girl lay back on the double bed, thighs spread wide, legs up in the air. Rusty got between them, knees on the bed, ringed hands on each side of the girl, working with her body so her cunt pressed down on the hooker's cunt, rubbing their pussies together. Rusty's flat stomach hard, her muscles clenching, as she worked, nostrils flaring, panting as her excitement grew. Always aware of the bureau with the $40 on it.

Rusty raised up while she worked and looked down at those breasts bouncing around, at the woman's thighs spread for her. The hooker turned her face, looking away.

Hard muscles tensed. The bed bounced, and now Rusty

was holding back, trying to prolong the moment. The girl's face turned against the wall, like stone. They don't kiss. Animal lust. Transaction.

The moon had moved two degrees across the sky. All the freaks and the poor tenants of this world had given up the streets. All the good gay girls in the bars had gone home, fiercely defending one another in each other's arms, or in groups, within whose circle is no room for strangers. Junkies nodded on fire escapes with no defense.

"Take it, baby," the girl whispered. "Take it." And her hips moved up to meet the butch, and her hands caressed Rusty's butt. Juice was wet on their legs and fire burned in Rusty.

"Take it, honey. Fuck me, fuck me." Talking to her, like she hadn't before.

Hot orgasmic rush was on its way.

"Fuck you, baby. Let me fuck you...oh, baby. I'm fucking you...oh, oh, baby."

The girl still had her face turned away like she was a million miles off somewhere else, but giving the thrust of her hip, giving herself so sweet.

"Do it, baby, do it. Let it cum, let it cum."

The imagined fire cum into being. For just an instant Rusty was pretending that the woman underneath her, moving with her, was cumming too, and an electric current shot through her. It was the best feeling she knew. Cum. It starts winding out from the center of her groin, from the core of her being. Straight as an arrow, a hot motherfucker, her clit was an arrow, she was fucking the woman harder and harder and faster, the woman beneath her grinding her hips, rolling around, her clit faster, a powerful sensation suffusing her whole being and the bed banging against the wall taking her higher.

"Take it, baby. Take it." Bang, bang. "Take it." Charged with a deep thrill like having climbed over the peak of a huge mountaintop, bed rocking, shoulders shivering under her jacket and the woman's hands pressing her close, grinding her sex down in a scene of dominance and release.

They lay there, both facing the empty future, Rusty thinking she would be lonely now. That's what happened once she was over the mountain.

Girl, she had to face the remainder of the night. Working. Empty streets, few cars riding, looking.

Pile of underwear, pants, socks, boots. Slowly put it back on. Tired, drained, she wanted only to climb into the truck and head away.

Girl put the $40 in her stocking. "Now, don't go seeing none of them other girls. Them no-count ho's out there still ain't broke luck, like me." Peeping into the mirror over the bureau. Hastily reapplying lipstick from a purple tube.

Dusty walls, carpet under their feet, boots, and high heels, silent footfalls, and the bustling about of two people ready to leave it once more. Despite what the girl told the other women of the street, yes, she did eat cunt, because she wanted the whole 40 bucks. Wanted to keep the trick coming to see her regular—that thing there, trick, butch, whatever it's called, not a person but a dollar sign. Whose body she knew every inch of and how to please. Keep turning it like a wheel driving on the road till she hit prosperity.

A scene of degradation. Pain of the soul. But of freedom also. It's all about freedom and power and control. It's all about going fishing in the night and coming back satisfied, instead of sitting up all night on a red-cushioned barstool alone, nursing a bottle of beer.

Girl stood near her, long leather coat buttoned. Light off, bed still made, like nobody'd been there.

Girl's eyes sparkled with dreams of stardom. "I had a bulldagger like you. She fucked me the same way you do. I treat you the same as anybody else."

"You were real good, honey. I'll be back to see you when I can afford it. I'll look for you."

Girl straightened her coat. "Well, keep coming back to see me. I like you butches."

They opened the door, stepped out into the street. People on the outside, looking in.

*Issue: March/April 1992*

# The Strength of Trees
by Anna Svahn

*A loud bellow sprang from her lips as she bucked once and orgasmed, great splashes of cum coursing down her thighs.*

She was flipping through her mail when the distinctive voice on the answering machine caught her attention: "Be at the Third Street entrance to the park at 9. Wear the black leather lace-up, your flat black boots, and nothing else." A brief pause. "Don't be late."

Putting aside her bills, she rewound the machine and listened again to the harsh whisper as moisture gathered in the throbbing crevice between her legs.

She knew immediately it was Denys, even though it had been months since the last siren call. Lena took a deep breath and sat down, her fingers picking at the leather armchair as she recalled their past.

For several years she and Denys had been involved in a relationship based on commitment and trust and a mutual taste for the violently erotic pleasures. Over time, though, Denys had increasingly devoted herself to the pursuit of sophisticated sadomasochistic arts, becoming internationally known as a skilled dominatrix. Her lifestyle left little time for friends and family. Finally, she and Lena had parted, and Lena resigned herself to more moderate passions with less adventuresome partners.

Intentions were no defense against emotions. Each time Lena heard the whispered commands issue forth from her answering machine, she longed for the strength to deny them.

Her heart racing, Lena stifled a sob. "I won't do it this time," she vowed, knowing she would. Rivulets of black mascara slid down her face.

Much later Lena struggled to her feet, feeling weak. She stretched, wiped her face with her hands, and shook out her hair. Walking like a woman just awakened from a long sleep, she made her way to the bathroom, leaving a trail of silk on the floor as she shed her clothes.

The tiled room was a cloud of steam when she stepped into the bath. She caressed her body with a sea sponge, carefully cleaning between her legs and beneath her pendulous breasts with a fragrant lather. With a razor she smoothed her legs and underarms to the softness of a baby's bottom.

She stroked lotion onto her skin and inhaled the scents of lotus and patchouli. She thought of Denys touching her with hands nearly twice the size of her own. Hands that could be gentle and brutal in turn—tender as they caressed her face or stinging with a backhanded slap.

Lena studied her reflection in the mirror, the light from a table lamp illuminating her body. She moved her hands down around her breasts and across the slight curve of her belly to cup the warmth between her legs. Her groping fingers swirled silky wetness around her clitoris.

Reaching for a breast, she felt for a spot of hardness in the erect nipple. Pinching it, she rummaged through her jewelry box and found the treasure shining in a corner. She moaned as she pushed the small silver ring through the half-closed hole in her nipple. The tiny diamond suspended from the circle of silver glinted in the dim light. Matching earrings soon swung from her earlobes.

Adorned only in diamonds, she went to the closet and retrieved a pair of thigh-high black leather boots that were perfectly suited for walking through stony brambles in the park.

The black leather minidress was a sheath that laced up either side of a narrow center panel from mid thigh to just above each breast. Bending over, she shifted her breasts until they were perfectly placed, nipples peeking from between the laced seams. Light caught the diamond nipple rig. The white of her skin through the crossed lacing starkly contrasted with the leather's dull sheen.

Admiring herself in the mirror, Lena smiled seductively and pulled on a pair of black leather opera-length gloves. Denys had said nothing about gloves; reconsidering, Lena took them off. She might be able to get away with the nipple ring, but the gloves would be too obvious. She removed the pins that had kept her hair up during the bath and watched it tumble down, a cloud of light around her shoulders. She was ready.

The park was 10 minutes away. Lena was grateful for the wool lining in her raincoat as she kicked through swirling piles of leaves. She saw the panther statues guarding the Third Street entrance and quickened her pace, but no one was waiting for her beneath their watchful gaze. Hugging herself, Lena looked around. Traffic noises broke intermittently through the sound of rustling leaves, but she was all alone.

"I want to do you up against a tree."

The voice came as a surprise; she hadn't heard approaching footsteps. She felt a silk scarf slipping down over her forehead, covering her eyes. She sensed Denys moving in front of her, blocking out light from the streetlamp. She could smell the familiar scent that followed Denys wherever she went, the subtle fragrance of lemon verbena.

"Will you join me?" Denys asked.

Lena knew that with a single word she could bring the proceedings to a close even before they had properly begun. Despite her confused emotions, she sighed and said yes. Denys softly chuckled and led her into the shadowy woods.

The moon was a waxing crescent, casting scant light over the landscape. Leading the way, Denys held aside the larger branches. "Step lively, there's a stone," she said, directing Lena's footing.

Lena walked with tentative steps, the night air chilling the sweat on her body. Her leather dress stuck to her, pulling at the skin of her thighs as she tried to keep up with Denys.

They reached the clearing deep in the wooded area, surrounded by dense undergrowth and mature trees still garbed in autumn splendor. A few scattered pine trees lent fragrance to the cool night air.

In the center of the clearing was a centuries-old oak tree, fully five feet in diameter, its roots exposed like crawling snakes at the base of its massive trunk. Even blindfolded, Lena could feel its presence.

Denys sat down on a large boulder. Brushing strands of hair away from Lena's face, she reiterated the rules of their game. "You will only speak when spoken to. However, if you say 'freeze frame,' I will stop immediately and escort you home." The deep tone of her voice raised the hairs on Lena's arms. "Do you understand?"

"Yes."

"Take off your coat."

Lena stood and shrugged the coat from her shoulders; Denys caught it with one deft movement and draped it over the boulder. She led Lena to the immense tree, positioning her against its rough bark. Lena had a fleeting impulse to run as Denys opened her "bag of tricks."

It was a large brown leather satchel Denys had owned since her public-school days in Britain. Lena had never been permitted to explore its dark interior, but she knew it contained many instruments capable of producing both pleasure and pain.

Denys took out a long length of thick rope. Knowing what was expected of her, Lena nestled her feet between the roots of the tree and held her arms on either side of her body, waiting for the rope's bite across her wrists. The knots Denys tied were loose as she slipped them over Lena's hands, but tightened when she pulled the tope snugly around the tree trunk. The bark scratched a sharp welcome into Lena's outstretched arms as she tested the rope's give.

"Spread your legs," Denys commanded. Lena lifted her feet and placed them a shoulder's width apart. "Wider."

Lena positioned her legs as far apart as she could, rooting herself in the earth alongside the deep tendrils of the trees. She tightened her groin muscles against the delicate invasion of the cool night air.

"Good." Denys reached out to caress Lena's thigh, exposed between boot and dress. Her hand moved gently, brushing almost casually against the clenched labia hidden beneath the leather dress. Lena moaned. Heat seeped out of her.

"Open to me," Denys said quietly.

It took all of Lena's powers of concentration to comply. She relaxed with a deep breath, her head falling to her chest as the tension in her cunt released. In an instant Denys's fingers moved deep within the cavern of her cunt, drawing out moisture to slick the smooth channel between Lena's lips.

"You're so wet," she said. "One would think you like this, Lena. Do you?" Her fingers created slow circles around Lena's hardening clitoris.

"Yes."

"What did you say?"

"Yes!" Lena's reply sent a bird screeching eagerly from its perch in a nearby tree. She blushed at Denys's amused laughter, waves of embarrassment engulfing her. Denys's two fingers, held tightly together, palpitated between her legs with increasingly rapid strokes. The beginning of a slow burn inched its way across Lena's cunt. Leaning against the tree, Denys moved her hand fiercely on Lena's clitoris. Her fingers penetrated deeply to draw more of the slick inner fluid out to the excited clit. She rested her head against Lena's chest, listening to the frenetic beating of her heart. Lena began to moan, softly at first, then louder as Denys's hand increased its staccato rhythm.

Lena pulled at the restraints, thrusting her hips into the air. She flung her knees far apart to afford Denys better access. Denys lifted her head from Lena's breasts, and with her lips close to Lena's ear, she asked, "What do you want, Lena?" She knew full well the answer.

"Please, Denys," Lena pleaded, "make me come." Denys's fingers became a blur in the darkness.

When Lena's trembling had subsided, Denys gently wiped the beads of sweat from Lena's face. Lena tried to kiss the hand caressing her and, failing that, simply rested her head against her shoulder. Her breath was forced between dry lips, her tongue too parched to speak.

Taking a water bottle from her bag, Denys drank a huge mouthful. She bent to kiss Lena and let it flow into her thirsty mouth. Rivulets ran down Lena's chin and neck, becoming trapped in the pool between her leather-bound breasts. Denys stopped to drink it. Her tongue probed between Lena's breasts and the leather minidress. When she reached the jeweled nipple, she stopped abruptly.

"What's this?" she asked and held it away from Lena's body at a sharp angle. "Very nice," she purred. "I compliment you on your taste." Pulling loose the scarf, she looked into Lena's eyes. Her voice changed. "Or was it a gift?"

Lena looked down, too embarrassed to admit that she'd bought the ring pretending it was a gift from Denys. Better for her to think it was a gift from a new lover.

Denys was flipping the bauble with seeming indifference. "I don't recall asking you to wear jewels tonight." She paused and a shiver of fear crawled up Lena's back. "Why did you?" She yanked on the nipple ring, causing Lena to cry out with pain. "Be quiet!"

Lena swallowed with some difficulty, her mouth suddenly dry again. Denys untied the leather thongs holding Lena's dress together. Partially unlacing the grommets to the waist, she freed Lena's breasts.

Moonlight caught the sheen from the blade of a small knife as Denys withdrew it from her pocket. Holding it against Lena's battered flesh, she traced the impressions left by the grommet holes and leather, scraping slowly up and down against the skin. Lena's breathing grew shallow as she tried to keep her breasts from rising into the knife's edge.

Denys threaded an end of lacing through the nipple ring and, pulling it toward her, completely unlaced one seam of the dress. The snaking leather thong popped free of the grommets and revealed flesh of thigh, cunt, belly, and breast as the dress opened but did not fall, trapped between the tree and Lena's stiff body. The night air caused goose bumps to rise on her stomach.

Quickly bored by the knife, Denys sheathed it and turned her attention to the offending breast, double-looping the string through the nipple ring and wrapping its end around her wrist. Holding her arm at some distance from Lena's body, she teased the aching nipple with quick movements. A sob caught in Lena's throat. The pain was intense but not enough for her to say the phrase that would make it stop.

Denys grabbed the back of Lena's head and peered into her eyes. With one hand in her hair and the other pulling on her nipple, Denys watched the expression on Lena's face. Lena closed her eyes as tears burned on her cheeks. The woman standing before her with a breast rein in her hand snorted derisively.

"Next time I ask you to meet me for a scene in the park, I want you to follow my instructions exactly. Do you understand?"

Lena nodded energetically.

"You will not wear any jewelry unless I ask you to. Do you understand?"

Again Lena nodded, her eyes still closed. In a hidden place

deep inside her she felt a shiver of delight. She couldn't resist challenging her captor.

"Can't I even wear earrings?" she asked timidly, wondering what Denys would find as a suitable punishment for this insubordination.

Using both sides of her hand, Denys slapped the extended breast repeatedly. Lena's other nipple tightened into a little nut as the beating continued without a pause.

The tender skin soon speckled dark red. Each whack of Denys's hand reverberated throughout her trussed body. By the time the slapping finally and abruptly stopped, she had lost count of the number of blows. She gasped at the sudden cessation of pain. Drawing ragged breaths, she tried to ease the pressure on her swollen breast by pulling her body away from the tree. Her tormentor recognized her intent and with one hand maintained the tension while the other stroked the flaming skin.

Each gentle touch was a new agony to Lena. She tried to escape by moving her consciousness deep within, but an inner voice kept insisting that she remain present and alert.

"Open your mouth," Denys commanded.

She tasted the salty bitterness of the leather. Her tear-streaked face closed into an expression of strong resolve. Denys reached into her bag, removed a bottle of lubricant, and smoothed some over her hands. The slithering sucking noise alerted Lena; the muscles of her cunt tightened of their own volition. This was what she really wanted, the reason she had come to be tied to the tree in the clearing. No one knew her body as well as Denys.

Opening her eyes, Lena met Denys's piercing gaze. Removing the leather from Lena's mouth, Denys came close and kissed her, lingering on full lips that parted sweetly. Their tongues met in a slow caress for several moments.

"You possess great courage, Lena." Denys whispered. "You give me much pleasure." She replaced the leather thong in Lena's mouth, gently pulling it between her lips to create a pleasurable tautness on the nipple ring.

Standing back to better view the bound woman, Denys ran her eyes up from the toes of the black leather boots to the pale skin of Lena's thighs and abdomen. As she stood spread-eagled, Lena's hands disappeared beyond the edge of the tree trunk, her breasts held high by the tension on her arms. The leather thong pulled cruelly on the nipple ring attached to the badly bruised breast. Strands of her hair were caught on the tree, streaming around her head like the petals of a desert flower.

An old familiar desire rose within Denys. Dropping to her knees, she pushed her tongue between the hairy lips of Lena's cunt. Her arms wrapped themselves around Lena's hips as she burrowed into the wet flesh, her tongue swirling and sucking the erect clitoris.

Lena felt weak. Her legs were barely strong enough to hold her body upright as she opened herself to Denys's ministrations. She felt the tackiness of dried lubricant on Denys's hands as they grabbed the cheeks of her ass to better position her for the seeking tongue moving between the swollen lips of her vulva.

Pressing her cunt into Denys's face, she leaned back into the tree, ignoring the bark sticking into her body. Her head moving from side to side, she bit at the leather thong attached to her aching breast, increasing its pressure. Denys nibbled and sucked on her throbbing clit, swallowing the moisture that came from deep within her.

Waves of pleasure rolled through Lena's body, crashing against the pain emanating from her pierced breast and sore shoulders. The dull throbbing ache of her upper body was in tantalizing contrast to the sharp joy radiating from between her legs. A loud bellow sprang from her lips as she bucked once and orgasmed, great splashes of cum coursing down her thighs.

"Oh, yes, feed me," Denys murmured as she lapped up the

mighty flow. Her hands held Lena apart as she sought every drop, her tongue pushing its way into damp recesses. Lena wept as her body quivered and came again and again.

"You are so beautiful when you come, Lena." Denys ran her hand against Lena's lower lips, their moistness bringing to life the waiting lubricant. Planting small kisses on the trembling belly against her face, she wet the full expanse of her hand in Lena's damp wall. Sliding three fingers inside the still quaking vagina, Denys began to gently thrust.

Lena let the leather thong fall from her mouth as she groaned with pleasure. This was the gift she really wanted from Denys. Diamonds paled in comparison to the intensity of the feeling building inside her. She moaned loudly, disturbing the quiet, but all the birds had long since fled.

Carefully observant, Denys gauged her movements to Lena's level of arousal, first with three fingers and then with four. It was several minutes before she tucked her thumb, and her hand and wrist were encased by Lena's body, the protruding knuckle having finally slid through the vaginal portal with only the slightest difficulty. Lena gasped as the fingers inside her curled into a tightly clenched fist.

"Ahh," she moaned, the pain a passing memory as she opened herself to Denys. She felt as though she couldn't spread her legs wide enough; she wanted to somehow discard them, to wrench them from her so Denys could have easier access into her burning core.

"Ohhh, yes, yes," Lena cried out in the stillness of the clearing. "Don't stop."

It was an impossibility, as Denys's hand was trapped deep inside Lena's body. Small movements caused ripples of sensation that came crashing out as groans from her gaping mouth. Reaching up with a free hand, Denys caught the leather thong as it swung back and forth, abandoned as Lena gave herself over to mindless sensation. Gentle tugs added resonance to Lena's cries of pleasure.

Lena felt herself loosen and let go, the fluid of her orgasms flowing once more down her legs, following dried paths of earlier pleasures. She felt the strength of the tree supporting her. Denys's fist inside her made loud sucking noises as Lena propelled a seemingly unending stream onto the ground.

With each shuddering release she was brought closer to that nameless place where time and feeling merge into one. There were no boundaries to separate her from the person she truly loved, the one she wanted to be, the strong and powerful woman who waited at the edge of her dreams.

Perhaps it was a change in muscle tone, but Denys knew that a part of Lena had left the clearing. Denys continued the rhythmic motions that propelled the bound woman into another realm. She knew that any change in her pacing would bring Lena back. She would simply have to wait out the journey unfolding her hands.

Lena was standing in a featureless landscape. From just beyond the horizon, an old woman approached, her garments moving about her body as if caught in a fierce wind. She gestured toward Lena. "You are gifted with yourself," she said, her voice echoing across the plain. "Remember, your strength is like a tree, steadfast through many a powerful gale."

Reaching out with bony, craw-like hands, she followed the hard contours of Lena's body from feet to fingertips, leaving the tingling traces where she touched the skin. Lena felt energy coming up from her toes, moving along the lines drawn by the crone. She felt bright with the light, invigorated by the touch.

The crone gave a rasping laugh and faded into the mist, leaving Lena once again alone. Looking down at her own body, Lena felt as though she were a stranger to herself, although at the same time familiar.

She felt herself to be firmly planted in the ground, her legs and arms extending the lines of the strength in her stance.

She became aware of a new rhythm beating between her legs, overriding the pounding heartbeat that had filled her senses. Remembering Denys, she said the words that brought the scene in the woods officially to an end.

It was but a hoarse whisper, but the waiting woman heard each one distinctly as though they resounded through the clearing. She first slowed and then gently withdrew her fist from Lena's limp body.

Denys used her knife to release Lena from the rope's restraints. Everything was thrown into the leather satchel as Lena struggled with her coat. Although obviously exhausted, her face was beatific in moonlight.

"You're very strong, Lena," Denys respectfully acknowledged. Then, carrying her as much as guiding her, Denys took Lena home.

*Issue: Sept./Oct. 1992*

## Absolutely Naked
by Lindsay Welsh

*Sue replaces her tongue with her hand; her skillful fingers
dance over my shaven lips as she moves up my body.*

I like shaving.

I like to seclude myself in the bathroom with the tall can
of cream and my silver razor. I like to cover my legs with
the perfumed whipped cream and then slowly scrape it off.
I like the long, continuous strokes up my calves and the
short, protective caresses around my knees and the bones in
my ankles.

My primary reason for all this is my silk pants. A couple
of years ago I treated myself to a horrendously expensive silk
suit. When my legs are freshly shaved those pants glide over
my skin like a whisper. When I go outside, it feels as if I'm
walking through the streets completely naked.

Sue generally leaves me alone when I'm shaving; I do it
slowly, after my shower, and the steamy bathroom is mine for
the better part of an hour. When I emerge, I'm ready to take
her into my arms. So she waits.

Today there's a knock on the bathroom door. I've just
rinsed the razor and put it away. Sue is waiting outside the
door, naked.

"Please shave me," she says.

I'm surprised by her request; her natural armpits are a

turn-on for me. She sees I'm confused, so she points to the soft mound between her legs. "Here," she says.

It isn't something I've considered before, but the idea becomes more and more appealing as I reach for the shaving cream and the heavy razor. Sue has already prepared the bed with thick towels to protect the sheets and placed a bowl of warm water on the table. She lies down and spreads her legs. I can't resist a final kiss on those sweet, hairy lips.

I begin by cutting the hair as close as possible with a small pair of scissors. Sue has long, bushy hair, and as her cunt emerges, I realize I have never seen it this close up. She obviously enjoys the feel of the cold scissors against the warm flesh, and I'm getting more turned on.

I admit I rub the thick cream over her pussy more than is absolutely necessary; I love the way it feels. She purrs deep in her throat and moves toward my hand. When I'm finished, a few black curls poke sharply through the cream, like porcupines buried under a fresh snowfall. I'm still naked. My hand strays to my own pussy for a moment; I push against my clit, and the sharp, pleasant wave starts between my legs and races up my spine.

I warm the razor in the water. While I'm actually shaving her, I don't think about sex at all; my only concern is the difficult task—getting all of the spiky hair, pulling her skin tight so that the razor doesn't cut her. But when I sit up and rinse the razor clean, the sight of her completely naked skin leaves me breathless, and it takes a moment to compose myself enough to finish the job.

When I'm done I wipe away the last of the cream. Sue asks for a mirror and lies there for a while examining her shaven pussy. I can wait no longer; I push the mirror away and lean down.

It's like experiencing a whole new kind of sex. I spend a long time just running my tongue over the area I've shaved, feeling her smooth lips and lovely mound. There's still a sharp

Lindsay Welsh

smell of perfumed shaving cream, but she warms to my touch; it's overpowered by her own aroma.

"Let me shave you," she says. I'm so intrigued by her hairless pussy that I agree immediately. She lays me down on the towel and performs the same operation, cutting with the scissors, rubbing in the lather.

I lie perfectly still as her fingers guide the razor. It's dangerous work, and even though I trust her, I'm waiting apprehensively for the rude steel to nick me. It doesn't, but the tension adds to my excitement.

My naked legs are nothing compared to this. When she's finished, I explore myself with my fingers, feeling a part of me I've never before known. I am totally nude, completely vulnerable.

When her tongue touches me I'm on fire. It's as if in the past she's been eating me through my underwear, and now they're gone. Like me, Sue spends a long time on my newly shaven skin, and I sigh with each lingering kiss. She's teasing me. I love it.

I feel every tiny move of her tongue, even the difference between the hot wetness when she laps at me and the cooler pointed motions when she uses just the tip. Without the protective hair, the contact is so direct that when she bears down on me, the sensation is almost too much. I have to learn sex all over again.

Sue replaces her tongue with her hand; her skillful fingers dance over my shaven lips as she moves up my body. We kiss for the longest time, our hands in each other's cunts. I can't believe how beautiful her smooth flesh feels. She moans into my mouth when my fingertips press on the swollen button of her slit.

Eventually she turns around and gets on top of me. We always love sixty-nining, but this time it's especially pleasurable. I feel like a virgin as I bury my tongue in Sue's wet flower, and shivers run through me as she applies herself to mine.

She is, as always, honey-sweet, and I delve. I know her

134

well—when she's close to orgasm I hold back to make it last longer. Three times I do this, until finally I concentrate my whole being on her clit. This is tough to do when she's just as eagerly going at me, but I do succeed: Her orgasm is long, loud, drawn-out, trembling, wet.

She uses her tongue and fingers on me until I come too. The fire builds between my legs and in my belly until I can no longer control it, and it races the length of my body, causing my arms and legs and even the ends of my fingers to tingle and burn. She's good, very good, and she knows it. She plays me like an instrument; I'm helpless in her hands. When the last shudders subside, I am completely drained, gasping for breath; I don't have enough strength to lift my hands.

We lie together in each other's arms. My hand moves down to cup her smooth pussy, still burning-hot; I love the feel of her, the new feel of me, both of us completely, absolutely naked under the blankets.

She tells me about an article she has read on erotic piercing. I hold her tightly and listen very carefully.

*Issue: March/Apr. 1993*

## Reunion
by minns

*She pulls me down to the mound of clothes and begins to move on top, wild, heavy, her hands seeking every opening, pulling me apart, me the butch wild child from the West...*

She actually read my book. She wrote to tell me. Now, it might not seem like much to you, but to a hungry author it was like a long, cool drink of water.

"I know it's been 15 years, and you probably don't remember me, but I thought I'd take the chance..."

Great opening, *non*? What writer could resist?

"I've been showing my photographs pretty regularly, and they asked me to bring my portfolio for the opening night's reception in the student gallery...like old times. I saw your novel in a bookstore on my way to the framers yesterday. I just had to have it."

She *had* to have it! Ha! Not even my publisher said that!

"...A lot has changed since we last saw each other. I gather from your novel that we have much more in common these days... Are you coming to the reunion?"

The reunion. Two graduates from a preppie women's East Coast college, all radical feminist energy and change-the-world intentions.

After graduation I'd gone on to drink and write my way across the country, trying to live out the female-punk version of Kerouac's *On The Road*. Lost touch with everyone but my best friend, and left her in New York with a kid, career, and her original husband. I learned how to travel long distances alone—stopping only for gas, new ribbons, and a few bad relationships.

Finally, the work clicked. The stories grew into collections, and the collections sprouted into novels. Now there was money (a little), a house (also little) in the West, and a new family of friends—none of whom had even visited the East Coast, let alone gone to school there.

Occasionally our alumnae newsletter would reach my various post office boxes, bringing news of the latest births, divorces, and promotions at Xerox. Seemed everyone was working for "Daddy's firm" and doing volunteer service between babies—well, almost everyone.

I'd thought about Kelly. Kelly of the green eyes and golden hair; the quiet, tall, Celtic refugee whose strongest voice was her camera. Kelly who looked like she lived madrigals and had been born in a castle. Kelly had once walked within two feet of me and Dr. Danielle Stone, hidden by the dance stage curtain, our clothes piled around our feet, our limbs entwined.

I doubt if she realized that one of the most intense, prolonged climaxes I ever had was a result of knowing she was doing arabesques just below us at the barre! I remember biting the edge of that cruddy curtain to keep from screaming, a century of dust and dancers' sweat filling my mouth, mingling with the taste of my professor. Yeah, I do remember Kelly quite well.

Before Kelly's letter I'd toyed with the idea of getting my best leathers Sanforized, hopping a late plane out of Los Angeles and landing ass-end-first in the midst of those aging 30-somethings, with 100 copies of my latest book tucked neatly into my suitcase. Hell, *Rhumba, Mon Amour* was getting decent reviews, some of them even mainstream. Of course, everyone would be bowled over by my bravado. Then, in the middle of the fantasy the mail would arrive, and there would be the latest update about "Muffy" or "Pissy," complete with a photo of her husband and the latest organizational board she'd been voted onto. Fighting nausea, I'd scrap the entire idea. Then another few weeks would go by, another good review or royalty check, and the fantasy would kick back in. Kept this up for eight months—until Kelly's letter.

Hell, what's a writer to do?

Write. Write back. Right away.

OK, so I left most of the leather at home. I carried only a single copy of *Rhumba* with me, already inscribed. Kelly had grown into more than a memory. More than remembered dance steps in a darkened hall. Kelly and I both knew, without actually writing it, that I was coming all right, but for her. Just for her.

Summer thunderstorm, lightning streaking and striking the face of the lake. Perfect backdrop for my arrival. (If I wrote it like this nobody'd buy it.) Put the rental jeep in the parking lot, hop out, make my way to the mossy statue of Athena that guards the front doors. Late. Everyone's been drinking for hours. The reception is in full swing as I open the doors, shaking the rain from my crew cut. I am looked at the way one would look at the proverbial drowned rat: Culture shock is instantaneous. So much summer pastel. So much "maternal suburbanite renovating the farmhouse while studying for a law degree while the children grow a bit." So much makeup and hair and espadrilles. Welcome home, Manilla.

I grin my best West Coast smile but don't remove my dark glasses. Feeling some kind of satisfaction at the muddy boot prints I track on the beige rug, I push past a woman trying to pin a neon nametag on my bomber jacket. Where the hell is the artist?

Then, behind the crowd of doctors and lawyers and congressfolk milling about, I see her, up front, beneath a huge blowup of this...this nude woman! At least it *looks* like a nude woman, parts of a nude woman. Of course, it could be sand dunes.

Has to be Kelly. I've done the research. Even found a review of her latest show at a small gallery in the Village. Now, her green eyes are shooting emerald sparks across the room. Her long mane is pulled into a French knot, her longer body sheathed in shimmering black beads and something soft. She is more than transformed—she is metamorphosed. Shit, maybe this is a big mistake. Maybe I've been reading too much between the lines. Then those killer eyes catch mine, and she shatters into a smile.

Goddess!

Garbo!

Instant wet. Meltdown. This has nothing to do with the rain. Sweet Mother of Christ. My cunt thunders inside, responding to the ex-dancer/photographer/angel-in-black in front of me. Electric, like the lightning. Instant connection. Gone, the shy, self-conscious, almost gawky swan child.

The crowd surges around her, hugs, well-spoken praise, all so proper. We'd all maintained our college manners.

I wait for the wave to crest and break away. The ever-present weak Chablis beckons from the sideboards. I pick up a discarded catalogue and move in as close as is prudent. By now Kelly has moved to a love seat, still chatting with a few folks.

"Uh, excuse me, Ms. Ferguson, would you mind signing this for me? I'm a collector and an admirer of your work."

I hand her the folder.

She looks up, her smile fainter, then gleaming again.

Maybe the dark glasses are throwing her, maybe the close-cropped hair? A pucker lays around the edges of those roseate lips. They seem almost swollen, tender, perhaps bruised. I want to caress them. Instead I offer my pen.

"To whom do I make this out?" Her voice is older, softer, a wee bit tired, a wee bit low. It's got that raw whiskey edge some city women acquire. Almost knocks me over.

"To Manilla..." I stop, liking the boom-boom gap in talk, the silent syncopation our hearts must be making, like the look that surfaces in those jeweled eyes.

"Oh."

My heart is pumping thunder again. All notions of cool have vanished. Practiced lines, swift abandonment of decorum, I've planned all along to do this, just sweep her away, into the blackened night, to the edge of the lake, the boathouse maybe. Past the crowd, laughing like maniacs, flying with each other, into and at and with each other till dawn. Ha! I've been sleeping with such images for months now. I am younger now than we ever were—tongue-tied and babbling.

Kelly reaches over, her prefect fingers trembling, and with a touch that burns, brushes my cheek.

Stomach falls into boots. Can't breathe. Think my cunt is going to explode (attractive image). All I can do is stand here, stunned and watering.

"Oh, Manilla."

Her husky voice is its own caress.

My breath slams back, stinging. It's obvious, as obvious as the tight knots of my hardening nipples. Thank God I've remembered to keep my jacket on.

"Manilla? Hey, look, it's Manilla! Look who showed! Oh, wow! Everybody, Manilla's here!" The fast-drinking entourage swarms back like a bunch of tipsy bees.

"I saw the review of *Rhumba, Mon Amour* in the book section. Haven't had a chance to actually read it yet, but..."

"My kid can't believe we went to school together."

"I saw you on that talk show in Chicago. Who would have thought..."

Chagrined, expecting only cold stares at best, here only because of Kelly, this has become my 15 Warholian minutes. Try to move away politely and just as politely get pulled back in.

Kelly is being gently shoved off the sofa, or maybe she's receding. One of the old music profs has her in a bear hug. His huge, hairy arm stays attached as he moves her away from the crowd, out of the gallery, into the hallway, and then, she's gone.

The sun is high when I awake. I sit up, wobbling in bed. My head's soft like a tomato. Shit. Last night—a blur after Kelly's disappearance.

Went to find her, but no luck. No one knew where she was staying. No way to track her in the storm. Could be anywhere this morning, maybe even with the—ugh—professor. I pull on black jeans, a black tee, the ever-ready cowgirl boots (now reeking of beer), and the black linen blazer. The Ray-Bans hide the vampire excesses of the previous night. I find the jeep keys and then go to find Kelly.

When I reach campus nobody's left in the dining hall. I bump into one of the summer interns in the kitchen, almost knocking a tray of gnawed bones out of her slippery hands.

"Where are they?" I gasp.

"Who? Hey, aren't you the writer? Manilla? Yeah, yeah, I got your book. It's way cool! Can't believe you actually went to this college! Hey, will you sign something, please? For me?"

She puts down the gruesome luncheon remains and pulls a black-and-white bandanna out of her back pocket while the sounds of steam cleaning and clanging silverware ring from inside.

"Here, I gotta get going." I scribble my name and hand the bandanna back into the startled girl's hands.

"Uh, I think half your class is in the lecture hall in the philosophy building."

I run, slipping in spilled barbecue sauce, the leather of my boot soles not getting the best traction on linoleum—real cowgirls rarely encounter linoleum. I smash out of the heavy dining hall doors into raw sunlight. I dash across green lawns, almost twisting an ankle on a sprinkler head, and take the steps of the philosophy building two at a time, sweat clouding my already cloudy vision. I dash inside only to have the prof look up from the lectern and the crowd turn around, aghast, like in a Woody Allen film. A bomb, a fire drill, a simple robbery? Their faces register the questions. I wipe my streaming forehead, remembering to remove my dark glasses, trying not to heave on the Docksiders and Papagallos. My fame has faded. No Kelly in the crowd.

I sit outside the Fine Arts Center, the smells of summer wafting by: suntan oil, barbecue, cut grass, clean sweat.

And then, out of the corner of my eye, a movement, not even a shape, something at an angle in the windows. Then a low, sweet, easy-sounding music wafting across the grass.

I'm in front of the Dance Building.

Sweet Jesus. Thank you, Jack Kerouac!

No time to see if I'm being followed, will get busted, will die before I reach the doorknob. Just follow the light, the music. Let it lead you by your lust, by your younger, headier, most outrageous self, back to a more heated time, when you were with the wrong women but always in the right places. I am at the door, and joy of joys, it swings open easily, quickly, and I am flung inside. The hallway seems to be alive.

Before my eyes adjust I hear the click of the industrial lock and the click of her heels as she kicks them across the hardwood floor.

"There's nobody behind the curtains this time," Kelly laughs.

My glasses are lifted for me. The blazer is ripped off,

falling silently like a broken feather. The music has stopped. The only sound is my breath, our breathing, our hearts. I know she wants me. This much. This time.

A quick intake of breath. She's been waiting, planning this out—for how long? Doesn't matter. Don't think, feel: Let this feeling burn straight to your core, carrying the burning to her; let her know the fire she's been banking all weekend; a scalding tongue against her clit; a flame licking her inner thigh.

I move behind her, reach around to loosen the soft chambray shirt from her sunburned shoulders. She sighs as it slips and joins my blazer on the floor.

"I was at the lake this morning, hoping you'd find me." Her voice is all sweet breeze.

Her breasts are soft-tipped surrender, then hard, the nipples waiting, slightly raw. My hands find them, finger them, pull and roll and move them delicately, just enough to make her moan.

I reach lower, unbutton the jeans, my fingers flipping the buttons one by one, to skin white and speckled. I move my own fevered crotch against her firm ass, my hands trembling as I ease the jeans over her hips, my lips tracing calligraphy across her shoulders, down her spine.

She turns to face me, wild, her hair down; the Amazon confronting this upstart who would reveal her. Her huge hands, infuriated, rip my black T-shirt with a ferocity that shocks and warms like a slap. Our clothes are around us, discarded skins. My boots are the last thing to go.

"Do you remember, 11 years ago, this place?" her voice is a low growl in my ear as she nips at the lobe, her tongue following the question inside.

My skin ripples. The air is hot, and we are very exposed. Outside, people are beginning to pass in the walkway, separated from us by only a few feet of rock and glass. They have dressed for dinner, are coming in early for cocktails and conversations about stocks and bonds. Here we are, vulnerable, exposed, exposing what we couldn't a decade ago—what we should have exposed even then.

Her hands tangle, low, pulling on each wet, mossy place, tracing my swollen lips as our mouths collide. We rock and sway, hips grinding, causing sparks to fly in the shadows. I am sure they must be able to see the fire through the darkening glass of the windows, sure our scents must carry over to the mowed lawns, our animal sounds rising over the volcanic bells in the tower.

She pulls me down to the mound of clothes and begins to move on top, wild, heavy; her hands seeking every opening, pulling me apart, me the butch wild child from the West, the crew-cut kid, the hellion writer who comes flying down in the middle of the night in black leather. This angel rides me sure and hard, splitting me wide, making me steam and scream her name over and over, rocking and rolling in the dark—which the dancing floor has never witnessed—her hands deep, pulsing, making a new music I cannot withstand.

I protest: This is not what I thought. But she won't hear it. She laughs, bites, draws blood from my lips, makes me taste it and bite back, explodes a second time as she thrusts and rocks even harder, making me moan her name over and over, making me sure it is her and no one else that I'm with, want to be with, will be with...will? Even later?

"As late as you want, cowgirl," she hisses, pulling me on top, her hair lashing and slashing me, our bodies streaming together, two rivers meeting in the sea.

And I am diving hard, fast, slick-backed, heaving from my own surrender but ready to gain honor again.

Kelly laughs, then moans, then swears in the hot darkness.

She is salt and sweet and good sweat, blond even here; even here she is the miracle woman, thrusting and pulling my head closer, my tongue pressed as deep as I can so my teeth only graze the hood of her clit, making her scream, making her name me now, coming in my mouth, coming again, and again, coming home.

"Coming home, Manilla." Kelly leans back, those old dancer's legs not so old, letting me go, for a minute.

"Kelly." What else to say? A writer made silent: What better compliment? She shuts me up. The first.

"That night, 11 years ago, when I came here to practice—remember?" She is propped up on one elbow, her graceful, long hands stroking my flank, as if I am some precious, dangerous, much loved beast.

"I remember."

"I knew you were here. I made myself come here, made myself stay. You two weren't as quiet as you thought, my sweet. I've been waiting since then."

Kelly finds my mouth, her lips bruised, swollen, tasting as much of me as herself. And then I feel the tear, drink in the tiny sip of salt as it slides between our lips.

"Happy reunion."

*Issue: July/Aug. 1993*

## Whips and Appendages
### by Mil Toro

*"I don't know what rumors you've heard about my species, but I'm sure the whips will come out tonight."*

Tonight I'm going to be trouble, female trouble, I thought as I walked into Live Wire, the local bar on the Zedder Space Colony. I knew everyone was buzzing about my recent arrival, but I had come to the bar for one specific purpose. I had my eye on the alien female bartender, since I'd heard rumors about her species. Her name was Nevia, and she was a Zedder. Tension passed between us when I sat down at the counter and ordered my drink. I felt it when she glanced briefly but pointedly at my breasts. I felt it when our hands made contact as she served me. I refused to elude her touch, and she made no attempt either. I would never back away from such a bold invitation.

As Nevia moved behind the counter to carry on with her work, I continued to stare at her in defiance and lust. It seemed to have absolutely no effect, though I can be openly defiant, arrogant, cool. And aggressive—underneath my cool exterior was a smoldering heat of passion ready to explode. Rumor had it that she'd never had a sexual encounter with a human woman, but I wanted to change that. I wanted to be her first. Just like a virgin.

It was difficult for me to continue staring, because when I did, my loins went into minor convulsions as I thought about her soft hands brushing against mine. I knew I was challenging Nevia, but I couldn't help myself. I had heard so many rumors about her physical attributes that I was beside myself with lust—but I refused to humiliate myself and admit my desire. Still, my thoughts kept wandering to the rumors about Nevia's appendage and the whips that made no marks.

I waited until the crowd had gone, and finally got up the nerve to talk to Nevia alone. Hesitantly I approached her. She was wiping down some tables close to the counter, and she smiled knowingly. I started to speak but was struck by humiliation. Usually I'm the aggressor, but with Nevia I found myself tongue-tied, feeling completely stupid. Finally, I stammered, "Are you closed for the evening, Nevia?" Immediately I blushed.

Nevia, who seemed to enjoy my discomfort, replied, "Well, I'm closing Live Wire. What would you like?"

As she spoke she hopped onto a barstool, gazed directly into my eyes, and, with her legs splayed, began stroking her appendage. I realized that the rumors I'd heard about female Zedders were true. It was quite obvious that hers was fully expanded and hard, ready for action. If she'd had on tighter clothes, all the universe could have seen her excitement. But right now only I was so privileged.

I strained to see the appendage through the material. I could not speak even when she asked what I wanted. I couldn't look at her or endure my lustful desires. What I wanted to do was collapse at her feet, lift up her robes, suck her appendage down my throat, then leap onto her lap and fuck the living starlights out of her. Instead I turned around and rushed out, seething inside. Over my shoulder I heard her laugh.

I wandered aimlessly around the colony grounds, not knowing what to do. I was coming unhinged with hunger and lust for Nevia. I, Bridget Linton, did not like being humiliated and made out to be a fool, but my aching desire refused to listen to my egotistical ranting. I was aggravated. How could I let myself get so out of control? The answer, of course, was Nevia's appendage—and her whips.

With human women, I was always the one in control, the aggressor. I'd never had to beg or ask for it; I'd always demanded it and got it. Easily. But this was different. This was Nevia, the Zedder woman. Lust won out over ego.

"Come in," Nevia sang out when I knocked on the door to her living space. I walked into the room and noticed her wild hair. Very few people had seen it; she usually hid it beneath her scarf. She sat topless in a chair, wearing only a loose wraparound skirt that concealed her appendage, which she gently stroked. Her position made her even more enticing and instantly caused me to avert my eyes. This was just too fucking humiliating. Her breasts were much bigger than I'd thought, and I wondered why she kept playing with herself. It was driving me crazy. I wanted to do it.

Nevia continued rubbing herself, even though she noticed my embarrassment. Her only words were, "You can take those clothes off now."

I was paralyzed, purposefully rebellious, resisting her. She repeated the directive. Angrily I started taking off my clothes.

"That's better," she said nonchalantly. She instructed me to kneel in front of her; this time I obeyed without complaint. I could smell the appendage as I knelt; this was what all the gossip had been about. Nevia had both receptive and extended reproductive organs. I whimpered, thinking what it would be like to run my tongue up and down both her organs.

I moved my face closer to the appendage, anticipating the feel of the bulging hardness in my mouth, but Nevia grabbed my hair before I reached my target. She held my head just inches from her breasts and said, "That's one of the things you're going to have to beg me for. None of this is free."

I gulped and had trouble breathing, but at this point I would have done anything to fuck Nevia and quiet my rage.

Nevia ran her hands over my body, examining the curves and

contours. She paused when I reacted, gasping when she touched my pleasure spots. Coolly she said, "It's been such a long time since a human woman has been this hot for me. I don't know what rumors you've heard about my species, but I'm sure the whips will come out tonight. My hands are tingling."

"That's just what I've been waiting for," I whispered.

Nevia told me to lie across her lap. She leaned over and pressed her lips to my mouth, pushing her tongue inside. Heat emanated from my mouth as I reciprocated her passion. At my sides I could feel Nevia's breasts leaning against me, and I moaned in pleasure as she pinched my nipples. I lifted my body up to meet her fingers, indicating that I wanted it harder. She responded harder than I'd expected, and I cried out. Her hand moved down to my pussy.

Nevia's breath quickened as she played with my clitoris, and she watched my body moving to the rhythm of her fingers. When she inserted one finger I moaned as my legs widened and tried to suck it in. She put in another finger, seemingly amazed at my ability to "suck." She murmured that she would like to feel her own appendage inside me, moving her fingers as if they were it. Then she abruptly pulled out.

"No," I whimpered. "Don't stop, please."

"Oh, so you do speak when you want something," Nevia taunted. "I thought you would suffer in silence. But all you need to do is ask."

I averted my eyes. This was even more embarrassing than her playing with herself on the barstool. I wanted Nevia to fuck me so bad, I ached with the need. But to ask her directly... Instead I squirmed and turned my face toward her breasts. I licked and sucked the huge dark nipples and moaned aloud, all the while thinking about that fucking appendage. In between licks I whispered, "Please fuck me with your appendage."

"You mean Proud Human Bridget Linton can only whisper for what she wants? You are going to have to do better than that, defiant one."

I was so frustrated at this point that I tumbled off her lap and sat with my head hanging down. Speaking directly to the floor, I fumed, "Damn it, do I have to humble myself? I'm not used to being treated this way." Looking up, I demanded, "Now, what do you want from me?"

Nevia smoothly pulled open her skirt, revealing her appendage and receptor, and said, "I want you to beg."

I groaned as I stared at the throbbing, bulbous appendage. I also noticed the glistening moisture oozing out of her receptor. Tossing my pride out the window and using the proper degree of humility, I begged Nevia to let me suck her appendage. She did.

I licked and sucked up and down the appendage. I liked the feel of it, both hard and soft at the same time. I had sucked appendages and had thoroughly enjoyed it, but this was the real thing—and it wasn't male. The smell of the receptor was driving me crazy with lust, so I reached down and licked along the sides of the opening. I was in a frenzy of passion, moving up and down. Finally, I settled on top of the appendage and sucked it down my throat, feeling a small measure of revenge when I heard Nevia moan. So she isn't so calm, cool, and collected all the time, I mused. It gave me the incentive to take over. Enough of the passivity bullshit.

I took my mouth away and grabbed Nevia's hands, pulling her into the sleeping room. I ripped off her skirt and dragged her onto the bed. My hands roamed all over her body and through her soft curly hair. Thinking only of what it would feel like to have the appendage inside me, I straddled my vagina on top of her and started fucking her wildly. Nevia pulled me close, kissing me ardently. My assertiveness seemed to arouse her so much that the whips from her wrists were beginning to inch out. Lightly she stroked my back.

Not moving off the appendage, I sat up. I wanted to see these whips I had heard so much about. They were dark, soft, and sensuous, measuring about a foot and a half in length. Not very many beings could make them come out, or so the rumor went. I could see why they had become a legend. I grabbed Nevia's left wrist and guided her hand to my breasts, wanting to feel them stinging me there. She obliged, whipping both breasts harder and harder to the rhythm of our fucking. Finally, I climaxed and collapsed on her breasts, sliding off the appendage.

While we cuddled and stroked each other, Nevia whispered, "You must allow me to climax also. The trigger is inside my receptor. It has nothing to do with my appendage."

Hungrily I licked my way down her body. I grazed the still-hard appendage and tongued my way down to the receptor that was oozing hot juices.

Eagerly I lapped them up, extending my tongue into her hot cave. Inside I found a hard knot and firmly ran my tongue over it. When I felt Nevia's whips slapping my back, I realized I must have hit the right spot. Rhythmically I slid over her hard spot while she whipped my back harder and harder. It seemed as though she was getting a feedback reaction to the sting of the whips, and together with my insistent tonguing, it intensified the hungry passion in her receptor. Finally, she exploded.

I leaned against Nevia's neck and gently kissed her. "Doesn't that thing ever go down?" I teased, surprised that her appendage was still rigid and stiff even after she came. Grinning, she said, "Not if I'm still excited, it doesn't. It can stay like that for days at a time if I have someone new in my life."

The next day I visited Live Wire and observed Nevia working behind the counter. We exchanged knowing winks, and I realized her appendage was fully extended beneath her flowing robes. I was grateful that her clothing discreetly hid the protrusion, or else everyone on the colony would have known what we'd been up to. No matter—soon everyone would know about me and Nevia anyway.

*Issue: July/Aug. 1993*

## Midsummer's Dream
by Robbi Sommers

*With one fast snap, Laurel's panties were ripped aside.*

"What a waste," Laurel muttered as she grabbed her knapsack from the small boat and headed ashore. The best day of the summer—shit, the best day of the whole goddamn year—and she was stuck with a Shakespeare Lit assignment that guaranteed a full day's commitment. Everyone else she knew was headed for the Women's Arts Festival.

Laurel followed the worn path up the side of the hill toward the forest. High in its midday ascent, the unveiled sun radiated piercing rays. When she had been rowing across the lake, the cool water had diminished the intensity of the heat, but now, completely vulnerable, Laurel was well aware of the persistent sun. The shaded shelter of the trees loomed invitingly, and Laurel quickened her pace.

Facedown, counting hurried steps, Laurel was caught off guard when she slammed into another hiker.

"Oh!" Flustered, thrown off balance, Laurel stumbled.

A strong, dark arm reached for her and steadied her. "You OK?"

"I wasn't watching where I was..." Laurel stopped mid sentence. The woman, whose firm, warm hand still held Laurel's arm, whose obsidian eyes glimmered with mystery, whose sultry scent swirled deliriously, stood before her. For a moment Laurel debated feigning a swoon—to tumble to the ground, to have this woman swoop her into a powerful embrace. She could only imagine the strength, the passion that those sculptured arms might generate.

"I'm so sorry. I wasn't watching where I was going." The woman hesitated, as if something more would be said—as if, perhaps, something more was *indeed* being said—yet she said nothing further.

"No, I was daydreaming," Laurel offered. Once again she discreetly appraised the stranger's magnificent build and sincerely wished she'd been knocked to the ground.

Almost as an afterthought, the woman released Laurel's arm. "Well, it was nice running into you." She flashed an amused smile then continued on her way.

Laurel stood motionless, unable to do anything but watch the woman, who had a walk that could bring marching bands to an abrupt halt, head toward oblivion. An overpowering urge to cry out "Wait, come back!" swept through her. And then what? Laurel argued with herself. Ask this stranger to hold me? Kiss me? Make love to me? As if such a thing were possible! As if such a woman would even be interested.

"Lord, what fools these mortals be," Laurel mumbled, staring across the now empty landscape. Her woman had disappeared somewhere down the hill. With a heavy sigh, Laurel kicked a rock down the path and begrudgingly headed toward Shakespeare and the waiting forest.

There was a place, not too deep in the woods, that Laurel called her own. One day last spring, while searching for blackberries, she had discovered her paradise. Encircled by a thick wall of bushes, down an overgrown path, Laurel had come across a small area seemingly unspoiled by the normal barrage of island hikers. Here she came to soothe her wounds, dream her dreams or, like today, read the I-don't-want-to, rather-be-at-the-women's-festival Shakespearean play.

She pushed her way through the thicket, not surrendering

to the persistent branches that challenged her with sharp, fast scrapes. Her reward—the big tree she'd lean against, the soft grass she'd sit upon—finally came into view.

From her knapsack Laurel unfolded a thin quilt. She tossed a pen, a pad of paper, and her copy of *A Midsummer Night's Dream* onto the spread blanket, gratefully kicking off her shoes. *Shakespeare, here I come,* she thought, leaning against the tree.

The forest was tranquil, so tranquil that a weary hiker could fall asleep—if the trek had been long, if the sun had been too hot, if the words from the play hummed like a lullaby. Laurel drifted in and out of Shakespeare's whimsical settings until she slipped, quite unaware, into a dream...

...and the air was hot. In a sheer floral dress, she danced in circles across the open clearing. Surrounding trees enclosed the field like tall green guards, and Laurel did fairylike pirouettes in the sun.

A seductive shadow—weaving between the trees, following her from the periphery? Laurel was uncertain, yet she sensed the dark eyes, those obsidian eyes, watching her from the forest. Around and around, Laurel, like a spiraling snowflake, twirled to please her hidden audience.

The shadow stepped into the sun. The heat sharpened, heightened, slowing the snowflake's dizzy dance. With a pace so exact, so steady, the mysterious spectator came to the center of the clearing, came to the lacy ballerina, and with one strong hand stopped the faltering spin.

At first the trees, the sky, the entire field still whirled, but even though she was temporarily disoriented, Laurel knew who had grabbed her from behind. She recognized the strength, the power, the passion in the gesture. The woman from the path had come for her.

"You," Laurel said softly. Pleasantly lightheaded, she turned to face the woman of her dreams, but instead a bewildering creature stood before her. The trim, muscular body and the onyx eyes were definitely those of the woman. But the face, the entire head, was that of a beautiful bronco.

The horse spoke in a low, clear tone. "I have wanted you from that moment on the path."

Speechless, Laurel stared into the horse's eyes, felt the distinct sensation of freefalling. Into the cool blackness, into the inky depths of those eyes, Laurel wanted to dive. The sun beat against her back. Too hot. Too, too hot. She felt suddenly weak, as if her legs would no longer support her, as if the grass-covered ground would soon give way.

In a swift motion, the horse-woman lifted Laurel and carried her across the field to a large, flat rock. The surface was rough, and her sheer dress snagged slightly as the horse-woman lay on the stone altar.

"Are your thighs as creamy as the dress you wear?" the horse-woman asked as she slowly raised the flimsy material higher on Laurel's legs.

Laurel moaned as her dress was pulled up to her waist. She glanced into the horse-woman's eyes, then to her sturdy shoulders, and finally to her upper arms. A dark tattooed tangle of black roses swirled across one of her bulging biceps.

The horse-woman separated Laurel's legs and stepped between them. She tore open the top of Laurel's dress to reveal thick, erect nipples.

"Your nipples," the horse-woman said as she plucked each one, then both together, "are incredible." She squeezed hard. Hard enough to cause Laurel to yelp in pleasured pain.

With one fast snap, Laurel's silk panties were ripped aside. Her legs were spread farther apart. Her pussy was completely exposed, and the sun—the delicious, pounding-hot sun—poured liquid heat directly onto her slippery pink sex.

"Yes," Laurel cried. "Oh yes yes yes."

"Do you want to go for a ride, my pretty princess?" the horse-woman muttered between short, quick breaths. Not waiting for an answer, she stretched the fleshy lips of

Laurel's pussy wide and sank a finger into the pearl sap. "How far? Huh, pretty princess? How far and how fast do you want to go?"

Two fingers, three fingers? Laurel was unsure. They were big, and they were rough; they filled her like nothing ever had before. Laurel raised her hips, attempting to push those fingers farther, deeper. But the horse-woman continued her fingers' journey at an excruciatingly slow, deliberate pace.

Four fingers? Five? Eyes closed, teeth clenched, Laurel tried to relax the involuntary tight clamping of her vaginal muscles. Now thicker, now larger, now wider, the hand pushed in. Laurel's pussy felt packed, as if that hand were more than a hand. As if that hand were much, much more.

The horse-woman, whose hand was now buried up to her wrist, let out a long cry and then broke into a fast plunge.

Laurel's cry rivaled the horse-woman's. She felt as if she were racing bareback, galloping, thundering across a wide-open plain on an unbroken stallion. It felt like her fingers, then a fist, and, finally, a solid, thick hoof up her pussy. Didn't matter. It was good, it was hard, and it took her far, farther than she could imagine. Farther than she had ever been before.

"Ride me good. Ride me good!"

Farther and farther. Harder and harder. She slammed down on the hoof. It rammed high into her, over and over until Laurel disappeared in a dust storm of violent pleasure...

...as Laurel slammed out of her dream. Her back pressed hard against the rough tree bark, felt scraped and raw. She felt dizzy, slightly disoriented, but completely satiated. Her book, still open on her lap, revealed pages that were crinkled and torn. The air was cooler, and the sun no longer occupied its midday throne.

Lazily, Laurel gathered her belongings. She'd go home and finish her reading tonight. Through the thick bushes, back to the main path she headed. Every muscle ached.

Down the hill, toward her small canoe, she walked. It was there, not too far from where Laurel had come ashore, that she saw the woman, apparently asleep on a large blue blanket.

Laurel approached slowly. The woman, who had removed her shirt and was sunning in a bathing suit, didn't stir. Perhaps 30, maybe 40 steps in that direction would lead her to where the woman lay. A hundred steps or so to the right was the boat.

Five steps toward the boat. Five more. Laurel stopped and took one more look at the sun-soaked sleeper. It was then that she noticed a tangled black tattoo on the woman's upper arm.

Laurel took another step. Then another.

*Issue: Sept./Oct. 1993*

## Hail Mariah
by Laura Federico

*"Don't worry, I'm not going to force you." I pin her, and she gasps. "Much as you'd love to play martyr, I won't make it that easy on you."*

For months now, Mariah and I have been playing a waiting game. I've watched her. When she didn't think I was looking, she stared back. I stand 5-feet-10 and weigh 170. I like to think of myself as a bold Viking warrior. Actually, I'm a truck driver. That's not a terribly heroic profession, but a lot of women, when they hear what I do, get turned on.

Not Mariah. In fact, her response to this information was decidedly scornful. She specializes in scorn.

Mariah manages the estate of a wealthy old man in Marin County, Calif. This strikes me as genteel, in keeping with the fact that she was born to a wealthy family in Andorra. Andorra is a micro-country in the Pyrenees Mountains. It lies between Spain and France, and Mariah speaks both those languages fluently, as well as Italian, and, of course, English.

What I am, in other words, is outclassed by her.

But not discouraged. She showed up at my house today at my invitation, which all my friends told me she'd never do. And she's been watching me now for hours.

I suppose I was crazy to invite her to an outdoor barbecue—expecting her to play volleyball and smack her lips on grilled shish kabob. It's almost comical to see her here, reclining on one of my rickety patio chairs, among my friends and me in our surfboy garb and Gap tees. She's wearing, as always, layers of formal black, fastened in needlessly complex ways. She means to let all of us—especially me—know just how unsustainable she is.

Apparently there's a lot she doesn't realize about desire. Staring at all those tissue-thin layers she's got on, which stir in the slightest current of air, only makes me think how easy they'd be to tear off. And after observing her all afternoon— the way she moves and the panther gleam of her muscles as she primly crosses her legs—I mentally remove that ascetic's dress altogether, outfitting her in animal skin.

Around 4 o'clock she says to me, "I'd better be going, Alex." Her accent is slightly French, but her command of English is flawless, even down to the idioms.

"As you wish," I bow to her, grinning. "Shall I have someone give you a ride?"

Instead of answering, she gives me one of her long looks, then with that gorgeous sneer says, "You don't talk like any truck driver I've ever known."

"How many have you known?" I counter.

She looks startled.

"All right," I smile, "you've stumbled upon my dirty little secret: I'm a poet."

"Oh, sure," she mutters. She folds her arms across her lush breasts, which are impossible to ignore, the way she's got them fortressed, and regards me skeptically.

"I am," I insist. "I used to be a journalist, got burnt-out on that, and decided to find a job where I could spend more time alone. And driving gets my juices going—creative juices."

"Hmm," she snorts. "And this poetry"—*zis* poetry. God, she's too much, a lesbian Brigitte Bardot—"is all about what? Life on the road? The American love affair with perpetual motion?"

159

I laugh. "Actually, it tends to be about women."

"Ah, yes." Her eyes narrow. "I might have figured."

I put down the beer I'd been drinking. "Come into the house with me. I'll show you some of it."

"You are very forward," she murmurs, taking a step away from me. But then she stops, looking at me intently. I take her gently by the elbow.

"Come on, I won't bite you."

"You insult me, which is worse," she says. Yet she's walking. Accompanying me into the house. "Do you imagine I don't know what it is you want?"

"No, I think it's obvious what I want." We are climbing the stairs, or rather I am herding her to the second floor, though I'm trying like hell to do so casually. When we reach my room, I stand aside so she can enter first. I realize I'm holding my breath. She hesitates on the threshold, then goes in. My breath escapes in a gust.

"And since you're here," I say, closing the door behind me, "it would seem you want the same thing I do."

"Don't flatter yourself," she snaps.

She investigates all corners of the room, like a cat. Finally, she turns to face me, standing against the wall. Head thrown back, teeth bared, not saying a word. She looks so magnificent that for a minute I'm rooted to the spot.

"Mariah," I say, "why are you here?" Silence. Her eyes glitter, and she looks so much like a cornered, outraged feline that my shoulders slump.

"Hey, listen, you don't have to do this. Or we can postpone it...whatever you want."

"Postpone it... Yes, Alex, let's do that." She laughs. Her teeth are perfect. "The way you've been watching me all day—you and your friends..."

I frown. "It's true, we couldn't take our eyes off you." Why is she trying to shame me? "And I wanted you to come up here with me. But you've got to want it too."

"Oh, do I?" she smiles. "What if you want it enough for both of us?"

I suck in my breath. "No, there's no such thing."

"Bullshit."

I realize I'm shaking—because I'm furious and because she's so close to me, and in spite of what I've said to her I want her so bad my bones ache.

Yet I meant it. I must have, because I'm going to the door and holding it open for her. "Take care of yourself, Mariah."

To my shock, she laughs.

"Oh, you're good," she says huskily. "That's very good. A dare."

"What?"

"Maybe all those rumors about your sexual prowess will prove to be true." I stare at her. Even from 10 feet away, I can see her chest rising and falling rapidly. Her golden brown eyes appear black: Dilated pupils don't lie.

"You want to, all right." I slam the door. "You want to, but you don't see why you should have to say it." I cross the room in three strides. "You're used to women getting down on their knees for you, right? Going so crazy over you that all you have to do is stand there like some goddamned suffering saint, sighing over all the vulgarity in the world."

I grab her around the waist and yank her hips against me. The sharp edge of her hipbone hits me dead center on the clit.

"I'd do it to you right here," I growl into her ear, "up against the goddamned wall—except you'd like that too much. I bet you'll like it wherever I do it, because you drip sex, honey. And you know it. So, no, I won't fuck you here then let you go around saying afterward how none of it was your fault. This is going to be as much your decision as mine, or I'll put a stop to it."

"Liar," she hisses. "You can't prevent yourself from starting."

I laugh, in spite of everything. She's quick, in addition to all the rest of what she is—prim and majestic, foul-tempered

161

and vulnerable. This will either be the worst fuck of my life or one of the best.

I pick her up and toss her onto the bed, She screams softly, and her arms fly up to cover her breasts.

"Don't worry, I'm not going to force you." I pin her, and she gasps. "Much as you'd love to play martyr, I won't make it that easy on you."

My hand slides under her skirt, which covers my wrist like the hood of an old-fashioned camera. My free hand is buried in the tangle of her hair when I realize all at once that I can't get at her. At *her*. *What is she?* I ask myself, silently panicking. *Some succulent bog from which I'll never escape? Or the opposite, an exotic country that I'll never quite be able to reach?*

I yank my hand out from under her filmy skirts, flex it in the open air, then reach down and tear the dress off her in a single furious motion. She flinches in surprise, maybe even fear, as all those tiny metal clasps hit the bed bouncing, like fleas. Her silver belt zings off with a whine and lands somewhere on the floor. I ball up the dress and shoot it across the room.

"Much better," I smile.

She reclines on the white bedspread, looking up at me, breathing hard and thoroughly acquiescent, in a thin white lace slip. Nothing underneath. I catch my breath all over again at the sight of her. I've never seen so much of her skin before. She has that smooth tight skin Mediterranean women have, its color and gloss like a pecan shell. Her black hair spills over her shoulders, and gleaming teeth grip her lower lip. There's nothing soft about this one.

"Well, Alex," her voice is hushed, "what are you waiting for?"

In a flash the reverence is gone, replaced with lust. I reach for her.

Her thighs jerk together. Squeezing her eyes suit, she snaps her head to one side, then lies motionless.

"What the fuck is it with you?" I explode. "What are you, some goddamned nun-in-training?"

Her eyes fly open. "Don't say that, Alex," she gasps. "Don't. It's a sin."

I gape at her. She's serious. "You should've told me you were Catholic."

"Why?"

"Because..."

Because I'm Presbyterian, and the deal we make when it comes to sex is that we'll just suppress it—get some work done instead. It took me all of my youth and most of my 20s to beat that one.

Catholicism is different; sexual at the heart, maybe that's why I have such a fondness for sloe-eyed Latin types like the one wriggling under me now. Spanish, Italian, South American—they all make my knees go weak, and they fill my blue eyes with tears of adoration. Catholicism says: *You'll do it. You must try to resist, but you're weak and you'll do it, and then you're going to enjoy it. Confess and submit to the ritual atonement.* Now, that's hot stuff.

"Because it matters," I say finally.

I press my mouth against her neck. She's salty and fresh and warm—and, to my shock, as soft as any other woman. Softer, in fact, than most. The bones under her skin are fragile and light. For the first time I feel a surge of tenderness toward her.

"Mariah," I whisper, "wrap your legs around me."

After a second's hesitation she does. I feel her sigh, and her hips rise ever so subtly under mine.

"Good girl."

I kiss her mouth. Again the tiny wait, and then her lips open. Cautious. And she's feeling everything, the surface of her skin alive with a fine prickling electricity that communicates itself to my fingertips. She ripples under me, and a breath pours out of her in a sigh.

My hands travel down the length of her. Everywhere I

163

touch reacts. She's panting already, and I've scarcely touched her. I marvel inwardly: What a fight she gave. Maybe it was worth protecting after all, this exquisite sensitivity and the bashfulness of a girl on confirmation day.

I slide my hands under her slip. She stiffens but doesn't draw back, then begins to moan. Almost inaudibly, involuntarily. Yet she hasn't really given in, and my blood quickens with the challenge of it.

Perhaps this too is part of her game. But what she doesn't realize is that even this, what she's giving me now, is better than I'd expected, so I can't lose.

My hands fit perfectly over her breasts. They're smooth and heavy. Her full nipples rise in the cupped heat of my palms. Her spirit and temperament may be virginal, but her body isn't. The way she arches her back, the way her black hair lashes at the white pillow, arouses a violence in me but also the opposite, something like worship.

The violence wins. My jaw clenches as the coiled force in my muscles builds. I struggle to keep my touch gentle, but my teeth graze the tendons of her neck, my hands thrust under her and grip her ass, and I know this is a battle I've lost. The hunger has been in me too long.

She writhes underneath me, her thighs grafted together. Her joined heels strike the mattress. She pummels my chest with her fists yet again. I sense that she doesn't mean it.

I catch her wrists neatly and pin them over her head. "You can't say it, can you? Not even to yourself. You can't admit that you want this as much as I do." I lean down into her face. The closed-eyes routine again. "It's fine if I take it from you. But the minute that word 'yes' crosses your mind—"

"Stop," she says through gritted teeth.

"Oh, no," I breathe. "Every little girl is taught to say 'stop.' It's the word 'yes' that women have been choking on for centuries."

I shove my hand sideways between her clamped thighs.

"Come on, Mariah, tell me. How much do you hate this, exactly?"

"Fuck you."

I grip one of her inner thighs, feeling the sweat and heat. "Don't you see? We're never going to own our destiny if we don't own our desire. It's who we are, baby."

She shudders all over then looks as though she might shove me off her after all.

"Open your legs," I say.

She whimpers.

"Oh, hell." I reach down and haul them apart. She's wet, of course—drenched.

"God, Mariah," I groan.

My fingers drive into her silky moisture, and the hot walls of her cunt fold around my knuckles, her acidity tingling my skin. I feel her inner quivering—a call beckoning me deeper. I follow; God knows I have no choice.

She arches her back. Her hips soar up off the bed, and her thighs stretch wide apart. I watch her hands reach down to grasp the damp bend of her knees, and a jolt races through me. She holds herself like this, lifting to meet my thrusts.

"Jesus, Mary, and Joseph," I gasp.

Liquid gushes out of her, filling my cupped palm and sliding down my wrist. My breath stops. I pump harder, hitting the same spot, demanding more. She gives. Again. Again. My thumb finds her clit. I massage it slowly, and her thighs fold inward around my hand.

"Too hard?" I ask. Her response is to fling her bent arm across her eyes.

So I watch her closely. She keeps her face covered, but when I get it right she parts her legs again shyly.

I smile down at her. What she's told me to do without words, I do. She swells under my thumb. I can see her pink nibblet nestled in her dark hair.

"Come on, sweetheart," I hiss, "give it to me."

I move my fingers more urgently, and she responds. Shoulders, ass, everything—rising off the bed and falling again; I'm swooning. The shine of her ruby labia, opening to my hand, dazzles me. I push my whole fist into her, and she shrieks.

"Yes, Alex, yes. Oh, God, please don't stop," she's choking. "Please don't stop now."

"I've got you, sweetheart." I cradle the moist back of her neck while my fist continues to drive into her.

Suddenly she clamps down. My fingers are squeezed to powder. God, she's ferocious, and I'm almost laughing. *Come on, baby. Do it.*

She does, in a final hot gush of fluid. I collapse against her raised knees, exhausted and jubilant. There's a stretch of time I can't account for. Each of us floats off alone. I'm dimly aware of her warm skin and hard bone under my cheek; my breathing returns to normal. We billow gently back to earth together.

Finally, without either of us having moved, I sense she's opened her eyes. I open my own to find her gaze full on me, soft now, and I smile at her. She drops her gaze shyly.

"I said it, Alex." Her voice is almost inaudible.

"Yeah, you did. It wasn't so bad, was it?" I ask. "So what now, eh? You're gonna spend all day tomorrow saying Hail Marys and Our Fathers, or whatever you fallen women say?"

She laughs. I realize then that I've never heard a real laugh from her. "You might have to give me more to repent for," she says, "if I'm going to go through all that."

"Baby," I tell her, "say the word, and I will stain your soul beyond reprieve."

She laughs again but covers her eyes with her hands. Luscious woman—and my fist still in her. I feel a poem coming on.

*Issue: Nov./Dec. 1993*

## Medusa's Dance
by Wickie Stamps

*Even here, with my lover below my whip, I chain my wrath, fearing it might break her back.*

As I sat by a pond I saw a dachshund trotting along the beach, accompanied by two young girls. The girls were laughing, touching, playfully shoving each other. The hound was pumping and panting, sniffing and snorting, all the while weaving in and out among the long, lean legs of his mistresses.

During his 73 years, my father owned half a dozen dachshunds, most of them when my brother, three sisters, and I were children. When not torturing his hounds he turned his rage on us.

At the entrance to my father's home—for truly it was not our home—hung a Medusa's head door knocker. When I opened the door it always swished as if I were breaking an airtight barrier between the outside world and his inside.

It was Medusa who marked the way.

I first heard of my father's existence through early whispered conversations with my sister. Huddled in his darkened hallway, she hissed that he had broken a milk bottle over mother's head. I imagined my mother with a crown of shattered glass. Christlike, lifeblood trickling down her forehead. Her glistening thorns were his touch of passion for her.

One day my eyes beheld him, feeding on his own offspring.

He was sitting at the table with my sister, forcing her to learn mathematics by counting black-eyed peas. With gritted teeth he would take each pea from its bag and place it before her, sometimes crushing it to pieces under his finger. He was hissing, "You idiot! *Count*, you fucking cunt!" Mid onslaught, as he pulled back to strike her again, his eyes met mine. She, dazed and muddle-headed, also looked my way, grateful that a new prey had diverted him from his feeding frenzy.

Riveted in the doorway, I could not then, nor now, determine whom I hated more: my father for his cruelty or my sister for showing her fear.

At this instant I knew what lessons lay ahead of me. My father would be my master. He and I would learn together the square root of age and terror, and I would seek the perfect equation for slickening that place deep within my loins.

I became my father's favorite. Now he was my favorite too. To sit at the right hand of rage was to be mine. Like a cobra mesmerizing its enemy with charm and viciousness, I began my Medusa's dance. As needed, I became more female than my mother or more male than my brother—for my brother, in my father's eyes, never qualified as manly. I took the remnants of my brother, a faggot boy whom my father raped of his masculinity, and re-created myself from the pieces of my father's carnage.

I had smelled my father's fear during our visits to his mother's home. She was the only woman who could bring him to his knees, praying before her Christian god each time before we left. On his knees with my grandmother, his tamer, he offered supplication to her and her god. On my knees I would study a photo of my father that sat on a table. He was dressed in a Little Lord Fauntleroy outfit. *Faggot child*, I thought, adding another knife twist to his heart.

So at times I became the image of his mother, sitting in chairs like she did, long and willowy, cool and impenetrable. I strove to castrate his raging spirit sooner than he could cut off mine. I coddled my father. I fawned over him. I became the female of his most horrifying fantasies: flirtatious, brilliant, and ruthless. Every fiber of my being was tuned to pleasing him. I crawled into his passion and his horror and wed them into a form bearing my name.

Then I, his most favorite, would strike with all my venom. I did my Medusa's dance, stinging every weakness he had. Then just like his mother I'd withdraw behind my veil of icy scorn. From my vengeful throne I'd watch him wring his hands, desperately wailing against the wall between me and his desire.

For I have become his most dreaded paradox. More manly than his greatest attempts at manliness, more female than his fantasies dared allow.

Like one who spitefully cuts herself in front of those who love her most, I made my body into a weapon to hurl at him. He dared not hit me, so I did it for him, flailing at myself just to steal his pleasure. It was with great glee that I journeyed into hell, my father in agony as he witnessed his favorite ignite before him. Daughter, lesbian, drunk, spinning downward.

I smeared my life with drunkenness, sitting in bars with men, in my father's shadow, plotting his assassination. After hours of booze, the men shoved their cocks, hard with our mad talk, into my pussy, slamming my rage out of me with each breath. I always wanted to come onto their bellies as they did onto mine, deposit my contempt for their desire on their bodies, to mock their impotent efforts at matching my father's game.

But all were mere interlopers and intruders in our paternal game.

I was my father's favorite. Deeply handsome, adored by women, I learned my passion for women by watching his ways with them. I became him: long, lean, mean. I became him—redneck-turned-patrician with a taste for the whore. As I watch a woman walk by and I gaze with desire, it is through my father's eyes that I have learned my lust.

And now I have a partner who has joined me in my childhood games.

"Changelings" is what I jokingly christened us when we first met. Truly, in my Daddy games, she is the child secretly put in the place of myself. When my lover calls out my name my father and I, standing in the darkest shadows of my brain, step forward with perfectly measured steps to play our Daddy games in tandem. My "boy" says what I refused to say to him.

"Daddy, please don't hurt me," she says, and I do.

"Daddy, please don't fuck me." And I do.

I do to her what he was too cowardly to do to me. I dare to say to her what he dared not say to me. "Spread your legs, you fucking bitch."

And together we dance into that place where rage, terror, and defiance set fire to our play.

Only once did I play the child in a Daddy game, and I was as limp as a junkie boy's heroin-sodden dick. My desire withered in my loins, for I did not know then what I know now: I have not finished my game with him. Now "Daddy" is a word that I will say only if it is beaten out of me along with my wetness.

I am now more than my father's favorite. For now I have become him. My mother's curse that "you are just like him" is truer than her wildest imaginings of me. In the mirror's reflection I see the spitting image of him. As I talk to my lover over dinner it is him that I mirror as I cross my legs. As I lie in bed and my lover flirts with me, I pelt her with lewd comments that make her blush. It is my father's words and ways that move my flirtation, not mine.

And when the rage rises from my gut, spilling out into the snakes that make my hair, I rise in the morning with my jaw clenched and fingers stiff from the serpents in my soul. I know I am my father's child. And I understand why bourbon was his nightly fare. It is the only thing—save brutal sex—that can untie my fury.

When I am mistress and my lover plays my boy, I strut and pace before her bound body in rhythm with my rising rage. I am at this moment the woman most feared by my father. With my boy I unleash the serpent trapped beneath my skin. It slivers from my mouth and transforms my pacing into a fury. My fury rises to a dangerous tide.

Even here, with my lover below my whip, I chain my wrath, fearing it might break her back.

At times men pay me to mete out the brutality that I learned at my father's knee. They pay me to dance my Medusa's dance. In my scene the vulgar language and the brutality that fits so snugly between my loins bears my father's handprint, my homily to only him. When I lean over the bastards groveling on the floor and torture their testicles, is it not my father, adept at crushing my brother's manhood, who trained me in my trade?

When I stand in low-lit dungeons and watch other groups of women play, I see not adults but young children playing their secret games, public now, daring us to watch. We are each other's siblings for the night. We must witness our respective games that kept us from our fright. Games that are like ground glass buried so deeply into the concrete of our sex that to remove their madness would shatter the whole.

Childhood frolics—is this not what I play?

But watch closely now. My Medusa's head is now turning, turning.

Throughout my games I must cover my ears against those hags who whisper about child abuse and screech that it was he, not I, who chose our game. He, not I, who conjured up our fun. But so foolish are they who try to distill to simple facts a game that taught me to dance so lovingly on broken glass.

Don't they understand that it is not for me but for my mother and sisters—and for my deranged brother who was nothing more than a sister in my father's eye—that I do my vicious dance? I used what he wanted most—my soul—to lead him away from my beloved family. I could snap my cunt around my father's desire and yank him from feeding on his female prey.

Can't those screaming crones who shriek about lost childhood see that my Medusa's dance is not, as they say, a monster that is destroying me? It is my only doorway into my tattered sexuality. Rather than pointing their accusing fingers at my dance, why won't they join me and celebrate my creation of this erotic dance?

But I was my father's favorite. And certainly he was mine.

A few nights ago I dreamt a dream. Half-awake and half-asleep, I lay in that place where motion and sound are suspended, a place as silent and terrifying as the eye of a southern hurricane. And in the stillness when I held my breath someone slipped into my sheets. My terror was not that it was my father, but that it might *not* be him. For to lie with another would betray that half of me, which, like a Siamese twin, is still bonded to my father's sexual needs.

From the moment I felt his presence in the dream, it was not "Father" but "Daddy" that the beast was named. Pay me a mere pittance and I will raise my dress, spread my legs and with a face carved from his seed I will masturbate with glee. For before me on his hands and knees, bound with the ropes he used on me, is my Daddy.

In my next life we will meet again, my father and I. There will be no Medusa at the door of my home. For then, strong from my centuries of rest, I will be the beast Medusa. And he must enter my door. But for now I leave him wanting. For is not the waiting worse than the act?

At my father's funeral, with the Salvation Army and gospel singers wailing, my brother exchanged a few words with me.

"He's dead," he said.

"Yes, finally."

But doesn't he still live, residing deep within my sexual needs?

I was my father's favorite. But he is no longer mine. As revenge against this man who worshiped the perpetuation of his seed, I will never bear a child. For will not that child carry our Medusa's seed? I was my father's favorite. And his madness will end with me.

*Issue: Aug./ Sept. 1998*

## Still Life With Dildo
### by K. Munro

*She was no-nonsense, meat-and-potatoes; the kind of kissing you see in the movies.*

"Have you ever been fucked?" she asks me.

I met her—we met; she appeared across the room and then at my side later on—in a bar. I saw her, talking and laughing with her friends as I was talking and laughing with mine, except her friends were all in black leather mob caps and chaps, and mine had with patched-leather elbows and corduroy pants. It's one thing I love about the city—you get a mix. The bar we were in gets everyone from tenure-track professors from the university to blue-collar workers and bondage dykes. We were both on home turf, so to speak.

I saw her, didn't recognize her, and thought nothing of her. It was a busy night; there was a lot going on. A friend of mine was trying to make a pass at a crew-cut college girl. One of the regular drunks was making her rounds, trying to see whose shoulder she could lean on without being brushed off. I had half an eye on someone I'd seen around before—someone I'd made a few inquiries about, someone who knew I'd make inquiries, and who was not looking in my direction consistently enough to tell me she might be interested. Mob caps and chaps weren't my thing. I paid no attention.

A while later she turned up at my elbow. I gave her the

glassy passing smile I thought was appropriate. She gave me a more purposeful smile in return, and I paused. Had I missed something? Did I know her from somewhere? She didn't look at all familiar, and I only just stopped myself from dropping a clanger and asking her if I'd seen her somewhere before.

She shouted something over the music, and I put my ear closer to her mouth, checking quickly at the same time to make sure my intended was still there. She wasn't. The woman at my elbow was shouting about buying me a drink.

I said, "Sure." She ordered it and another for herself, and we clinked the rims of our glasses and sipped our drinks and moved our heads to the music.

"Do you want to get out of here?" she shouted after we'd finished that drink and then another.

My friends were gone. The crew-cut college girl was dancing with her girlfriend, who was wearing a Brownie uniform with the beret folded and tucked into her epaulet. Two of my exes were petting pretty seriously in the end booth.

"Sure," I said, and we collected her leather jacket and my duffel from the coat check and left.

Outside there was a fine mist of rain and it was chilly. The weather channel had said there was a cold front moving in and the rain would be snow before morning. We paused by the door and zipped up our coats, then stood looking at the sky and weaving slightly to stay on our feet.

"Do you want to get a coffee?" she asked suddenly, and I wondered how old she was. I said sure. Then, as we walked, I changed my mind. She seemed relieved.

"Do you want to go somewhere?" she said. "I live close by."

I paused, I remember, for just a moment—just long enough to let the rain run its fingers down my neck, and to hear a horn wail, and to see the college girl and her girlfriend come out of the bar and walk away in the other direction, their arms about each other's waists.

"Sure," I said, and we went.

"Have you ever been fucked?" she asks me, and I'm not sure what to say.

She's asking for good reason. For one thing, she's about to fuck me—poised with the black leather dildo jutting from her pubic bone like a single misplaced horn. Something in her stance reminds me of a matador, though I don't know why— I was in Pamplona last summer, and I saw the fights: Matadors keep their hips back, protecting their vital organs. She stands with her hips thrust forward, the dildo standing at a kind of half-mast attention, quivering slightly as if in anticipation. I'm bent forward over the bed in front of her, my face pushed into the hump of her duvet, my pants around my ankles. I've turned my head slightly to the side to hear her question better—frankly, I wasn't expecting any talking from either of us at this point.

She doesn't live alone, of course, and two of her roommates are awake and watching a movie on television in the next room as we do this. I met them when we came in, and there was the usual moment of embarrassment when we did introductions, and she didn't know my name. Her roommates laughed in a way that told me it wasn't the first time. They lit another joint and offered it to us, and she took it and I didn't. When we left the room she put her hand on the back of my neck in the dark hallway and said, "I'm Beth." *Beth, Beth, Beth,* I thought, then forgot it completely until the next day.

We stopped in the kitchen, where she drew a glass of water at the tap, and I stood next to her in the semi-gloom and looked at the string of lit-up relleno chilis hung between the refrigerator and the windowsill. She drank some of the water and offered me the glass. She was lit from the side with chili-light, and she had a soft face, more rounded than I'd thought, almost moon-shaped. I drank some water and she put her hand on my ass and we went downstairs.

We hadn't kissed yet—her hand on my neck and then on

my butt, where it had only stayed a moment, had been our only points of contact. She didn't touch me in the stairwell or in the hall. She showed me where the bathroom was, and then the laundry room, as if I were a prospective buyer. I looked at her profile and at how far away from me she stood and began to wish, in a vague way, that I'd spent the evening pursuing the other one, the one who'd got away.

The door to her bedroom was open, and she stood aside politely to let me go in first. I went in and stood in darkness, feeling absurd. She came in behind me and closed the door without turning the light on.

After a moment I said, "Is there a light?"

She turned it on, and we stood there blinking. Her room was a mess. The drawers of her bureau stood open, spilling a tangle of Y-fronts and plaid flannel shirts and Beefy-Ts to the floor. Ashtrays overflowed on both of the windowsills, and a cache of half-empty beer bottles covered the bedside table and the part of the desk. A miniature cactus was dying in a bright terracotta pot in the corner.

For a moment neither of us said anything; then I cleared my throat and said, "Uh—" She reached out, caught hold of the corner of my coat, and reeled me in.

We kissed. She was no-nonsense, meat-and-potatoes; the kind of kissing you see in the movies. It's not usually my favorite style—I like to play around a bit, especially with someone new and butch—but she did it well. She didn't touch me, but when I put my hand on the back of her neck she purred.

We occupied a few minutes that way, stumbling back and forth through the beer bottles and undershirts and used Kleenex, groping at each other and moaning when we got something right. I was smiling. I like necking; I like to schmooze and spoon and fool around. Most of the time, if I'm doing it right, it makes me want to burst out laughing. This woman, with her hand in my crotch and her leather creaking every time she turned her head, was very serious.

Another time, it might not have worked. My giggling would have pissed her off, her getting pissed off would have killed it for me, and we would have pulled our belts closed and said good night. It's happened before—I've been bid a white-lipped and hypocritical late-night farewell at the doorsills of many apartments. It's a disappointment, but I try not to think less of the women who've done it. I've had one-nighters drive me nuts in a hundred different ways; it's never perfect once you've left the bar.

This time, though, I could almost hear her grit her teeth and bear it, which made it easier to like her and to take her seriously. I stopped giggling. She put her hand down my pants. We sat down hard and gracelessly on the edge of her bed.

I was dimly aware that I was half-sitting on something hard and boxy, probably a shoe, caught up in her sheets. I could smell the dead butts in the ashtray next to us, and the clean laboratory tang of whatever she used in her hair. She was still kissing me, directly and persuasively, and beginning to lean forward, so that I was pressed backward onto the bed. I let myself go, and felt a size-9 sole stamp my lumbar region. I stopped kissing her.

"There's a shoe in my back." She didn't say anything; without looking away from my face she reached beneath me and rooted in the sheets. After a moment she pulled out a blue Doc Marten and tossed it to the floor. Before I could say anything she reached in again, and in another moment pulled out the second of the pair and tossed it down beside the first.

We lay there for a minute. She was lying almost on top of me, her thigh between my knees, her face level with my breasts. She was looking serious. I could still see the corner of one of the shoes over the edge of the bed, and even through my duffel coat I could feel something else. I opened my mouth cautious, afraid I was going to laugh.

"Are you packing?" I asked her, and for the first time that evening a slow, sweet smile spread across her face.

"Have you ever been fucked?" she asks me, and now I really must consider the question. It's a serious matter, to her at least—I can't see personally how it matters or what difference it could make. Fucked or unfucked, or somewhere in between, are all about to become one. That's why we're here, after all. That's why I'm sprawled in such high state, my ass tipped in the air and my face somewhere down in the sheets; that's why she's standing behind me with her hands on my hips and a critical, appraising look on her face, as if she were standing in front of a late-night refrigerator, debating between dill pickles or Gruyère. I fuck, you fuck, she fucks, we fuck. I don't understand the question.

I discreetly fish a feather out of my mouth and consider my possible answers. Does she mean, have you ever been fucked by a boy? Is she worried about splitting my hymen—popping my cherry, they used to call it—about blood blossoming red on her creased white sheets? I think of a boy I used to know, in high school and in college, and our seven-year tryst, sweet and nearly celibate. I never could get used to that idea of sex, and he was the only one I ever tried it with. But that's serious, it's almost secret—it certainly isn't something I talk about with a one-night stand, whether or not she's wearing a wand. If that's what she wants to know, she's going to be disappointed.

Does she mean, have you ever been fucked by a girl? Meaning, do I do this a lot, am I into dildos, do I know how they work, what they feel like? I glance back over my shoulder at the dull black contraption hooked around her waist and want to giggle again. It reminds me of the panty girdles my mother used to wear and tried to force me to wear once I was old enough. The only real difference is the long dick prong hanging out of the crotch, nodding to itself like an old man dropping off to sleep. She sees me looking, takes it in her hand and rubs it slightly, up and down. A misunderstanding. I can't take it as seriously as she can.

Does she mean, have you ever been fucked like this—as well

as I'm going to fuck you? This is the rhetorical option—this is her talking to herself as much as to me, talking to hear herself say the words, to turn us both on. Since I haven't been fucked by a girl before, I don't know the rules; I don't know if I'm supposed to reply at all to this kind of question, and I know that if I say the wrong thing it will all be over. The boy never presented questions like this. I don't want to think about it—if I think about it I'll either laugh or I'll snap at her, tell her to get on with it already. She's the one who pulled the thing out of her fly like it was the Grail.

"Have you ever been fucked?" she asks, and now she's had to repeat herself. Her eyes are narrowing, she's getting suspicious. Suspicious of what, I don't know. I search her tone for a new emphasis to tell me something, but I still don't know what to say. I can hear the television in the next room playing the credits of the movie her roommates were watching, the soundtrack swelling. I can hear them getting up and moving around, talking and laughing. Her fingertips are warm on my hips.

*Issue: Dec. 1998/Jan. 1999*

## Chip Gets a Bum Rush
by Kate Sorensen

*I licked your asshole. I carefully stuck my tongue into your asshole.*

I hate it when lesbians wear baseball caps backwards. Frat boys wear baseball caps backwards. Wearing a baseball cap says *I need a haircut.* If your hair is not behaving, don't point to it with a baseball cap. Be proud of your big hair or get it cut. Now, some people might think this harsh. But I think people are just promoting the myth that looking like a frat boy is cute. Frat boys are generally gross bigots with big stupid egos and bad haircuts.

My lover walked into my house one day wearing a baseball cap...backwards. I started calling her Chip, my frat boy. We set up a scene. We met in a frat bar. Chip swaggered over to me with his rutting strap-on, belched Dos Equis in my face, and tried to pick me up. I took him home and let him grunt on top of me until he came and fell asleep.

After she moved across the country, I sent her this letter:

Hey, Chip,
    Dude, I miss you, bro. You were the best part of Penn, really. I'm glad we're out, but I do miss the brothers at the house. We had some crazy times at Cap Cappa, didn't we? Remember when we sneaked Sylvia up to our room and we both fucked her? What tits—enough for both of us. You were so excellent

for settin' that up. I gotta say, you were the best roommate I had there. But you know, I gotta tell you something. I wasn't going to tell you, but you're like my brother, so I feel like I need to.

Remember a couple of months ago when we tried all night to pick up chicks at Walsh's? And you threw up all over the toilet? We were soooo wasted! We barely got home. And when we got home we couldn't get our pants off, and we passed out kinda halfway on the bed. I didn't pass out. I couldn't sleep. I was so horny from tryin' to score chicks. And you were snorin' so loud, dude! So I started to mess with you in your sleep. I started rubbing your ass, and you stopped snoring. You were still asleep, but you were mumbling. You mumbled your girlfriend's name, and I thought that was noble. I thought, I wonder what does Jez do to Chip's ass to make him groan like this? I stroked your balls. Then I played with the hair on your thighs. You were whimpering, man. So I pushed my fingers along your butt crack. I was dying to know what you were dreaming. I licked your asshole. I carefully stuck my tongue into your asshole. I was so afraid you would wake up and find me there. You would have kicked my ass until I was dead. But you didn't wake up. You just kept whimpering and groaning in your sleep. I fucked your dream for what seemed like hours. I had the biggest woody of my life just imagining what was going on in your head. Finally, I had to roll over on my stomach and beat off. I guess I was goin' at it too hard because you woke up. So I pretended to be asleep, but I was still watching you. When you sat up on the edge of the bed, man, your dick stood straight to the sky. You looked at me sleeping, came over, and pulled down my boxers real slow. And you fucked me with that rocket. I don't know how I did it, but I pretended I was asleep the whole time. I didn't make a sound. You grunted into my ass until you shot your wad, then you passed out again.

You thought you raped me, faggot, but I wanted it.
I love you,
Deke

*Issue: Dec. 1998/Jan. 1999*

## Convoy
by Diane Anderson-Minshall

*Bert was on top of me, straddling me. She made me keep my legs tight against each other, so every push of her strap-on had to move through my fat thighs to get inside me.*

I'm sitting in my truck on the overpass with my legs spread and my hand inside my Levi's. My fingers are parting my lips and battering my clit like an ambitious lover. It's my sixth time on the overpass this month.

My ex-girlfriend drove an 18-wheeler. Everyone called her Bert. I don't know if it was short for Bertha or Roberta or what. All I know is she drove an 18-wheeler and she brought me to this shit-hole town in the middle of the Nevada desert and dumped me. Winnemucca, Nev.: population 6,000; lesbians: four (if you count my male neighbor who tells me he "feels like a lesbian").

After Bert left, I started parking on the overpass, watching the semi trucks pass underneath me. I'd close my eyes and put my hand on my nipple, flicking it gently as I heard the first truck pass.

Brrr-bumm. Brrr-bumm. Brrr-bumm.

Then I'd move my other hand in. In and out of my mouth, over my breast, between my thighs.

Brrr-bumm.

Semis make a special sound as they cruise along the interstate. Brrr-bumm. Brrr-bumm. It's the sound of the truck caressing the folds in the road. Each time I close my eyes and hear that brrr-bumm, I want to caress a fold in my own body. So I masturbate.

The first time I masturbated, I was watching the trucker movie *Convoy* on television. I was sitting alone on the couch in the downstairs family room. The house was empty. More and more trucks kept coming on screen, and Kris Kristofferson kept driving along: stoic, steely, silent. I closed my eyes and listened to the brrr-bumm, brrr-bumm of the trucks. I moved my hand inside my training bra and touched my nipple. First tentatively, with just one finger, in case I got caught. Then I wrapped my full hand around it, moving my fingers back and forth over my now-hard nipple.

After I was aware of nothing else but the blood rushing to my crotch, I moved one hand down to my cunt, parting my lips and moving my fingers across my clit. Every few minutes I stopped to shove my fingers deep inside my cunt and pull them out, rubbing the juices on my sweaty thighs. The other hand thrashed about across my body, teasing my nipples, my belly button, my fleshy thighs. Then I threw my face into my underarm—dark, damp, musty—and bit down as I came.

Brrr-bumm. Brrr-bumm.

It wasn't Kris Kristofferson that got me hot. It was the feel, the look, the *sound* of the trucks that got me hot. It was the cacophony of the trucks pummeling down the highway that got me excited. So I started masturbating, and I've never gotten the brrr-bumm out of my mind.

The first time I fucked Bert, we were in the tiny cab of her 18-wheeler. The engine was roaring ("You never turn off fine machinery," Bert told me), and heat was rising from beneath me. Was it the engine or our passionate union that heated me so? I never knew, but I was roasting. Sweat was beading up on my brow, my breasts, my cunt. Bert was on top of me, straddling me. She made me keep my legs tight against each other, so every push of her strap-on had to move through my fat thighs to get inside me. With my legs closed like that, my cunt was tight, and as her dildo moved in and out of me, I struggled to keep my limbs together. When I came, I filled the air with a deep guttural growl, and I tossed my head violently back into the side of the cab.

My first girlfriend knew about *Convoy*. She'd sing lines from the theme song as she moved her fist in and out of my cunt. "This here's Rubber Ducky," she'd sing in a deep voice. "We got ourselves a convoy."

In and out, in and out of my cunt.

So now I fuck myself. It's inevitable. I can't stop.

I came to Winnemucca, trucker heaven, with Bert. "The best runs in the West," she told me. I got a secretarial job at Nays Trucking. Everybody knows I came here to be with my girlfriend, and she left me for someone younger, cuter, firmer, and, I'm sure, better in bed.

So now I can't stop parking on top of the overpass, listening to the brrr-bumm, brrr-bumm with my hand moving in and out of my cunt. Sometimes I'm rougher, aggressive. Sometimes I'm softer, lazier. It's been six years since I've been with a woman.

Well, OK, it's been five years, but I hardly think one night with my boss's wife counts.

My best friend Janie is a lounge lizard. That's what they call the women who hang out at truck stops like Flying J, waiting to score with a trucker. A lot of people think she's a hooker because she hangs out there. She's not a hooker; she just has a jones for truckers. Maybe I'd feel better if I had a thing for truckers, but I've only met one female trucker in my life—Bert—and I definitely know I don't have thing for men of any occupation. Janie thinks I should give up this "thing" for women, find a simple trucker man, and settle down in Winnemucca in a nice double-wide.

But I don't want a man. I want to sit on the overpass and masturbate.

I've got my legs spread and my hand inside my jeans again. One hand is moving in and out of my cunt. The other is rubbing my breasts. I close my eyes and listen to the highway. I'm waiting for the brrr-bumm.

There it comes. Brrr-bumm, brrr-bumm. Whirrrahh.

I jolt back to consciousness, my eyes wide open and fixed on the beast that had made that unusual sound. Whirrrahh. I've never heard that sound before.

It's a huge 18-wheeler with a vibrant purple cab that just passed under the overpass and switched into the right lane. *It's getting off,* I thought. I knew the truck would end up at Flying J. I had to see the owner of this truck, had to see if it could be a woman. I mean, purple. What kind of guy drives a purple truck?

I rev up the engine and speed to Flying J. I pull up alongside the purple truck, but the cab is empty and both doors are locked. A bunch of drivers are milling around the gas pumps, but no one's near the purple truck. A driver is heading into the store.

I follow the driver into the truck stop, still trying to figure out if he is the driver and if he is a man or a woman. I glance around the restaurant. No women. I search the aisles. No women. I head back to women's restrooms. Empty.

Suddenly, trying to find a woman in a truck stop seems so ludicrous. The building is cavernous and filled with two of everything—one for truckers, one for regular folks. I weave my way through the truckers' lounge, the women's lockers, and the drivers' showers. Most of the showers are locked. I still don't find her, though I do get a proposition from an unlocked shower's occupant. I make a speedy retreat.

I hear a truck pull away from the gas pumps, so I rush out to the glass doors to see if it's the purple one. It isn't.

I head back to the lounge just as I hear another truck take off. I rush to see if it's her. It's not. I keep peering out desperately, just in case I can get a glimpse of the driver who may belong to the purple truck. The pink-haired cashier is busy doling out Beefaroni and chicken wings, but she takes a minute to point to a sign that reads NO LOUNGE LIZARDS. The truckers like to put the sign in their trucks. Well, the married Christian truckers, at least. Pink Hair thinks I'm a hooker too.

There are no women here, I decide. I'm an idiot. A perverted, obsessive, idiot secretary living in the middle of the desert, trolling truck stops for Mrs. Right.

I rush to the bathroom, tearful, disappointed. I can't hold back the tears. I look under all the stalls to make sure they're empty (hope springs eternal), and then I lock myself in the farthest, biggest stall. I undo my pants, sit on the toilet, and cry. Then I hear another truck take off, and I decide not to rush to the door. But the roar of the truck is strong, and my heart begins to race. Blood rushes to my clit. My nipples harden. So I masturbate. Moving my hand in and out of my pants, I forget all about my foolish trek through the truck stop. I forget about my desperation. I just think about the prickle of my skin and the smell of my sex filling the air. I bite down on my hand as I come and let out a tiny peep.

I flush the toilet (for appearances) and look beneath the stalls to make sure I'm still alone. I am.

I fix myself in the mirror, straightening my clothes and wiping my eyes. As I round the bend toward the door, someone jumps from behind the partition and pins my arms behind me.

All I can smell is Old Spice. All truckers wear Old Spice. My mind is racing. The trucker covers my eyes with one hand, rips my shirt open with the other. I'm too scared to scream. Then I feel it. A bulge. Not a cock, thank God; it's her breasts bumping up against me. Fleshy, large breasts. This is my mystery woman.

Old Spice? What a cliché.

I want her.

She keeps me pinned behind the door, with my eyes covered. I don't make a sound. Her tongue is moving across my breasts, putting each nipple in her mouth, sucking, nibbling, ravishing them one at a time. At the same time, her hand tugs open my jeans and moves quickly down to my cunt. Her fingers are big, leathered. With ease she slides two fingers into me and cups her other fingers around my clit. With each push inside me, her other fingers pull my clit up and down, sending shock waves rippling through my body each time.

She moves her hand from my eyes, and I see her for the first time. Tall, big, brown hair, piercing blue eyes, baseball cap, big hips with a key chain hanging from them. With her hand inside me still, she lifts me up and presses me against the wall. I wrap my legs around her waist, and she moves her hand in and out of me; moving a bit deeper with each thrust.

When I start to come she pulls her hand out and moves me—still wrapped around her—to the sink, where she props me up and removes my jeans completely. I glance furtively toward the door. She bends down on her knees, spreading my thighs and pushing her head between them. Each movement of her tongue on my clit seems to last an eternity. Up, down, up, down. Every few minutes she swirls the tip of it. Just a bit. Just to tease. Then she goes back to the long, heavy slurping. Just as the shivers rush through my body, she forces one hand inside me, the other reaches up and grabs my breast, and she does her final swirl.

I come with a ferociousness that makes me fall off the sink. This has been years in the making. Coming? Making.

"You want to go somewhere private with me?" she asks.

I nod. She helps me dress, buttoning my shirt, pulling up

my jeans. Then she leads me, flushed and happy, out of the bathroom and out of the truck stop.

I'm aghast. The purple truck is gone. Mrs. Right leads me to the last aisle, to a red Toyota Celica with Oregon plates. I get in, choking back a chortle but grinning nonetheless. As she revs the engine, I hear a slight whirrr-ping. She grabs my thigh.

Whirrr-ping. Whirrr-ping. I think my overpass days are over.

*Issue: Feb./March 1999*

## Cowpoke
by Mary Tidbits

*Her black boots creaked with the slap-slap-slap of flesh on flesh.*

My first crush was on Arrow, a Pinto my neighbor let me ride when I was seven. After Arrow, my love of horses only grew. Other girls replaced the horse pictures in their rooms with pictures of MTV idols, but not me. It seemed totally normal to me that I liked horses better than boys. It still does.

A little later in my life I started getting it bad for cowgirls. If I see any lady on a horse I'll look twice. If she has her horse moving forward on the bit, I'd probably be wet just watching her ride. If she's a redhead, it's all over.

I like redheads so much because Rita Roselock is a redhead. She won the barrel-racing event at the Montana State Championships—a day I'll never forget: Rita, sitting erect in the saddle, her horse dancing beneath her. When the gun went off, her whole body contracted. She busted through the gate to win the Cup and left me in the dust, gasping, waiting to get a chance to congratulate her and maybe get a handshake.

A few beers later I walked to her trailer as she was packing up. What to say to her? I racked my brain as I stood there fixated by her body. "Nice ride," I said lamely.

Rita turned to me, her face expressionless. To my surprise, it lit up. "Hey!" she said, "You're Diablo's owner, aren't you?" She reached out to shake my hand. "I just love the way he moves."

"Uh, thanks. Yeah, he's got a real nice lope. Part Mustang, part Arabian. Makes him a real fireball, but once you get him going good he's smooth as can be."

There was a long silence that she did not seem to find uncomfortable. Rita reached up and put her hand on my shoulder. "I've had my eye on you. You've got potential, and so does your horse, but you're both real green. I rode on this circuit for five years before I ever won a medal. I could teach you what you need to know. I've got the equipment, if you know what I mean." She took a handful of my hair in her fist. Her breath smelled like coffee. "Do you really want it?" She breathed into my ear. "I can give it to you."

Holy fuck! I put my hand on her thigh to make sure we were on the same wavelength. To my amazement, she smiled. "That's right, cowgirl," she purred. "We could have a fine time together, you and me."

Her fistful of hair pushed my head toward hers. Our belt buckles clicked together as we ground each other hard. She had me on my tiptoes riding her thigh when we heard voices.

Rita smiled a little half-smile and pulled me inside.

She didn't have much in her trailer except a bed and a couple of sawhorses in the corner. She took my hand and sat me down. "First you watch."

Her tank top came off, revealing her taut stomach, white as a baby's butt next to her face. She dropped her bra to the floor. A tattoo of a lasso wound lazily from one small breast to her other nipple. She unbuttoned her jeans, and a patch of reddish hair peeked out. With her left hand she reached into her pants while tracing that lasso tattoo. She licked her lips and looked down as she stroked the candy-pink line in her crotch.

"So do I get to touch?" I asked.

"Be patient," she replied. "It gets better."

Rita peeled off her Wranglers one leg at a time and sat naked except for her snakeskin boots. Her thighs, like all barrel racers', were rock-hard. I tried to pull her onto my lap, but she resisted.

I sat back, a little dismayed at what she wanted. As an answer, she pulled a shiny black dick out of a bag. "So do you like toys?" she asked.

"It depends on who's using them," I replied.

"How about you bend over that sawhorse right there and tell me if you like how I use it on you?"

It sounded all right to me, but I was aching to put my fingers inside her. "OK," I said, "but first you have to come over here."

She took a step, and I started to get up. With both hands she pushed me back into the chair. "You stay put," she hissed.

I snaked my arms around behind her and grabbed two fistfuls of ass. She put her hands on my shoulders and let me slide two fingers down her crack and into her wet cunt. I licked her belly and sucked her nipples. She pushed herself onto my dripping wet hand, and I straightened my fingers until all five were surrounded by a lovely, warm, slippery gush. Her hips released my hand with a shudder.

Rita stood up and pointed at my dusty Wranglers. "Strip."

My sleeveless denim top fell to the floor, followed by my 1967 State Roping championship belt. Rita calmly watched. I kicked off the boots and tossed my cow boxers in my heap of clothing. I felt clumsy and dirty compared to such a polished seductress.

She attached her dick to a black leather harness and cinched it around her waist. It looked like a good size, with a fun little crink on the end. "Ready, cowgirl?" she asked.

I had a good view of her boots when I leaned over the sawhorse. I lifted my ass high in the air and never took my eyes off those boots as she entered me, slowly at first. I squeezed, resisting, making her slide it around in a circle before she found the right angle. When she found that spot, that sweet orgasmic spot, I arched my back and relaxed and let her enter me.

She had both hands on my hips and moved slowly at first, then slammed the breath out of me. My head hung low over the horse, blood rushed to my head, and her black boots were creaking with the slap-slap-slap of flesh on flesh. I lost control of the rhythm and felt a warm orgasmic flutter spreading from my cervix outward. The boots stopped. Silence. I groaned and collapsed on the sawhorse with my legs apart. She left the dick in there for a minute and kneaded my lower back. My body was spent. It felt damn good.

Rita was still standing there wearing her strap-on.

"Wanna switch?" I asked, hot to fuck her back.

"Later, cowgirl. We can't blow our wad in one night. Why don't you bring your toys over tomorrow and we'll see what happens?"

Thus ended my first night with Rita Roselock, and began my thing for redheads. It's been with me ever since.

*Issue: Aug./Sept. 1999*

## Cool Blue Suit
by Fetish Diva Midori

*Something snaps inside me. I think it's the scent of her pussy finally registering with my brain.*

Is it ice water that runs through your veins? You always look so cool. Your pale skin never flushes, never blushes, and certainly never seems to sweat. Oh, pardon me. I forget. Women like you don't sweat, you glow. Except you don't do either of these. Fuck, you're too damned cool. I want to see you sweat sometime. I want to see that long black hair stick to your flushed and sweaty face. You never even let your hair down. Always coiled tightly on the back of your head, your long jet-black hair rests like a sleeping serpent. One silver hair stick is precisely pierced through the bun as if it were keeping the serpent from leaping out onto some unsuspecting passerby. I've never seen you laugh. I've seen a tight and patronizing smile stretch your lips across your cold face as some poor undergrad tried to warm up to you. You just barely tolerate them, don't you? But they keep trying for you every semester, every year.

Your demeanor brings down the room temperature around you by at least five degrees. This must be good for the books and the specimens on the shelves around you. This must also be good for protecting your heart from any passions too hot to handle. Or is it? I wonder.

Your fashion m.o. is the same as your manners. Cool and crisp. Your suits are always perfectly tailored. Never too tight, never too baggy, and certainly never trendy: Your suits fit you perfectly without any fussiness. The colors are always cool: navy blue, gray, slate, and charcoal. I know when there's an academic dignitary coming in: That's when you bring out your pinstripes. Your blouses are always an impeccable cream silk. Your stockings are a slightly lighter color than your suit. The shoes you wear are always terribly sensible—the heels are never over two inches and are never adorned in any way. Year in and year out you wear your damned uniform of cold authority over your domain of books and knowledge. I've never seen anyone wear a wool suit like armor the way you do. Even your ever-present pearl necklace looks likes it's a mandatory piece of insignia for your profession.

After two years of daily visits to this library in my efforts to finish my thesis, you seem to register a barely noticeable recognition of me. At least now you know I've got a brain under this rough shell. At first I'm sure you didn't take me for much more than a class-skipping slacker. You may have your uniform, Ms. Sakamoto, but I have mine too. The old leather jacket that my first real girlfriend gave me protects me from bike spills and dyke spills. Maybe you've noticed the gravel marks and beer-bottle slashes? Maybe not. My Wranglers are always beaten up, but my T-shirts are always immaculate. These black boots have taken me around the block a few times, you know. I keep my hair short in a crew. I want every-one to know exactly who and what I am. Today is special. I dressed with something special packed just for you.

I watch you today. You don't know that I've finished my thesis two weeks ago. I've just been coming in to watch you. My hot-blooded body needs to see you to keep from sponta-neously combusting. There's only a few more days until grad-uation. I gotta make this count. It's a Friday afternoon, so there are only a few grade-desperate geeks around here now.

Other than the rustling of papers and some keyboard tapping, the air is filled with stillness. Your face is perfectly still as well—without any emotion, without any passion.

I want to see you sweat.

You get up to put some books back in the stacks. The WILL RETURN SHORTLY sign makes its appearance. You must have a lot of books to reshelve. I pull out my stacks pass from my back-pack pocket, shove my pack and helmet on my chair, and stride past the sleepy intern who barely checks for my authentication to enter. Enough waiting. I'm going to enter because I want to.

I find you two flights down in the steel stacks in the back, near the forensics section. Perfect. As I approach, I cough. You don't even turn around. Yeah, you're cool. I walk up closer to you. You're still putting those damned books away. I wish you'd turn around and look at me. I want you to look at me. I want you to see my need for you burning in my eyes. I come up a step behind you and stop. You still haven't stopped working.

"I heard your thesis was well-received. Congratulations," she says suddenly. She doesn't even turn around or stop working. What? My mind tries to take in the fact that she spoke to me...then it tries to wrap itself around the fact that she knew about my thesis being finished. The implications make my head spin. All I planned today slides right out of my dyke dick and drains right down my feet and out of my body.

She has me.

I thought I had cornered her today. Now she's cornered me alone here in her cold domain. Jeez, what else does she know? I've lost all nerve to do what I planned.

"I suppose you've come to say goodbye to me." She speaks coldly.

"Ummm...yes...well...you've been very helpful." I sound like a fuckin' kid. I can't stand myself right now. She's turned around now and looks down at me from over her black-rimmed glasses. Damn it. I feel like a schoolboy. Damn it!

"You're welcome. If that's all, I have work to get back to. Have a good day." With that she turns back to the shelf. I mutter something like a defeated boy and start to walk away. My dyke dick is definitely deflated right now.

"Wait a minute, there. There's one more thing. You forgot to give me something," her voice rings at me. I suppose she wants that ever-treasured stacks pass back now that I'm graduating. I stop and turn around only to find her face inches from mine. I just realized that she actually wears perfume. I've never been this close to her. My throat is suddenly dry. I think I'm going to spontaneously combust. Her gold-brown eyes pierce right through my mind.

"Didn't you come here to give me something?" Her left eyebrow rises in a Mr. Spock–like query.

"Um...yes, ma'am...I mean no, ma'am." God, I sound like a fucking idiot.

"Well, which is it?" she snaps—but she's now pressing her tailored-suit-clad body into me. I lose balance and fall back in to a bookshelf, dislodging a few tomes on criminal psychology. Damn, I'll be in trouble for that one. Except she's not scolding me. She's still pressing her lithe body into mine. Her musk and night rose perfume scrambles my brain.

"I can see that you've come here to give me something, and I think you should follow through," she snaps in my ear as her delicate cold hand slides down my torso to my hip, then crosses my thigh and rests on my dick. Without moving her body away from mine, she effortlessly slips out of her navy-blue jacket and tosses it aside.

What the hell is happening now? I thought I was here to show her what I had for her. Sweat beads at my brow. I still haven't moved. Her gaze locked to mine, she leans back. Her left hand is on my dick again, but her right hand slides up to the nape of her neck. With one graceful motion she plucks the silver hair stick from her bun, releasing a cascade of blue-black silken hair over her shoulders. I'm mesmerized by the waves of black before me that I've only imagined late at night as I've jacked off. What I didn't ever imagine was what she did next. With a flash her butterfly hand held the silver stick firmly with the point planted solidly on my jugular.

"So, are you going to give it to me or not? If you don't have the balls to do it, get out of here right now and I don't ever want to see you." The stick is still in my neck. Then she moves the femme weapon away from my throat as if challenging me to make a decision. In desperation—not entirely knowing what to do with this new turn of events—I wrap my arms around her and kiss her as if my life depended on it. I think it did.

Her lips are burning hot...not cold as I thought they'd be. Her body seems so slight in my arms. God, she smells divine. Her painted mouth bites back at me, eating my kisses as fiercely as I give them. I hear the stick drop to the floor. Her hands force my jacket off and tug at my belt. Keeping one arm wrapped around her, I use my other to assist. The belt buckle undone, the fly now undone, her hand gropes in my boxers. Her small body manages to push me down to the floor where I sit unzipped, horny as hell and looking up at her straddling me. She unzips her skirt behind her back, and it slides down her lean legs. She's wearing stockings and a garter belt. Has she always worn stockings and a garter belt? Next thing I know she's taken off her postage-stamp-size underwear and is standing demandingly before me. I must look like a scared schoolboy to her.

Something snaps inside me. I think it's the scent of her pussy finally registering with my brain. I lean forward and nuzzle her mound covered in a fine layer of silky straight pube hair. Her musk is divine. My tongue reaches out to taste her. She thrusts into me. I drink from her hungrily, holding her ass cheeks in each hand. I can hear her sighs. I can feel her grinding into me. God, she's soaking wet. I could drink from her for hours—no, days—but she pulls away.

I would have begged her to let me keep going. The only thing that stops me from the indignity of begging is her swift hand pulling out my black silicone dick, already condom-covered and ready for action. Noting my preparedness, she grins and then laughs at me. My God, she's laughing. Before I know what's happening she takes all of me into her. I feel her weight crashing down on me, and a wave of heat rushes through my body. I hold on to her soft thighs in an effort to affirm that I'm really here. She's taking me and my dick. She's kissing me with abandon. My hips thrust up to meet each stroke. My cunt is so wet and hot that I must have steam rising from my crotch. Her black silk hair flies through the air. A silver streak of sweat runs down her cheek. A strand of hair clings to her flushed face.

I always wanted to see her sweat.

*Issue: Oct./Nov. 1999*

## Flowergirl
by Kirsten Flournoy

*I would bend her backward over my arm, pour red wine into her cleavage, and drink it through my rolled tongue, eat nasturtiums from her belly, violate her violet cunt mouth.*

She's there across the street, short and round, tiny and stacked. Her ass jiggles impossibly when she walks. The flowergirl has water balloons for breasts, hard 20-year-old wonders that creep toward her perfectly columnar neck as if to strangle her. I like to imagine the lush, damp creases beneath her arms, a mouth-watering smell of wet gravel rooming there.

Marooned on the island of my desk, I think of her, she of the innocuous name and missed cues. I must invent Very Important Business that requires profligate floral arrangements, cards to be bought, corporate clients to impress with unwieldy sprays of birds-of-paradise and gaudy red-wax leaves, like a baboon's butt with an obscene rippled yellow stamen shooting forth. I wish she worked in a coffee shop, where my increasing presence would not be so noticeable, not as much the subject of her raised eyebrows and unsubtle commentary. *You again?*

Today I am determined to make a move. I enter the shop, inhale its aroma of loam and rotting greenery, stagnant water, green scummed ponds. Spindly gnats flit through the humid air. I browse the floor-set pails of mixed bouquets, bundles of wilting roses, turgid powdered lilies. She's in back, puttering, muttering, joking with the fellows, her shorts and T-shirt absurdly tight even for someone of her age, revealing every curve and indentation of her callipygian body. I follow the line of elastic bra strap around her ribs, over her shoulder, then put my face into the refrigerated cabinets, breathing in fragrant long stems, my hot blush steaming against the cold. I can hear my breath rasping, catching, the old-fashioned watch on my wrist ticking loudly. I know what I want to buy.

I would bend her backward over my arm, pour red wine into her cleavage, and drink it through my rolled tongue, eat nasturtiums from her belly, violate her violet cunt mouth. The air here is too much for me, too close, too suffocating. I retreat. In the office restroom I lock myself in the big handicapped stall and slide spit-slicked fingers deep into my hole, drag them out against my eager clit, plunge them salty-sweet between my own lips, pretending it's her come flooding my mouth.

I enter the shop. She's there in the back room. Moving toward the cutting counter, she sees me, stops, scissors suspended mid bite, the ferns in her grasp trembling imperceptibly.

I shove her onto the counter, snatch the shears from her willing, weak-fingered hand, cut off that vile lime-green shirt, the cruel jeans keeping me from her. Flowergirl's supple mouth, heart-shaped, and her slack, startled gaze liquefies, her arms rising round me as I tongue her brown nipple, feeling the flesh tighten and pucker. She is as sweet as sugar; her saliva runs like warm maple syrup into my mouth as I drink her down, flesh pressed to fiery flesh. We don't care that the front door is standing open, that a prim granny is waiting at the cash register to be rung up. The oscillating fan swipes us with its breeze. She's smiling, no longer shy, afraid of what her boss might think. I see her confidence bubbling up, her cries wild and guttural as I part my long suit jacket to reveal my own projectile stem, my lavender latex pollinator cleaving her pocket of wet red petals. Moving beneath me, thrusting upward in mad abandon to impale herself on my burning spear, I laugh, fucking her on the counter; it's lunchtime and I'm dining well. She comes thrashing, knocking gift cards astray, kicking over silk flowers in plastic vases. The granny stands with one horrified hand to her aghast mouth as my flowergirl bellows out her delicious agony.

In the big bathroom stall I come on my hand and lick my fingers clean. I pull down my dress, smoothing it at the mirror behind the sink. My cheeks are flushed and pretty. I pick up my pocketbook, again counting out my wrinkly bills, making sure I have enough to buy a bouquet. I'm heading toward the elevators, crossing the street on my lunch break, on my way to the flower shop.

*Issue: Oct./Nov. 1999*

### What They Do
by Rachel Heath

*They—the lesbians—do it with their fingers.*

"Say you're Italian."

I don't know how old I was when Mom first told me that, but it must have been early. She'd say it as a reminder whenever I started a new school or went to a new church, though she didn't really need to. I knew you had to fib sometimes if you wanted other people to like you, and I never used to be one of the kids who got picked on.

Although I wasn't good at the book part of school, I loved hopscotch and tetherball and dodge ball, later softball (I made several home runs in high school). I never had a real problem getting along—I always knew when someone was starting to get weird.

By high school it was important to make myself look pretty, and that led to a lot of fights with Mom, who didn't like me to wear the type of makeup that was popular in those days.

"You want to make yourself look like a ghost?" she would ask. "Do women have white lips? What's pretty about that?"

"Oh, Mom," I said. I'd wave a hand at her. I didn't expect to make her understand.

The thing we really fought about was skirts. "It's dirty to

expose your knees," she'd say. "Dirty. Do you want to be *marime*\*?"

"It's not dirty," I'd answer. "Everybody does it."

"The *gaje*\*\* do it. We don't."

"I don't want to be weird," I said.

"Do you want to be dirty instead?" She'd shake her head, and her eyebrows would pinch together in an ugly way.

I didn't want to be dirty, but I didn't want to be weird either, so a lot of things were a struggle for me. I could never eat at a *gaje*'s house, so I became good at making excuses. Then there was the time I was visiting a friend—most of my friends were *gaje*—and her cat came over to me. I froze, and my stomach knotted up. The look of distaste must have been evident in my face because Eve asked, "What's wrong?" and I replied, "Nothing," but I said I had to go to the bathroom so I could get away from the cat because cats are such polluting animals with the way they lick themselves, bringing dirt from their outsides into their inside.

In my senior year at Lincoln High—it was the only year I went to that school—I was only friends with one other Rom girl (besides my cousins whom I lived with). There were other Rom kids at the school, but I stayed away from them (except Rom gatherings) because all the *gaje* knew what they were and made fun of them, calling them "dirty gypsies" and pretending they were afraid the Rom kids were going to steal their stuff. Worst of all, guys would come up singing "She Was a Gypsy Woman" to the girls they knew were Rom and ask, "Is it true all gypsy girls are whores?" when we weren't even allowed to *date* like the rest of them and we were supposed to keep our knees covered. I can't believe how the *gaje* reverse things, seeing Rom as the immoral ones when they live their whole lives in pollution.

---

\**Marime* describes the shameful condition of those who are Rom—usually called "gypsies" by most people—who have become "polluted" and therefore shunned by other Rom.

\*\**Gaje* is used by Rom to refer to anyone who is not Rom.

Mary/Yvonne was my best friend. Mary was her name around *gaje*, and Yvonne was her Rom one, just like Dana is my name for *gaje* and Sofie is for just Rom. At school, even in the girls' restroom with no one else present, we always called each other by our American names. We weren't real good about going to class because we weren't planning to go on to college; our parents thought even high school would be too corrupting. But when we cut class we didn't go home because our moms and grandmothers would put us to work around the house (although they wouldn't get mad that we weren't in school).

Yvonne and I would drive around, usually in Yvonne's grandmother's old yellow Cutlass, to nowhere in particular, just talking. It was on one of these times when we were cutting our last class of the day and riding around that Yvonne told me she knew what *gaje* do on dates. "Lori told me about it," she said in Romany.

Lori and her were like best friends, but not completely, because Lori was *gaje*. "Lori told me *everything* a boy did with her," Yvonne claimed. I looked over at her; even though it was her car, I was driving. She let me sometimes, and I always wanted to.

My heart tripped. I felt my mouth go dry, then water just as suddenly. I was excited but also scared because it might make me *marime* even to *know*. But I wanted to know.

"She told you..." My words ran out. From the look in my eyes, Yvonne must have known I wanted her to continue. My hands on the steering wheel got clammy.

Her voice went down. "Find a place to park, and I'll show you, Sofie," she promised. In our cars and homes, when we were certain no *gaje* would hear, we called each other by our Rom names.

My heart beat excitedly as I drove. "Where?" I asked.

"That lot that's down the block from your cousin's auto repair shop."

But I'd already thought of it before Yvonne said it.

I stopped the car and parked. I was afraid to look at Yvonne, but I had to.

"First, the boy just takes your hand, like this, Sofie," she said, taking my hand. I felt a warm glow begin. "And for a while, that's all they do, just hold hands."

Silently I looked into her large, dark brown eyes. A wave of inchoate yearning passed through my flesh.

"Then he starts just...moving a little bit, up and down, like this..." Her palm went lightly up and down the inside of my arm.

"Oh," I said, scared, but with a fear that wasn't all bad, more like watching a scary movie.

"Then he'll kiss you," Yvonne said. Yvonne put her hand on the back of my neck—my heart tripped again—and she wanted to see if I would stop her.

I did not.

Yvonne kissed me on the mouth, close-mouthed and not for too long.

I giggled nervously when she pulled away. My face must have been red.

Yvonne giggled too. Then she said, "Now, what usually happens is the girl tells the boy to stop."

"Stop," I whispered automatically.

We both giggled again.

"And he does, for a while. They just sit there, and he goes back to this"—Yvonne held my hand—"and this"—she slid her fingers up and down the inside of my arm, half-tickling.

A pause followed. We were still holding hands. Yvonne intermittently caressed my arm.

I looked at the windshield, blinking and swallowing hard.

She kissed me, very lightly, just on the side of the face. "Then he starts again," Yvonne said. Her tongue licked lightly against my ear. Hot chills raced up and down my spine. She paused again. She put her hand on the back of my neck. My face turned toward hers, and we kissed on the mouth again—open-mouthed this time, her tongue thrust inside my mouth. A warm pulse beat between my thighs, in my woman's parts. I squeezed against her arm, and my right leg lifted up automatically.

Yvonne pulled away from me. I saw I had smeared her pink lipstick and knew she'd pinked my white. "Then they usually say something like 'I love you, Sofie,' " she went on.

"I love you," I said, very softly, hardly audible, not quite knowing the words were coming out of my mouth.

Her hand brushed lightly against my breast.

"Oh," I gasped.

She waited. Then her hand cupped my breast, through the blouse and bra, not directly, and, looking through the car windows at the sky just beginning to get dusky—it was November and getting dark early—I felt sweat burst hotly from my armpits. My nipples burned and stung with a furious arousal. I started to grind my hips around on the seat.

" 'I love you,' he says, and 'Baby, baby' and 'Oh, Sofie, I love you,' " Yvonne murmured. "And then he puts his hand under here like this." Her hand went to my leg, up my skirt.

"That's polluted," I said, suddenly and genuinely terrified. "Stop!"

"Yeah, but that's what the *gaje* guy does on a date—he puts his hand up there to your...parts," Yvonne explained. Her hands rested on my skirt. "People can find out when a boy does that," she said, musing slowly. "The girl can get pregnant. But if I...no one has to know except us."

*No one has to know except us.* I would clean the parts extra special. Yvonne would clean her hands. No one else would know and make us *marime*.

I didn't say anything. Yvonne's hand went tentatively to my knee. I looked out the window—our parents might be mad if we came in late; they might even think we'd been with boys!—and I closed my eyes. "Yes," I breathed softly.

She heard. Her hand went slowly up between my legs. I felt a curious pinched, even painful, tension in my woman's parts, and my hips started to move as her fingers touched the most forbidden place and I let out a little cry of frightened joy as my breathing sped up and a wondrous shiver of purest pleasure shook me from the scalp of my head down to the bottoms of my feet.

A single tear ran down my cheek afterward. I brushed it away. I drove myself home.

When Yvonne's hands touched the wheel, I thought: *Oh, no, it is marime.*

It wasn't too long after that, at a big Rom get-together, that I found out what lesbians do. Maria Yonko knew. She was a real smart girl, especially in the ways of the *gaje*. None of the *gaje* knew her true ethnicity; since her name was Maria, she always told them she was Mexican.

All of us girls were together in the den, away from the adults and the boys, when Tina told us. "They—the lesbians—do it with their fingers. Put their hands into the woman's polluted place."

A collective gasp went around the room. I gasped with everyone else but looked down at the floor. My face went dreadfully hot. Yvonne was sitting on the floor right next to me.

"Terrible," Yvonne murmured.

My heart skipped a beat. *No one needs to know.* I would never be *marime*, I told myself.

"Lesbians," Yvonne said slowly, in a voice filled with horror. "Those awful women," she added as she squeezed my hand.

I squeezed back.

*Issue: Feb./March 2000*

## Thank Heaven for 7-Eleven
by Kate B. Nealon

*I notice short, dark hair under a baseball cap, muscular arms, and hands that look small enough. Please, god, let it be a girl.*

The front doors beep as I push through them, and the balding man behind the counter glances up briefly before refocusing his stare on a tiny television in front of him. I make my way past the rows of candy and the racks of girlie mags toward the refrigerated cases lining the back wall. I've always found something comforting about a 7-Eleven at night, with its familiar aisles of processed treats and its bright lights to keep all the darkness outside.

A stock person is unloading a box in the next aisle, and I feel an instant leap of attraction. I notice short, dark hair under a baseball cap, muscular arms, and hands that look small enough. Please, god, let it be a girl. My heart skips a beat as she turns around: yup. The girl, who looks even better from the front, notices my look, and a slow smile spreads across her face. I blush and spin around, pretending to be suddenly preoccupied with my beer decision. Hmm, so many choices nowadays.

But when she moves again I can't keep my eyes from following her. She's going slower now, showing off because she knows I'm watching her. She flexes as she picks up the now-empty box and heads through the EMPLOYEES ONLY door. I gaze wistfully after her for a moment before gathering my wits, grabbing a six-pack, and stopping by the freezer case to get a "pizza for one."

At the register I look down with slight dismay at my selections, which scream, *Alone tonight? You bet.* I hope that if the cute stock girl notices, she'll find it endearing instead of pathetic. As I furtively try to see if she's coming back, the man behind the counter interrupts with a grunted "Cash back?"

"Huh?" I say, "Oh, no, thanks." He hands me my receipt, and I grab my bag.

I'm headed toward my car when her voice stops me: "Hey."

I turn around. She's leaning against the wall, smoking. God, is she hot. When I finally find my voice, it's shaky.

"Hi," I say, slowly walking back to her. I'm trying to be casual, like it's every day that girls wait outside stores to meet me.

"Are you off work for the night?"

"Cigarette break," she answers.

Ah. That would explain her standing outside smoking a cigarette. My heart races. Please, let her be trying to pick me up. I stand next to her, aware of the traffic sounds from the freeway and the way the shadows from her hat hide her eyes. She takes one last drag of her cigarette, stubs it out, and turns to face me. I feel her hand at the small of my back, and before I know it, we're kissing. I guess she doesn't believe in long formalities. Little sighs and groans escape my mouth as I revel in her soft lips. Her hands travel down to my butt, scooping me up and pressing me closer into her. Then the headlights of an approaching car play over us, and she pulls back.

"Come here a second," she says, grabbing my hand. She leads me around the corner to a door marked RESTROOM with universal man and woman symbols. She slips a key in the lock and flicks the light switch.

Even though convenience store restrooms do not rank high on my list of favorite spots for trysts, I know by now that I want this woman so bad that I'd fuck her just about anywhere: even standing in a puddle of pee, where I realize we just might be as I look down at the damp floor. The yellow light bulb overhead casts an unflattering light on the small dingy space with just a toilet, sink, and paper-towel dispenser. But this woman wants to be alone with me here, which means that this is heaven.

Her hands fumble to the door lock as I press her against the wall, running my hand between her legs. She reaches under my shirt to brush my nipples, and I moan into her mouth, rubbing up and down on her thigh.

She lifts me up to the sink and unbuttons my fly. We're kissing this whole time, and she can't take me fast enough. I lift one butt cheek to help her take off my jeans and underwear. The sink is cold beneath my butt, but all thoughts of fear and discomfort quickly disappear as she runs her hands up my bare thighs, pausing for a long, long moment before her thumbs come to rest gently on my clit. I hadn't expected such finesse in a 7-Eleven bathroom.

I become one big nerve ending as she slowly strokes me, becoming acquainted with my wet folds. Everything in my body begs her to keep going as she slips more and more fingers inside me. As she finally starts thrusting, my back arches and I bump my head on the mirror. I hardly notice; I'm getting louder and louder and can't help myself. Her breathing is getting heavier too, with her soft groans providing a subtle bass line to my gasps and breaths.

She somehow loosens herself enough from the vise grip of my thighs to slide her face down my body. She looks back up at me as her head gets between my legs, and I feel time stop. My face clearly shows all my emotions, but I don't care. I want to be even more obvious so that she can see exactly where she's taking me. I rest my thighs on her shoulders, and her mouth softly closes around my clit.

Oh.

"My god," I murmur as she licks the underside of my clit, her fingers still inside me. She keeps her tongue moving, lightly at first, enjoying the responses she's provoking in me. I am completely at her mercy. She moves her hand inside me again, curving her fingers to find my G-spot and stroking it steadily until I make animal-like groans. Finally, she senses I can't take it much longer and sucks me full force. I jerk, so stimulated that it hurts. My mind becomes a fog, but my body adjusts to her increased tempo, climbing higher and higher to its inevitable peak. I let my legs fall wider and wider apart, totally relaxing my muscles, begging her to go deeper and to bang her head harder against my cunt. A wave of heat starts in my belly, and then my mind blanks out, my body shakes, and I come with a final shout.

After a moment, she lifts her head and I feel suddenly naked. She kisses her way back up my body, and when she reaches my mouth, I taste myself on her lips.

As I slowly regain control over my movements, I feel shy and sheepish. Here I am, half naked and in love with this girl who has just shown me heaven in a skanky public restroom. Maybe she notices my sudden modesty, because she picks my jeans off the floor and helps me to put them back on. I search for something to say as I button them, something brilliant that will forever emblazon me in her memory.

"Will your boss be mad?" I finally ask, feebly.

She grins lazily. "Nah, but I should probably get back to work." I get off the sink and grab my plastic bag with its thawed pizza and warm beer as she unlocks the bathroom door. As we step outside, I hear crickets chirping, and the air smells like summer nights used to when I was a kid. She walks me to my rusty Toyota, and I fumble with the keys, trying to think of some excuse to see her again.

"Um," I finally ask, "can I give you my phone number?"

"Sure," she says, and I scramble among the empty food

cartons and debris in my car to find a scrap of paper and a pen. I finally hand her my number and look into her eyes to see what color they are. It's too dark to tell, really; hazel or brown, I think.

"Thanks," she says before walking back toward the store. I watch her as she takes off her hat, smoothes her hair quickly, and pops her cap back on again, pausing for a moment before disappearing inside. I wave one last time—with my car door (and my mouth) still hanging open. After she's gone, I listen for another moment to the crickets, then slowly start up my car to head home.

*Issue: June/July 2000*

## Damp Panties
by Jennifer Jen

*Obediently I rubbed her pussy, spreading her juices over her labia.*

My girlfriend Jeannie is a lingerie junkie, and sexy lingerie has a simple and compelling message that can be summed up in two very direct words: Fuck me. Her dresser drawers are overflowing with camisoles, peek-a-boo bras, and crotchless panties. She owns at least two dozen teddies that lace up from her delicious mound to her luscious breasts. She treasures her hundreds of black silk stockings that hug her long legs, held up by garters decorated with rosebuds and bows.

Jeannie takes precious care of her lingerie. But once in a blue moon she'll take her most pristine pair of panties and defile them for me. As much as she launders her treasures, the sweet scent of her pussy still clings to them, traces of her emissions embedded in the silky fabric.

For Jeannie, putting on lingerie is the same as foreplay; it primes her body for sex. She cannot squeeze her breasts into a plunging red lace brassiere without her nipples stiffening. As soon as her pussy feels the tickle of satin, it begins to respond.

Jeannie's lingerie tells me not just that she wants me to fuck her; it tells me how. If she's in the mood to be teased, she'll slither into one of her virginal white teddies and invite me to reveal her body in tiny steps. First her nipples, taut with sexual tension. Next her tummy, glistening with golden down and the faint glow of wetness. Then her hips, just beginning to writhe and twitch with anticipation. Finally, her pussy and its golden curls spring into view.

By the time she's fully undressed, the pink of her pussy is shiny wet. I lay her down and make love to her.

There is, however, a danger to having a lover who's a lingerie junkie.

Jeannie and I were having dinner one night at a popular restaurant. After sharing a platter of oysters and enjoying an after-dinner liqueur, the seduction began. Leaning over, she took my hand and guided it up her dress. My fingers, touching the crotch of her panties, told me she had been thinking naughty thoughts. Beneath the fabric, her pussy hairs were warm and wet.

"We've got to get out of here," she whispered hoarsely. "I'm horny."

We would've dashed out the door without paying the bill if a waiter hadn't walked by. I tossed my credit card on the table and took hold of Jeannie's arm, and we hurried for the exit.

We almost didn't make it to the car. As we approached the parking lot, she wanted me to make love to her on the grass behind some bushes. But I persuaded her to wait. We climbed into the backseat, and she raised her dress all the way up to her waist. She opened her legs, grabbed my wrist, and pulled my hand to her crotch.

"Here," she rasped. "Fuck me."

Obediently I rubbed her pussy, spreading her juices over her labia. She slid forward to the edge of the seat. "Do it," she groaned, and I slipped two fingers deep inside. "Oh, God," she moaned, and as I started to move faster, I felt an orgasm starting somewhere down in my own groin. Then I remembered my credit card.

"Holy shit!" I blurted. "My credit card!"

Jeannie grumbled as I pulled my hand out of her, swung open the door, and dashed back into the restaurant. Luckily, my credit card was still on the table, with a receipt ready for me to sign. My fingers still smelling of Jeannie's pussy, I signed the receipt, put my credit card back in my purse, and raced outside to the car, where I found Jeannie playing with herself. I flung open the door.

"Save it," I said. "I'm back."

I slammed the door behind me and slid beside her. "You're a slut," I whispered in her ear, and as I started to finger-fuck her again, my own stirrings returned. I crossed my legs and squeezed as hard as I could.

Right at that moment, as I was diddling Jeannie and squeezing myself into ecstasy, somebody was tapping on the glass. I froze. I didn't know whether to laugh or cry, but Jeannie didn't give me a chance to decide. She was obviously in the middle of her own orgasm, grabbing my wrist and jamming my fingers harder and deeper into her cumming cunt. "Screw it!" she was screeching. "Screw me!" So I ignored the tapping and went back to work. It felt terrific too, coming as I was with Jeannie, my spasms joining with hers. But then I heard a woman shriek.

"Hey, bitch," said a man's voice, "do that shit in private."

Mumbling something about fucking assholes, Jeannie threw her arms around my neck and pulled me to her, kissing me and preventing me from seeing who it was who had invaded our privacy. But I was thoroughly pissed. I broke off the kiss, turned my head, and shouted, "Fuck off, asshole!"

"Calm down," Jeannie whispered. "They're gone."

Unwrapping Jeannie's arm from my neck, I sat up straight and found a wet spot on my dress. I had peed my panties in the midst of my orgasm, and the mixture of coming and peeing had soaked through and onto the seat.

"Shit," I said. "The upholstery is ruined."

Jeannie just laughed. "Don't worry about it. Here, we might

as well do it on this side too." She opened her legs wide, gathered her panties, pulling the red silk tight against herself, and started peeing. "Love it," she said. "God, it's warm. It's swishing around my clit." Her panties were turning to a darker red as the pee squished into them, oozing through and seeping out, trickling between her legs.

When she was finished peeing, she pulled off her panties and told me to take off mine. I did. We cleaned each other up as best we could, and finally drove out of the parking lot and back to our apartment.

*Issue: Aug./Sept. 2000*

## Double D Fantasy
by Blaize Tempest

*Oh, my poor baby. I've let you go so long without feeding...*
*You rest in my arms and let me nurse you.*

Liz watched her reflection in the mirror as she pulled on
her stockings, fastened the garters, and slipped on her panties.
She pulled her front-clasping bra over her head, leaned forward, and hoisted her ample breasts into the double-D cup
bra. Her breasts ached. She didn't like to let so much time
pass without seeing her lover Gina. Gina would be nearly
starved, she thought, as she puffed some perfumed powder
onto her deep cleavage before fastening the hooks of the
tight-fitting bodice of her dress.

At the front door, Liz beamed broadly at her beloved.
"How's my baby been?"

Gina returned her gaze for a moment, then let her eyes settle on Liz's cleavage. "Baby's been hungry," Gina replied
emphatically.

Gina waited patiently as Liz unclasped the brassiere and
released her right breast. Gina's mouth fell open, and her eyes
glazed a bit as she relaxed her head completely into the crook
of Liz's right arm. The sight of Liz's breast, rounded and soft,
almost as large as her head, made her heart ache and cunt
throb. This heavy orb crowned with a large, brown-pink nipple, a half-inch long standing erect, puckering at the end like

a small mouth, held her elixir. Liz guided the large nipple deeply into her waiting mouth.

The smell of Liz's body and the warmth of her cleavage made Gina's body shiver with small orgasmic contractions almost the moment the nipple was lodged in her mouth. Liz's right hand cradled Gina's head and held it firmly. Gina sucked, wrapping her tongue around the bottom of the nipple, pressing her face into the breast and pulling out its contents with urgent, deep suction.

Liz felt her own cunt contract. "Oh, my poor baby. I've let you go so long without feeding. I won't withhold from you, baby. This is all for you. You suck now, baby. You rest in my arms and let me nurse you." She stroked her lover's hair and held her tightly, feeling an amazing warmth and release in her own chest.

Soon Gina's sucking became less urgent, more long and deep. Without warning, Liz slipped her finger into Gina's mouth to release the suction, then she pulled her breast away.

"I need you," Gina whispered into Liz's ear as she put her arm around her waist.

Liz felt a thrilling tingle at her responsibility to keep her lover well-fed.

As if reading her mind, Gina confirmed her intention with a solid tone of voice. "I'm gonna drink my two weeks worth, and I'm gonna hold you steady to do it, Liz." With urgency, Gina unzipped her pants and pulled out her long, thick cock. She lifted Liz's skirt up around her waist.

Liz felt her vulva become slick at the sight of Gina's urgency. Gina raised her eyebrows sternly. Obediently, Liz stood and removed her panties, then sat back on the soft velvet sofa. The sofa was low, and Gina urged Liz to the edge with a beckoning finger. Liz took a deep breath and spread her legs wider, opening the pink wetness for Gina's approving gaze. Gina held her cock firmly and lifted her eyes.

"Do you know what I need?" Gina asked rhetorically, and

Liz nodded. "I want your tight little cunt to suck this," she pulled the cock forward, "while I suck those."

Gina moved forward and buried the dildo deep into Liz's cunt, thrusting slowly for a few moments, delighting in the gentle movement of Liz's breasts. Liz moaned softly at being so well-filled, but she whimpered a bit when Gina stopped moving. Gina pushed Liz's thighs farther apart to nestle her body as close as possible between Liz's legs, her cock buried inside Liz as deep as it would go. She looked into Liz's eyes and said, "Hold me now."

Liz wrapped her legs around her lover tightly and lifted her left breast, nipple pointing toward Gina's eager mouth. She held the back of Gina's head with the other hand and guided the nipple deep into her waiting mouth. "I've got you, baby. I've got you," Liz cooed, her cunt squeezing the cock as tightly as she could. Gina felt so completely possessed—engulfed and surrounded. She sucked hard, drawing the nipple into her mouth deeply and forcefully, issuing muffled moans from deep in her throat. Liz held tightly, her hand in Gina's hair, her cunt tensing, her fingers offering that breast, squeezing it as Gina sucked, trying to drown her lover.

"Oh, yes," Liz continued in a low, soothing voice. "Is that good, baby? Are you getting what you need?" Gina nodded slightly, eyes closed, at Liz's cooing questions. "Is my pussy taking care of you, baby? Are you taking as much as you need?"

Gina sucked hard, biting the nipple, frustrated that she couldn't take the whole breast into her mouth at once. Liz felt her nipple sting with those bites, and she arched her back to take her lover's forcefulness.

"It's OK, baby. I've got plenty for you," Liz admonished, pulling the back of Gina's hair when she became too rough. Gina took this guidance but quickly sucked hard again. She knew she must protect Liz and her beautiful breasts if she were to be well-fed and cared for in the future, yet she wanted to possess Liz. She wanted nothing held back.

Liz arched her back to enjoy the slight pain and pulling, and she squeezed her cunt more forcefully and steadily. As she felt the contractions in her cunt, she knew she'd soon burst, and she desperately wanted Gina's cock pounding inside her when she came. Gina too felt her cunt contract in time with her deep sucking. She heard Liz's breath coming faster and knew Liz's orgasm would bring her own. Liz held Gina's head so forcefully against her huge breast that she had to suck air periodically around it. And then came Liz's request, soft and pleading, starting Gina's orgasm deep inside, the sensation moving out toward the dildo, all the way out to its tip, deep inside Liz.

"Please fuck me, Gina," Liz begged. "Don't make me hold it any longer. I've squeezed it all I can. Take care of my pussy. Fuck me hard, baby."

Gina removed her mouth from that breast, letting it fall so she could cover Liz's mouth with her own to muffle the voices erupting from their throats. She did as she was asked, holding Liz's hips, thrusting inside her hard and fast as their orgasms rushed over them.

*Issue: Oct./Nov. 2000*

## The Long Parallel Tracks
by Peggy Munson

*People who ride trains know how to linger, and she took her time.*

It may sound like a romantic artifact from a Russian novel, but in my country the sleeper car is just a haven for aviophobes willing to pour their yearly savings into a trip that takes 12 times as long as by airplane. A well-engineered little cubicle that resembles a mausoleum with a toilet. There, rumbling past the dizzying faded paint of freight cars, I always relearn the lost art of patience. When I asked the conductor when we were going to take off, he said "Do you see a runway out there?" and told me to relax.

So I bore down for a thousand games of solitaire, not expecting to have a good time at all. But then, as we rolled out past Boston's periphery, I saw the woman strolling though the passageway, wearing chunk-heel dyke shoes. I've been all over; I know the regional differences in queer mating signals. In the Midwest, dykes tattoo their own arms using needles sterilized in whiskey. In the West, people have flawless haircuts, and they wear them like trophy hunters. In the East, dykes have shoes that can ground lightning.

All it took was a glance from her and I knew I wanted to come on sudden and furious. She was looking for nothing but a good night's rest.

Her eyes measured the parameters of my cubicle. I was reflecting back on all those games of Seven Minutes in the Closet I missed in junior high, when I wanted so badly to kiss a girl in a dark, dusty hideaway, high on mothballs and musty coats.

Without the shoes, I ascertained, she was probably just another Midwest transplant like me. I wondered how her Protestant work ethic might hold up in bed.

"Where are you headed?" I asked her as she passed.

"To the end of the line," she said. "Chicago. Actually, to a town you've probably never heard of."

"Try me," I said. "I'm going to Joliet, Illinois."

"Hey, I'm landing outside of Romeoville," she answered. We both grinned. "Right behind a grain elevator."

As I watched her maneuver into a sleeper car down the hall, I noticed the rainbow triangle on her bag. A Midwest dyke with a butch swagger, wearing assimilationist shoes and muscling her own bags. I was ready for trouble. I was ready to be run out on a rail.

When *The Avengers* came on my index-card-sized movie screen, I called her out of her car. "Hey, do you want to watch Uma Thurman put on tight costumes with me?"

"Oh, yeah. I'm all over that," she answered, and we both squeezed into my sleeper. To watch the movie, one of us had to sit right on top of the covered toilet, so I volunteered, trying to be chivalrous. We pretended we weren't violating the laws of proxemics, but we were marvelously close, the denim of our knees rubbing together.

She held out her hand as introduction, cramping it back because we were so close. "Civ," she said.

"Civ?"

"Used to be Cybil. My sister had a lisp. It became Civil, as in disobedience. Now it's Civ, as in sieve."

"How very Marxist," I said. "Or Betty Crockerish. So let's

watch this Kremlin-edition movie screen and eat the pretzels I brought."

"Great," she said, laughing, even though my joke was nervously weird, and I couldn't even remember if Marx wrote *Civil Disobedience* or if it was written by some '60s guy, like Abbie Hoffman.

By the time Uma was wearing something fit for deep-sea diving, Civ and I had our hands dangling close together, brushing against each other. We weren't watching the movie, but rather talking about how people from the coasts never see geography from the ground. How they don't see the utter flatness of the plains as real topography, even though the mystery of that space—the ground, the roots, the soil—has such rich texture. I was starting to really like her. I was starting to fantasize about her topography.

"Hey," she said, glancing at my ass, "you're going to have to move for me. I gotta pee."

"Do you want me to leave?"

"Just look away while I go."

Since adolescence, when the intimacy of locker rooms was my only door to desire, it has turned me on to listen to women peeing. I love the snap of belts, the rustle of jeans, the way I can sense their self-consciousness or bravado. I faced the long, panoramic windows and watched the rolling scenery of Pennsylvania—unremarkable hills, the perfect asymmetry of trees. Spread-eagled against the window, I listened to her relieving herself. I heard the crinkle of the denim being drawn up, the zipper sliding closed. But then instead of latching her belt, she pulled it out of the loops. I didn't turn around, just heard the leather catch on air. We were both really quiet for a second. Then I felt the weight of her whole body against my back as she stretched the belt out around my waist and against the window to pin me there.

"Got you," she said.

My cheek was flat against the rattling window, where outside two scrappy kids were running alongside the train and waving. "Do you think people can really see in?" she asked, when she reached one hand around to unbutton my shirt and crack it open so the glass chilled my belly. I didn't think she wanted me to answer. She reached down to unbutton the fly of my jeans, with her fingers grazing the cotton of my underwear. "I bet they can," she said. "I bet they can witness everything."

Then she pulled my jeans down quickly so they hung halfway down my thighs.

"But you know how those backwoods perverts are," she said. "They love a lesbian show."

I felt her pressing my splayed body against the glass, trying to flatten me into a cheap porn caricature for our Pennsylvania audience.

Then she started slowly biting and kissing my neck. People who take trains know how to linger, and she took her time licking the backs of my ears. I was curling my arms in like formative wings. She wrapped the belt around them, then began cinching it to hold my arms in place, the way people used to fasten suitcases or carry schoolbooks with leather straps.

Without my hands to steady me, I felt out of control as the train rocked and careened through Dutch country. But she worked me like an old butter churn, then licked the sweet corners of my shoulders. We passed a car lot, a backyard full of trash, a spray-painted building. She frisked my sides, moving her palms down the round edge of my breasts. We passed a gap-toothed picket fence, then an intersection with flashing lights and cars watching us. There, she turned my head and kissed me demonstratively on the mouth, deeply, licking the ticklish ridges of my palate. Then at a junkyard, bright colors melting together in the sepia of the sunset, she slid one finger down the crack of my ass. When I moaned a little she said,

"You have to shut the fuck up, really. We don't want to get kicked off the train."

Some migratory birds formed a V next to the train just as we passed under a tunnel tagged with bright graffiti, and she slid one finger into my wet cunt. We buzzed past a rusting metal scrap yard, the train rocking like a maternal primate, and her hand began rocking too, rocking into me, one finger at a time, harder, more intensely. A sign said DEMOLITION with a big picture of a crane, and her fingers pushed up into a ball, curling and pressing into me. Just then, the train gradually hummed to a stop at a station platform, and she had me pinned there with her hand squeezing up hard into me. Everybody waiting for the train in Podunk wherever, wherever we were, could see our show. I tried to turn my head away.

"Oh, shit," she said, when we both noticed the gawkers. She reached around behind her for the light switch and turned off the compartment light. Then she began pushing into me really hard, just the way I like, rocking rough and feral until I came for her, suppressing a scream and shuddering and moving my weight down onto her hand.

"Is this one of the eight states with sodomy laws?" I asked her between heavy breaths.

"This isn't sodomy," she said, but just then she slid a finger from her other hand into my waiting ass. "*This* is sodomy."

Then she began fucking my ass so exquisitely and said, "You Bible Belt Midwesterners can never get it right."

"Oh, yeah," I said, and gasped. "Now I remember Sodom and Gomorrah."

"Yeah," she said. "I bet you came out in a gay men's bar, just like every Illinois dyke, with the drama club fags."

"Someone once said to me, 'That's just a bundle of wood, a faggot.'"

"That's because sticks and stones...you know, but words can never hurt you," she said sardonically, losing her focus for a minute but then pressing up so hard into me I steamed half the window when I moaned.

We both knew that was all wrong, the thing about words. We both knew their injurious potential. That's why we didn't talk. That's why, later, we would use words as a form of redemption, to explain what happened. That's why I wanted her hands to speak soliloquies. That's why I loved it when she was all action. That's why she held me rough like I was a gay hustler, pressing my pretty cheek against the thick glass and pumping hard into my ass. That's why she said, her voice getting gravelly, "I bet you're good on your knees too."

And why I got down on my knees so quickly, I can only explain one way. Women taste savory, not sweet. And I like to savor. I like the long, hard effort of a 22-hour trip before I arrive at my destination. I like to beg to be taken back home. I like the long line of indiscretions that lead up to atonement.

I propped her up on the two sterile pillows and unzipped her jeans slowly. I kneeled between the two facing chairs and unlaced her dyke shoes, working my way back to her earthen roots, smelling my way up the rubbed-in, work-worn scents of her Levi's, and then I pulled them off. Underneath she was wearing indigo boxer briefs, old worn cotton, and I could smell the perfect autumn spice of her cunt. I massaged her thighs with both hands and said, "Comfortable?"

I wanted her to be comfortable. We still had about 16 hours.

"Yeah," she said, stroking my head. I worked her briefs down her legs.

Just then the train jerked forward and my face slammed into her cunt. I was smeared with her juice, and she just whimpered with surprise. My instinct was to gasp for air, but she held my head down, like she was pushing my face into a mud puddle, making me taste the damp earth and all of its minerals and desecration. I could tell she loved how humiliated I looked.

"No cockpit," she said, smirking. "Just the long, parallel tracks."

And then I slid my tongue up the lips of her cunt, savoring the metal, savoring the glint of coal. I tasted the years of civil disobedience from loving women, from phantom dicks and amputated desire and the furrowed rows where beauty is planted. I worked my tongue up to her clit and flicked the tip of it, then kissed and sucked on it, until I felt her thighs flinching. I worked hard with my mouth and tongue, tasting her, licking the damp wild fiddleheads of her pubes. And when I felt like she was about to come, I became the little engine that could, chuffing up a hill with so much heady affirmation.

"Do you think you can come for me?" I asked her, raising my head and licking her briefly off my lips.

"I think I can," she answered, and I just smiled and went back to work. I hoped she was repeating the little engine's mantra in her head, because I wanted to make her feel good. I wanted to fuck her all the way back to her Americana steam-engine roots. And when she finally wailed for me, it had the pull of nostalgia and the sweet taste of everything familiar. Then I pushed her hard against the chair back, forcing her to kiss her own juices off my lips, so hard she knocked me away and wiped her mouth with her hand.

"You're pretty uppity for someone from a desolate little farm town," she said.

Then she stood up and turned the crank on the sleeper car bunk above us, pulling it down and latching it into place.

"Well, get up there and lie down," she ordered when she saw my uncertainty. "So I can fuck you in Ohio. I need another pin in my map."

*Issue: Oct./Nov. 2000*

## Chaka Masturbation Fantasy #29
by T.J. Bryan, a.k.a. Tenacious

*And she takes it all, takes every musky, sweet drop of jizz in her mouth.*

There's one place where I can always find her. Where the blues in her voice ride me. Stroke me rough and raspy like a winter wind before the storm. There's a song she belts out: "Ain't nobody...loves me betta... makes me happy... makes me feel this way..." And I know she's talkin' 'bout me.

Yeah, this is where she lives. So I come, a pilgrim seeking. Waiting patiently for those high notes to rip right through the heart-a me again. Giving me goose bumps on my goose bumps. Making every hair on the back of my neck jump up and stand at attention.

Those high notes of hers turn the insides of my thighs to Jell-O. And I can feel her mellow tones wrap 'round my hips and surge up into me. I'm alive in this place. Alive as I can only be with the sound of her screams and moans.

The soulful current of her voice brings about a change in me. I am myself and much, much more.

Nerve and blood meet muscle and sinew...woman/boy create cocoa-brown cock.

It starts off soft but soon hardens, thick and erect with blood and lust. It throbs, responding to her highs and lows.

My balls shrivel up close and tight underneath me in anticipation of her touch.

And then she appears. My diva queen appears before me on her knees. She wants it. I can tell by the way her big, dark eyes roam hungrily over my nakedness. And by the way her voice drops low, real low as she calls out to me, moaning "Baby."

I tangle my fingers in her thick, red, weave-on hair and pull her up 'til her face is level with my erection. At my command she takes me in her lipstick-reddened mouth. To steady herself, she grips the cheeks of my ass with both hands and spreads her knees apart. I watch all this through eyes half closed. My cock presses against her forehead as she sucks, bathing one of my nuts then the other in her spit. And it's all I can do to keep standing when she uses the tip of her tongue to play with the soft, kinky hairs she finds there.

She's extremely skilled and obedient too. I knew she would be. But that ain't enuff. I'm not satisfied 'til my meat is thrusting against her lips. They open, yielding to me, and soon I'm fucking her. Stroking with ever-increasing force in and out of her mouth. There are no high, clear notes now. Only gurgles and sighs as she struggles with the mouthful I have given her.

At first I try to go easy on her. I mean, deep-throating my whole 10 inches would be a lot for any woman, right? But this one is too much for even me to handle. The sight of her down there, between my legs, cheeks hollowed out with the pressure of suction, luscious lips rolling back and forth, back and forth 'round every delicious inch of my rod unmakes me. Sends me over tha top, so's I end up grabbing her by the sides of her head and pumpin' like crazy.

My knees are buckling, so I brace my back against the wall and allow a violent jumble of emotion, vision, and touch to possess me. In that desperate moment I promise her my life, the world, the sun, and the moon. I gift myself with another look at her, taking all of me, sweaty and rock-hard, down her throat. Her mouth sliding furiously in a slick of spit up and down my cock 'til I don't wanna hold it no more. 'Til I gotta let it go!

I try to pull away, so she doesn't have to, you know, swallow. Some say it just ain't safe these days. And 'sides, a lot of the women I know can't deal with the bitter-salt taste of my cum, anywayz. Not her, though. She's all over me like a second skin. But it don't matter. Even if she wanted to pull back, it would be too late.

It hits. My body is jacking and bucking. From deep inside it comes rushin' over me with a slow rhythmic force like nuthin' else I know. And it's all concentrated at that point where her demanding lips meet my engorged tool.

And she takes it all, takes every musky, mucousy, sweet drop of my jizz in her mouth. Tasting what her mouth can hold. Letting the excess drip past her lips and down her chin coming to rest finally at the tip of one erect nipple.

Satiated, panting, I reach down to pull her up into my arms. She moves fluidly from knees to feet. Morphin' into mist, then evaporating into nothingness...

Ain't nobody...nobody...

I want more of her. Need more of her.

Loves me betta...

Her sweetness stroking the insides of my ears...

Makes me happy...

This is how I show her my devotion.

This is where I...feel this way.

*Issue: Feb./March 2001*

## Adventures in Capitalism
by Muffin Dobson

*All I want is to be knuckle-deep in pussy. I want to hear her whimper, feel her cunt squeeze my hand as she comes.*

Good software engineers are studs. The other programmers look up to them. Just like apes, the highly skilled programmers are the alpha males. When you're working on a project, you have your team of engineers and everyone is important, but the head of the team, the guy who can write the really smooth code, he's the head ape and everyone knows it.

I like that I get to be that guy. The other guys like it too. It's funny how a group of ex frat boys with degrees in computer science can get used to having a dyke around. They get a kick out of me. They joke around with me about girls, make comments about the ass on the new admin (so high you could set a drink on it).

We have a few things in common, these Silicon Valley boys and I. Rebecca, for instance. Every single member of this team wants to fuck her, including—or maybe I should say especially—me. We may all have the same cropped haircut and Gap khakis, but I've got an in that the rest of the boys don't. Rebecca, bless her perfect ass, prefers muff. I'm sure of it.

I haven't told the boys. I hate to break their little hearts. They'll never believe it anyway. What the hell do they know about dykes? They think all dykes look like me: cropped hair, khakis, and biceps.

I've been lingering around her desk a little too much lately, and I think she's caught on. Not that she hasn't thrown a few looks my way. I noticed her skirts got a little tighter after we were introduced. She prances around the office, hand-delivers memos to me whenever she gets the chance. She sends me E-mails asking if I need any office supplies. I ordered some of those little rubber fingertips, as a not-so-subtle hint. Apparently she got the joke, since my fingertips never showed up.

It's Saturday morning. Software engineers work on Saturdays, especially when they have a product that's about to go to beta and it's still full of bugs. I may make a shitload of money, but I work my Gap-clad ass off for it, I assure you.

So here I am, at work on a Saturday, and lo and behold, so is she. Something about catching up on some filing. Uh-huh. Right. No one else is here. We have the place to ourselves. Looks like that bug isn't going to get fixed before we go to beta. Oh, well. E-commerce can wait. I'm about to make one overpaid administrative assistant earn her keep.

She's not in her normal uniform. Baggy jeans and a T-shirt have replaced her usual bitchy skirt-and-pumps ensemble. No bra—I can just make out her nipples. She's uncharacteristically demure, almost shy, pretending to work at her desk. She barely nodded when I came in. Acted like it was the most natural thing in the world to be here on a Saturday. I'm hunched over my screen, determined not to make the first play, when I hear her walk up.

"Hey, Samantha. I was going go grab something to eat. Do you want something?" Her voice is husky. It's obvious she has something on her mind besides lunch.

She's got her hands on her hips. Her long brown hair is down and a little messy. She's not wearing makeup. She looks edible. She looks delicious.

"Um, yeah, how 'bout a Coke?"

"Whatever you like."

"Wait, here's some money." I reach into the pocket of my jeans and pull out some wadded-up bills.

"Just get me when I come back." She says, and saunters out the door.

I certainly can't work. In fact, my crotch is already damp, and my mind is clouded with thoughts of her hair, her face, her body. I'm tempted to blow off the whole thing, sneak off to the bathroom and get it over with, do it myself, come back to my desk, and get to work. But Christ, who am I kidding? All I want is to be knuckle-deep in pussy. I want to hear her whimper, feel her cunt squeeze my hand as she comes.

When she finally walks back in, I nearly jump her at the door.

"Here's your Coke," she says. And for a moment I imagine she spills it. I see her T-shirt sticky and wet, clinging to her breasts, her nipples hard through the fabric. But no, this is not a porno flick. This is my life. She sits down on the edge of my desk, a little too close.

"So, Rebecca," I say, "what the hell are you really doing here on a Saturday?"

"Waiting for you to show up." She grins at me as she says it.

Who needs foreplay? I like a woman who gets to the point.

"C'mere," I say as I stand up to face her. I wrap my hand around the back of her head, pulling her hair a little as I kiss her. She presses her mouth hard against mine then pulls back and bites me. Hard. A drop of bright red blood wells up on my bottom lip.

This is going to be fun.

I run my hand across her breasts, over her T-shirt. Her nipples are stiff. Her breasts are very small. Her body is incredibly soft. I'm afraid of bruising her, or maybe I want to. Her hair and skin have the same amazing scent, a musky floral. I press my face to her neck and bite her. I'm pleased to see a half moon of bluish teeth marks when I pull away.

"Oh, God, Sam. I've wanted to fuck you for ages. What the hell took you so long?" Her voice is very breathy. Femme fatale-ish. I know it's an act. I don't care.

"I don't know. Maybe I know better than to fuck girls I work with."

As I finish my sentence she steps back and pulls off her T-shirt. Yum. No more second thoughts. Oh, God, I think I'm in love.

I push her backwards and down, onto the floor. She practically loses her balance, but catches herself, lands softly on her butt with her hands behind her to catch her fall. I grab the front of her 501s and pull. Her fly opens right up. She groans a little as I pull her jeans off, raising her hips to help me. She's in just her panties, a little breathless, quivering with need and lust. This is why I love femmes. Their desire, the way they respond to being touched. Her skin is superconductive. She tingles everywhere my fingers touch her. I want her so bad it's almost sickening.

I spread her thighs and press my face against the cotton crotch of her panties. She wiggles against me and cries a little. She tries to press her crotch against my face, but I hold her thighs apart, directing the action.

She practically snarls at me. "Fuck, Sam, put your fingers inside me. Now."

I press my tongue against her clit, lightly, through the fabric of her panties. I can feel her heat and wetness against my face.

"You bitch," she whispers, "hurry up."

Her pussy is wet, right through the cotton. I hook a finger under the crotch and pull it to the side. Her lips are puffy and swollen.

"Don't worry, Rebecca. I'll fuck you, I promise." I blow lightly on her clit then lick it slowly, lasciviously. She grinds her ass into the floor and exhales loudly.

She's impatient, and I can't help enjoying torturing her a

bit. I run my fingers lightly across the swollen slit of her pussy, barely tracing her clit. She moans with pleasure and jerks her hips. Finally, I can't wait any longer and push a finger between her lips. She sighs loudly and pushes back against my hand. She's so wet and open that I decide to venture another finger. It slides in easily, and I can tell she wants another. OK, babe, you asked for it. I withdraw my hand for a second then push three fingers in her cunt. She bucks her hips against my hand, and I feel her body tensing. I love how badly she wants me.

I curl my fingers upward and press them against her G-spot while my thumb lightly flicks her clit. The sounds she makes as she rides my hand are exquisite. Suddenly I'm afraid it'll all be over too soon. I slow down my movements, pace myself. She opens her eyes and groans in protest. Inspired, I grab her by the hips and flip her over.

"What? Oh, no, don't stop," she moans, but I insist and eventually get her on her stomach, back arched, with that perfect ass in the air, just begging for attention. I lean over her and stuff four fingers into her pussy from behind. She's so slippery that I'm able to slip my thumb into her ass. She moans loudly, and I decide to go for it, sliding it in a little deeper.

"Oh, fuck, Sam, don't stop. Whatever you do, don't stop."

She's fucking my hand like crazy. Four of my fingers are in her pussy, my thumb moves in and out of her ass, and she's pushing back against me for all she's worth. My arm aches from thrusting. My fingers are cramping, and I'm afraid of losing the rhythm when suddenly her whole body tenses and her pussy clamps down on my hand. She's making noises, not words exactly, just utterances. Monosyllabic sounds. Fuckfuckfuckfuck. OhGodOhGod.

I feel her pussy crushing my hand. It's almost painful. The feeling in my crotch is incredible; I could almost come just from her cunt on my fingers.

"You are incredible," I say. "Come for me, baby. You're

beautiful." I whisper encouragement until she finally calms down. Her body twitches, like miniature electric shocks are hitting her. When she relaxes, I carefully withdraw my hand from her soaking cunt. She turns around to give me a look, like a bad little girl, then curls up tightly against my body.

"How exactly are we going to work out this particular relationship?" I say as I stroke her hair. "How am I going to get any work done with you around to distract me?"

She just smiles in her naughty-girl way and presses her hand against the soaked crotch of my khakis.

*Who the fuck cares?* I think. E-commerce is overrated anyway.

*Issue: June/July 2001*

## Sex in the Stacks
by Wendy Hill

*I'm suddenly wet and reaching up to stroke her waist, her breasts under the shirt falling forward. I grab her belt loops and pull her in.*

She's wearing her packing pants.

That's the good sign. Everything else points to trouble. Tonia's leaning against a column on the library stairs, legs crossed. Even her backpack, sitting lumpily on the marble, looks annoyed. The hands casually in pockets are just a decoy. We've been together eight months now, and I can spot *pissed* from a mile off in a blizzard.

I'm late, and wearing jeans, which is totally counter to the plan. The plan is: sex in the stacks of Widener Library. It sounded fun when we plotted last week over brunch, full of postcoital endorphins and fountain Pepsi. Now it's just another thing I'm doing to prove I'm all here, in this relationship. Well, I'm here, but I'm late and wearing jeans.

"This is your thing, not mine," she says flatly.

That's true, strictly speaking. I'm the one graduating, who's supposed to have sex in the stacks in the grand old tradition. She has a year more of school to make this trip again with someone else. But really we're doing this for her—her public sex fetish, her test of my constancy.

In the face of her packing pants and pissed-off eyebrows,

I realize too late that my outfit is the perfect symbol of passive-aggressive. I wore a hot bra and a sweater that shows it off, but what she needs is to get into my pants expeditiously. The library screw is a down-to-the-second, risky venture, danger lurking around every shelf in the form of voyeuristic divinity school students. At least this is what I imagine as we head inside.

"What?"

"What?"

"Nothing. Go in?"

"Sure. What?"

She just shakes her head.

Get past the guard, check. I guess ABOUT TO HAVE HOT LEZZIE SEX IN THE STACKS isn't stamped on my forehead after all.

In the lobby she asks quietly, "Why aren't you wearing a skirt?"

True answer: Because I never wear skirts, so if I did today, I'd be doing it just for this, just for you, and though I'm doing this for you I'm going to make it a little difficult. (Even as I think this, already I feel dumb—it'll be my circulation getting cut off when my jeans are around my thighs. Some rebellion.)

Out-loud answer: "It's too cold."

If she were really invested in this fledgling fight, she'd say, "Like some people I know." The fact that she didn't is as good as a date to have it out later.

First two floors of stacks: too many people. Fourth floor, southwest corner: bingo. I had said I wanted to do it on one of the desks they assign to graduate students (comfort factor), but she walks to the middle of an aisle and stands in the dark, waiting. She's looking at me, but I can't see her expression. On this floor there isn't really floor exactly. It's metal grate; you can see people in the aisle above and below if the lights are on. I lie down in the aisle between the dusty shelves and, pressing my shoulders against the grate, wiggle my jeans down. I feel suddenly insecure and exposed, not because of the open space above and below, but because Tonia, kneeling by my feet, is looking at my cunt but I can't see her cock.

In a second she's on top of me, heavy breasts pushing mine, one hand propped by my shoulder and the other, spit-licked, pushing the head of her cock down to rub against my clitoris. As she breathes on my throat, her head down with concentration and fuzzy yellow hair brushing my chin, I'm suddenly wet and reaching up to stroke her waist, her breasts under the shirt falling forward. I grab her belt loops and pull her in.

But I can't get it, the angle isn't right. With my jeans around my shins, I can't get my hips high enough for her to settle in. I reach over to the shelf next to my head and pull out as many books as I can fit in my hand. They keep the oversize books and folios on the bottom shelves. Some of these books have probably been here since slavery. They're probably worth something. I thrust up my pelvis, dislodging the unwarned Tonia, and slide the stack under my ass. Breathing hard, she pries open a space between my swollen lips with her fingers and pushes in, thick, no more friction because I'm so wet; she pushes almost all the way in, and oh, right now I love her so much. She moves just a little, trying to get in all the way, pulling the head back each time so it catches on the opening of my cunt. My muscles react, trying to grip her and hold the firm plasticky ridge of her cock. And then she pulls out.

"No good. Turn over." Panting, we push books out of the way, and I get on all fours. Shit, my knees on the grate. "You should have worn a skirt."

But now we're fucking; she's in so deep it almost hurts each time. I think it might be too much, but I push harder against her. I know she tries to fuck me harder than men, every goddamn push, every time. She doesn't have anything to worry about. Men don't come in silicone. If I can make it hurt a little more, it'll be so good. I arch my back, tilting my pelvis to feel the pressure on every inner wall. I'm almost licking the grate, my head down and my mouth open to suck someone who's not there. I push my shirt up to my armpits to feel my nipples brush against the cold grating.

Her thighs are smooth against my ass. I can see their rounded sheen, a vision from heat and memory. For a dreamy instant I try to remember when she started shaving her legs.

The light flips on in the aisle under us. I recognize the buzz cut and blazer of my Chaucer professor. I hold my breath to keep quiet, but we can't stop. I'm pushing against Tonia like a mindless machine, no longer meeting her rhythm, and finally throwing my head back, pushing the breath out into the musty, echoing air.

Tonia collapses onto my back, gasping and stroking the fragile undersides of my breasts. She must have pulled up her shirt too; the sweat we don't remember making coagulates stickily between us.

In the tiny elevator down, all I can smell is sex. We're still panting, and kissing for the first time today, when we stop on the third floor. As Tonia, my professor, and I descend, I wonder if my nipples are noticeably hard. I can't look, though; the elevator is so small that no movement is casual. I glance at Tonia, since I can't kiss her. She looks relaxed. And slightly smoother, with the tool detached and safe in her backpack. I concentrate on regulating my breathing and holding the wetness that's dripping down my thighs.

Silently giddy, we head out of the elevator and past the security desk, where a tired student checks our bags for stolen books. Rooting through Tonia's pack, he stops, his hand closing around something. Holds it in his fist for a moment as he looks at Tonia's tight shirt, bleached-blond hair on brown skin, army pants. She looks back, that same indifferent look I know that's not really indifferent at all. It's just an instant, then he withdraws his hand and nods for us to go. As we walk out, I see his reflection in the glass doors, holding his fingers to his nose, frozen like an addict.

## About the Contributors

When *On Our Backs* published "What She Did With Her Hands" in 1988, **Dorothy Allison**'s award-winning book of short stories, *Trash*, was about to be published by Firebrand Books. Allison went on to write the critically acclaimed *Bastard Out of Carolina* and the Lambda Literary Award–winner *Cavedweller*.

**Diane Anderson-Minshall** cofounded *Girlfriends* magazine (in 1994) and *Alice* magazine (in 2000). Her work has appeared in dozens of national magazines, including *Curve, Femme Fatale, Diva,* the *Utne Reader*, and *Seventeen*. She and her wife divide their time between Idaho (where the politics suck) and California (where the cost of living is too high).

A lot has changed in **Red Jordan Arobateau**'s life—most notably his gender—since *On Our Backs* printed "Cum E-Z" in 1991. At the time, Red described himself as a "lesbian butch porn writer and sometime trick." He has gone on to publish and self-publish many novels, including *Lucy & Mickey, Satan's Best, Dirty Pictures*, and *Daughters of Courage*.

"Yes, white queers challenged society's erotophobia, but radical queers with views informed by race and colonization are set to again redefine sexual politics," says **T.J. Bryan, a.k.a. Tenacious**. T.J. is a black Caribbean femme living in Canada, who has been published in eight black/queer/erotic/wimmin's anthologies and is currently creating two collections, *It Takes Ballz* (nonfiction) and *Tales From the Rainbow Side'a Tha Dark* (short stories).

**Gina Dellatte** was a frequent contributor to *On Our Backs* in the late '80s and '90s. She was a young writer living in the New York suburbs, where worked as an ambulance driver while "attempting ceaselessly to avoid stress." As of 1989, her first novel was in its final draft.

**Muffin Dobson** is a writer, reader, and dyke with an attitude problem. When she's not writing smutty stories, she's busy working on a MFA in fiction at San Francisco State University. She's also a computer geek, but don't tell anyone—it might damage the studly rebel image she's trying to cultivate. She digs motorcyles, hair bands, and keeping the ladies happy. "Adventures in Capitalism" is her first published piece of smut, and she likes the feeling.

In the era of "Hail Mariah" (1992), **Laura Federico** was a freelance writer living in San Francisco and doing various squalid day jobs to support her madcap lifestyle. Her first collection of fiction, *Owning Our Desire*, was debuting soon.

Some fiction is truer to life than others. Author **Kirsten Flournoy** says of her story "Flowergirl": "I wrote it in the throes of a mad crush on the hot little florist across the street from my office." Kirsten has recently completed her first novel, *Fresh Hell*, based on her experiences as a stripper in San Francisco. She now resides in Denver.

Although the Internet had yet to boom, at the time of "Exchange Highway" (1987) the upstate New York–based **Gwendolyn Forrest** described herself as "a terribly boring computer programmer who gets off on compu-sex with strangers" and who had a "faithful feline and huge phone bills."

The very first issue of *On Our Backs* (Summer 1984) describes contributor **Jewelle Gomez** as a "former member of the *Conditions* editorial staff whose work has appeared in many feminist, lesbian, and third-world publications. She is currently working on a collection of black lesbian vampire stories." In 1991 Gomez's award-winning collection came out under the title *The Gilda Stories*. She is also the author of *Don't Explain: Short Fiction* and *Forty-Three Septembers: Essays*.

**Rachel Heath** is a prolific erotica writer whose works have appeared in several magazines, including *On Our Backs, Bad Attitude*, and *The Spanke Shoppe*. One of her short stories was featured in the anthology *A Movement of Eros: 25 Years of Lesbian Erotica*. She lives in Atlanta, where she enjoys lying in bed and listening to the radio—among many other things.

"Sex in the Stacks" (2001) was the fiction debut of **Wendy Hill**, a repressed Southern girl who spends a lot of time in libraries. Her first novel, a mystery, will be published in 2003.

In 1989 **Home Girl** wrote "Faith" as a "swan song to a dream lover who turned out to be a nightmare."

A freelance writer for nearly 20 years, **Jennifer Jen** has published her work in a wide variety of magazines, ranging from *Arizona Highways* to *Cats*. She has been in and out of the hospital lately, mostly in, which means she hasn't had time to do much writing.

Many lesbian readers are familiar with **Lee Lynch**, the popular Naiad press author of *Old Dyke Tales, The Swashbuckler*, and many other lesbian novels and collections. At the time *On Our Backs* published "Cactus Love" (1989), the best installments of her nationally syndicated column "The Amazon Trail" had been collected into a book.

Internationally known **Fetish Diva Midori** graced *On Our Backs* with her very first piece of erotic fiction ("Cool Blue

Suit"). "This is the first piece of fiction I've written since I was maybe 8 years old," she says. "Back then, I wrote about adventures of princesses, but they were actually me. So I guess nothing much has changed!" Midori was raised *hapa haole* (half white) in a feminist household in Tokyo and moved to the United States at age 13. She has worked as an Army intelligence officer and in the corporate world ("I still fetishize power suits"). Today she lives and works as a professional dominant and fetish model in San Francisco. Educator and writer on S/M, fetish, and human sexuality, Fetish Diva Midori travels the world, presenting to universities, the S/M community, media, and the greater society. Learn more about her at http://www.aphrodisios.com.

When **Martha Miller** submitted "Obsession" (1990), her short fiction had appeared in several lesbian and literary journals. She wrote that she "looks for diversity, writing about characters who don't fit the formula." She quit smoking years ago and has finally stopped looking at rooftops. She is the author of *Skin to Skin: Erotic Lesbian Love Stories* (New Victoria, 1998) and the mystery *Nine Nights on the Windy Tree* (New Victoria, 2000).

The prolific Californian writer **minns** has been published a handful of times in *On Our Backs*. In 1993, when the magazine published "Reunion," she had completed two novels, *Virago* and *Calling Rain*, and was about to be anthologized in *Herotica 2*.

"Dildos have been popping up a lot in my work a lot lately," notes Canadian **K. Munro**. True to form, her piece "Still Life With Dildo" features a dildo-wielding dyke and a realistic view of a one night stand's blend of awkwardness and lust. "I find it difficult to take the more romanticized stuff seriously," says Munro. "I enjoy fiction more when it's rough and quirky." Her work has also been published in the magazine *Bad Attitude* and the recently released *Midsummer Night's Dreams*.

When *On Our Backs* published "The Long Parallel Tracks," **Peggy Munson** said that the trip that inspired her story was long and tedious but admitted to a passion for train travel. "I believe that slowing down, being observant, and noticing details from the ground up really is what makes good sex good." She was born in 1968 in Normal, Ill., and her work has appeared in five volumes of Cleis Press's *Best Lesbian Erotica*. She has also been published in the anthologies *Perceiving the Elephant* and *Hers3: Brilliant New Fiction by Lesbian Writers*. She is the editor of a collection of writings on chronic-fatigue immune dysfunction syndrome, *Stricken: Voices From a Hidden Epidemic* (Haworth Press, 2000). She has won residency fellowships at the MacDowell Colony, The Ragdale Foundation, and Cottages at Hedgebrook, and is learning to play electric guitar.

**Kate B. Nealon** is a freelancer living in Portland, Ore.

Author of two collections of writings, *A Restricted Country* and *A Fragile Union*, and the editor of seven others, including *The Vintage Book of International Lesbian Fiction* (1999) and *The Persistent Desire: A Femme-Butch Reader*, **Joan Nestle** is still active with the Lesbian Herstory Archives and is currently working on her third collection of writings, *The Last Refuge*. Her latest anthology, *GenderQueer: Voices From Beyond the Sexual Binary*, coedited with Riki Wilchins and Clare Howell, is due out from Alyson Publications in spring 2002.

Well-published by Naiad Press, **Robbi Sommers** is the author of nine novels, including *Behind Closed Doors, Kiss and*

*Tell,* and *Uncertain Companions.* When she submitted "Midsummer's Dream" (1993) to *On Our Backs* she was "thigh-high in research for her novel *Personal Ads,* asking, 'Is it hot in here or is it me?' "

AIDS activist **Kate Sorensen** lives in Philadelphia and wants everyone to know she'll be staying there for at least the next 20 years. Her story "Chip Gets a Bum Rush" was inspired by her dislike of the backwards baseball cap. "I really do hate that look, but it's on its way out, fortunately for me at least." She has published her own small magazine, *Joy,* and her work has also appeared, among other places, in *Girljock* magazine.

**Wickie Stamps**'s "Medusa Dance" (1993) was her second contribution to *On Our Backs.* She submitted it as "a lesbian sadomasochistic transvestite communist who writes for a number of gay and lesbian publications," including *Doing It for Daddy* and *Brothers and Sisters.*

When "The Strength of Trees" was published in 1992, **Anna Svahn** described herself as "a New York–based writer who works as an editor in Manhattan and lives alone in a plant-filled apartment in Park Slope, Brooklyn."

**Mary Tidbits** lives in San Francisco and works as a landscaper, and her story "Cowpoke" was inspired by her life experience. "I've spent a lot of years working on a lot of ranches," she says. "I even worked for a wrangler for a while when I lived in Montana, and I've been riding since I was little." This is her first published story.

In 1993 **Mil Toro** told us she was "a banker by day, a sci-fi writer by night." At the time, she was completing "a novel about a lesbian vampire cab driver."

"A great storyteller and prolific fantasizer" is how frequent contributor **Mickey Warnock** describes herself in the Nov./Dec. 1989 issue of *On Our Backs*. She has also been published in the *Herotica* series.

**Jess Wells** is the author of 12 volumes of work, including the novels *The Price of Passion* and *AfterShocks*. She is the editor of *Home Fronts: Controversies in Nontraditional Parenting and Lesbians Raising Sons*, both Lambda Literary Award finalists. Her five collections of short fiction include *Loon Lake Duet* (pending publication) and *Two Willow Chairs*.

In 1992 **Lindsay Welsh** "couldn't act, dance, or sing, so she bought a typewriter, hoping to write her way to fame." As the author of several erotic books for Masquerade's Rosebud imprint, including *Provincetown Summer and Other Stories*, that's exactly what she did.

When she wrote "The Dead Air Between Stars" (1990), **Stephine V. Wilson** was a freelance writer and composer living in Delaware. She was also "working on an opera about things that go bump in the night."